MW01138865

The Last Bad Job

a novel
By Colin Dodds

ROYAL PULP

Where Great Literature Meets Cheap Thrills
RoyalPulp.com

This is a work of fiction. Names, characters, places and incidents either are products of the author's imagination or are used fictitiously. Any resemblance to actual events or locales or persons, living or dead, is entirely coincidental.

"Every journalist who is not too stupid or too full of himself to notice what is going on knows that what he does is morally indefensible ... the writer-subject relationship seems to depend for its life on a kind of fuzziness and murkiness, if not utter covertness, of purpose. If everybody put his cards on the table, the game would be over. The journalist must do his work in a kind of deliberately induced state of moral anarchy."

—Janet Malcolm, *The Journalist and the Murderer*

Well, we live in a trailer at the edge of town
You never see us 'cause we don't come around
We got twenty-five rifles
Just to keep the population down

—Neil Young, *Revolution Blues*

1.

VADO, NM—"I want you to start sucking my dick," Jack yelled as he threw Mary Beth off the pontoon boat.

Mary Beth surfaced after a moment and gasped. She brushed her wet hair from her face and slapped her hands down on the surface of the water. A long moment passed. She didn't say anything, didn't swim for the shore or for the boat. She just looked up at Jack, who was flanked by his fellow devotees at the dark wood railing of the boat.

It was a normal day off, much like people in the World would have planned. The phone banks were closed for the day, as were the administrative offices. Most of the people who lived at the ranch were on the boat or sitting out on the lake shore.

Dizzy was the exception. It was the fifteenth, so he was either locked in his bungalow or out past the fences in the desert, speaking with the divine couriers. Though Dizzy had prophesied to the people all around me that the world would last only another ninety or so days, it was a normal day off, out on the lake, until just then.

"Oh baby," Mary Beth sneered from the water.

She didn't budge from her spot in the water. She looked up through Jack and spoke with a flatness to her voice that amounted to sarcasm. It struck me that I hadn't heard sarcasm in public for a few months.

"You know I want it so bad," she said to Jack. "You know how bad I want you."

No one in the boat moved. I imagined the devotees playing it off as a joke, maybe even some kind of provocation to enlightenment. Jack's nostrils flared. I noticed a sweat stain begin in the center of his back, darkening his white, short-sleeve, button-down shirt. He flexed his muscles, but stood stone-still, under the spell of the raw anger that made him the sheepdog to Dizzy's sheep.

Some people walked away from the railing. No one on the boat knew what to do. No one did anything and so no one did anything. Everyone on the boat, except me, had abandoned all the old notions of how to behave and what to expect from one other. I think everyone expected Jack to get embarrassed in all that silence. I did.

Only Mary Beth seemed to know what to do.

"Come on, *lover*, I know you'll be able to get it up *this* time. That's right, Floppy. I want you to *do* me right now."

Jack was too angry and too stupid to come up with anything. I stayed by the railing and turned to him, hoping to speed his embarrassment. But he just stared wrathfully down at Mary Beth, like he was going to dive into the water and hit her. His face tried on the beginnings of several expressions, discarding each before it could take hold. His muscular, clean-shaven jaw clenched its way through the situation. A breeze blew. He sweated more heavily.

8

Could he still say it was a joke? A lesson? Dizzy was sometimes cruel and even violent, and no one doubted his holy credentials, at least not on the ranch.

"Oh yeah *stud*, you know you're the only one who can fuck me right. Why don't you show all of them how you do it," Mary Beth continued, firing her barbs at him from the water.

Her sarcasm shocked the people on the boat more than Jack's violence. It seemed more effective and more vicious.

Mary Beth started to say something else. But she stopped herself and exhaled hard. It sounded like a big sigh or a little scream. Then she bobbed her head under the water. Bubbles the size of hard-boiled eggs came up.

Jack walked away from the edge of the boat and got a little plastic cup of water from the red-and-yellow thermos cooler. The stain on the back of his shirt had fattened and grown wings, straining to reach each of his broad shoulders. No one spoke to him. He took his time with his little plastic cup of water, determined to show how little Mary Beth's tirade bothered him. He walked back to the edge of the boat, cup in hand and looked at the spot on the lake where the bubbles had come up.

I watched that same spot on the water as it flattened out. On the boat, someone tried to change the subject, to start a conversation. Someone awkwardly tried to keep it going. The rest of the people left the wooden railing of the pontoon boat, except me. My face burned and my hands went numb on the railing. Mary Beth never surfaced.

Jack was still with us, however, and still in charge of the outing. He was at the controls of the boat, turning on the engine, the sweat stain on the back of his shirt now reaching almost from his neck to his waist. He muttered that the bitch will turn up sooner or later. But I knew better. I don't know what the others thought or knew.

Then Jack drove the pontoon boat back to the floating aluminum dock. And we all quietly climbed off the boat and scattered without making eye contact, to go meditate or fuck or read or do whatever we could to deflect the always-uneasy swath of free time that just had opened up.

At the dock, I fought to keep my face expressionless and avoided all eye contact. I took the long way back to the shed they let me use as an office, around the back of the cafeteria, to avoid speaking with anyone. My hands were still numb and it felt like I could only take tiny sips of the air. All I could think was that I was no student, no believer, no ascendant-in-training, and as such, I had no excuse.

No one followed me, and I turned around more than once on my walk to make sure of that. It wasn't paranoia. I had just seen something I wasn't supposed to see. And maybe that, not cowardice, explained why I'd done nothing on the boat. I was on the ranch as a professional observer, a transparent eyeball with press credentials—like on a nature show. The National Geographic guys don't whistle to warn the wildebeests they're being stalked, after all.

But my credentials couldn't have fooled me or anyone much. I'd hidden my pretensions of objectivity too well, slacked off too long, fucked too many of the girls on the ranch, took too many privileges, too many liberties, drank too deeply from Dizzy's cup, and stayed too long. And that was merely unprofessional up until then. Suddenly it was dangerous.

If my conscience still had some sway, I would have sat down that afternoon and written an elegy for Mary Beth or a scathing article about the sad failure of Dizzy's assault on heaven, or a polemic against the toxic whisper of transcendence. I might have at least skipped dinner. The rice and beans in a thick brown sauce was okay.

That night was cold, windless. I wanted to go for a walk, but I didn't want to look at the lake. One by one, I checked off all the things I didn't want to look at on the ranch, until I just stood outside behind the dormitory, listening to the deep quiet and the sounds of Jack and the others taking target practice under the bright lights down at the rifle range.

2.

Lying on my bed in the heated dorm, I listened to the early-evening humping all around me. The room was big and open like a gymnasium. The beds were steel frames, with nets of springs and thin mattresses. No one was careful not to be heard. No one was careful with sex at all on the ranch. I'd turned away the charmless advances of an athletic, middle-aged woman with a massive braid of hay-colored hair and crooked teeth. Saying no is another liberty afforded me as an outsider.

It was a tense night after the incident on the lake. So the devotees in the open dorm screwed longer and louder than usual. It wasn't sexy. The springs, loose bed frame fittings and sex noises sounded like the sad mewling of a thousand house pets. The dorm was also brighter than usual. Jack and the others in charge kept the sodium-arc lamps outside on until dawn. I guess I wasn't the only one on edge.

And all night, Mary Beth's sarcastic end replayed in the criminal court of my skull.

Mary Beth didn't get a funeral. I heard it whispered that they found her under one of the boat's pontoons a few days later, her arms and legs still clutching it. I heard she held on so hard that she'd put a dent in the aluminum. But people tend to exaggerate. Aside from a few whispers, though, no one talked about that day on the lake.

But nobody made much of a fuss over suicides on the ranch. The World and our lives in it were such a doomed enterprise in Dizzy's religion that no one's death was a sad thing, exactly. Sometimes after a suicide, there was a short ceremony, sometimes not. It depended on what Dizzy thought of them. There seemed to be one or two suicides a month.

After Mary Beth died, a week went by, and the jury in my head softened. It said maybe it's not Jack's fault, maybe it's not anyone's. There were a lot of desperate people here and Dizzy kept them all on edge. Unlike the other cults I'd researched, his had no dancing, singing, no speaking in tongues. There was no catharsis or release for all the turmoil that his cosmology encouraged. It was serious, quiet, and intense on the ranch, like organized despair.

And I pretended to work, napped the afternoons away, and came to feel more like the people on the ranch—as though I was besieged by something enormous. Dizzy said it was the World that had us cornered like this. He told the devotees on the ranch they'd escaped, for the time being, and that soon they would escape for good.

Before Mary Beth, and before I lost my journalistic compass, I went to the funeral of a suicide on the ranch, took notes and transcribed them. It was for an obese woman, Jen, who worked as a telemarketer and whose most notable trait was that her eyes would fill with tears whenever she spoke to anyone face to face. Jen wouldn't cry, her eyes would just well up and drip. At the service, Dizzy told the devotees that even on the ranch, the World was still ravenous, that it could still find and destroy them. But he said their suicides weren't necessarily a defeat. Sometimes suicide was a triumphant escape. That was how Dizzy explained Jen's suicide.

I never heard him say it, but supposedly Dizzy gave a sermon in which he likened suicide to premature ejaculation— bad form perhaps, but hardly a tragedy. If a person was fully trained for the next step, the best thing he could do was to commit suicide before the World sucked him back in. It was Mary Beth who told me about the sermon, after I'd prematurely ejaculated one afternoon.

I've got vulture ears, reporter ears. So suicide talk is like gold to me. I can see my readers, trundling kids off to school and going out to earn a living, savoring the morning paper's fresh dose of outrage. The headlines write themselves. "No-Nonsense Newsman Describes Death-Dealing Doctrine (in Disbelief!)" Advocating suicide? Cover the children's ears! Tell me more!

But Dizzy's bald-faced embrace of suicide was hard to swallow, even for a true believer like Mary Beth. That same afternoon, alone together in my shed, we talked about it.

"I guess he's right. He's always right, right?"

We were naked under army surplus blankets, the dim mildew smell of the scratchy green fabric. I pursed my lips, but nodded so that she'd continue.

"But it just seems like you ought to help people to be happy and help them stay alive," she said. "I don't know. I mean, just about every other great teacher said to do that, right? But I guess they didn't help much, did they? Maybe even they were too corrupted to understand death, or how you can hurt people by helping them keep living. You can hurt their souls, you know? This is a new teaching that he's giving us. Maybe the teachers who told us to help each other were just tricking us, tying us down and making us think we were doing the right thing."

Mary Beth and I were alone that afternoon, which wasn't encouraged. We were having a conversation we weren't supposed to have. The sex was allowed, but the moments were stolen, which made them sweeter.

"I don't know. Maybe Dizzy's just wrong," I offered, and wished momentarily for one of the many things I couldn't get on the ranch—a drink, a cigarette, a person who didn't take everything so seriously.

"Maybe. But I can't think so. I ... I think I'm just having a hard time untying myself from the World. I'm snared, you know, by everything. It's a whole lifetime of conditioning to overcome, especially when it comes to something like death."

"You really think so? You don't think maybe the whole suicide-is-okay thing feels wrong because it *is* wrong?"

"You wouldn't understand. You don't even want to understand, really. I just think Dizzy is on a higher level. He's strong enough and he sees enough that he knows that death is just, like, the harsh medicine that we need to swallow to get well."

"Is that all you have to swallow?"

"Ha ha. You getting jealous, lover boy?"

"I don't know. Maybe."

"Don't get cute. You know the rules."

"Okay. Forget it. You were entertaining doubts about Dizzy—keep going."

"It's not doubts. It's just hard sometimes. Dizzy just seems so petty with his rules sometimes, and all the work, the way they make you stick to those telesales scripts, and then Jack flexing his muscles and bossing everyone around for him. It gets scary."

"Like how?"

"It just seems like, if someone slips up here one day, or challenges Dizzy, or just Jack, that in a few weeks they make their 'willed departure.' And no one says anything about it. It just seems suspicious. And I know this is just the paranoid part of me. And I know it's just the World trying to hijack my soul. And at bottom, that's really what I think this, like, doubt, is. But sometimes I wonder if all those people really did kill themselves."

"Like when a company says a guy resigned, but he was actually fired. You really think Dizzy's having them killed?"

Mary Beth's big brown eyes widened at that moment. I remembered her tangled hair and her bare face, alert and alive. She was excited to hear me say what she wouldn't.

"I don't know. Probably not. I've spent most of my life lying to myself and then going in all the wrong directions because of it. I'm not what you'd call a trustworthy source, even to myself. But this suicide stuff still makes me wonder if I should be trying harder to live, maybe get out of here. But that's just the bullshit side of me, trying to get me to do the wrong thing again."

Part of what made Mary Beth so beautiful was how she seemed to be alive to all possibilities at all moments. But it was also probably part of what made her life so unbearable.

"There's nothing all that wrong with living," I said.

"Yeah, you're supposed to say that. You actually get paid to say it. You're a visitor here, and the whole keep-on-living thing is where you're from and where you're going back to. But I can tell that even you don't really believe it."

Then she winked and gave me a conspiratorial little chuckle. You couldn't tell if she was being insightful or just playing a trick. But I liked what I heard in her dark little laugh.

Anyway, that's what pillow talk sounds like in an apocalyptic suicide cult, if you were wondering.

I met Mary Beth the first time I visited the ranch. There was something about her that stuck with me, though we hardly spoke. The assignment could be a career-maker, but I think she decided it for me.

After that visit, I had a long talk with my editor, Mo. I fed him a bunch of Dizzy's dark rhetoric. I wanted out of New York, out of the daily grind, out of life in an office where they knew me all too well, out of petty favor trading, out of coaxing sources to say the obvious five days a week and having to thank them for it.

Mo was damn excited about the story.

"Are you kidding me? This *motivational speaker* and his people are ab*solute*ly batshit crazy enough to do it. They are way off the reservation. Kiddo, I think we have found our winner in the Holy Loser Lotto."

"The savior in our Suicide Star Search?" I added. We talked in bad headlines when we got excited.

"Or the suicide in our Savior Star Search. I really think we have it. Jonestown without the international travel. Right in the middle of the American West. It really doesn't get any better than this. I want you there, on the ground, before it happens. I want close-ups. I want you to be able to give the readers something to cry about for every one of these doomed, crazy fucks."

Mo had a detailed map of where the bodies were buried at the paper. So, a month later I had the assignment. He'd negotiated me all access on the ranch for the six months leading up to Dizzy's scheduled apocalypse.

A few weeks after I arrived at the ranch, I told Mo that my situation was tenuous, and I could be expelled or worse for a wrong turn of phrase. We began rescheduling our regular phone meetings until we forgot about them entirely. And with deadlines of his own to tend to, I became a chore, and then an afterthought. And that suited me.

But two weeks after Mary Beth, I began reporting again. I stopped the devotees on the ranch with all sorts of asinine questions. *Do you miss baseball? Do you miss talking on the phone to people you used to know? What candy bar would you eat if you could? How do you feel about cosmetic surgery?*

Truth is, after Mary Beth, I was a little afraid for my safety. I hoped my stupid, man-on-the-street questions would make Jack and the others take me less seriously than they already did. And I wanted someone to answer one of my inane questions by saying something, by accident or necessity, about Mary Beth. But no one did. In the World, we have condolences for the awful things that leave us numb. On the ranch, no one would even say they were bad.

One day, in the cafeteria, I was in the middle of taking notes as a young Spanish devotee with a wispy mustache on his upper lip struggled to answer a question about his favorite movie, when Jack took me aside.

Jack was a big guy, played football at Michigan before blew his knee out. Still built like an athlete, he had the violent, unbalanced smell of an enforcer to him. He liked the power, but lacked the foresight, self-control, and confidence to be a leader. He was a classic number-two, and more dangerous for it.

Outside the cafeteria, Jack gripped my shoulder, alternately massaging it and tightening his hold. As intimidation, it worked well enough that I can't give any verbatim quotes. But to paraphrase: He said that if Mary Beth couldn't swim, she should've just asked for help. He said boating accidents happen all the time out in the World too. He said it with the menacing obliviousness of an enforcer.

They say more suicides are the result of spite than despair. And when it comes time to break out the pistols and the poison here, Jack will do it out of spite. I saw him give a sermon once when Dizzy was out talking with the divine couriers. And I've never seen anyone talk about enlightenment with so much rage.

3.

Dizzy doesn't make me work—another perk I get as an outsider. I'm not allowed into most of his smaller audiences, and I don't bother going his sermons anymore.

That leaves me with a lot of time. And free time on the ranch somehow isn't as bad as free time in the World. There isn't the sense that you could be doing something better. You don't feel so almightily entitled to be bored.

But the desert is merciless. The air never sits right on my skin. It's too hot in the day, then too cold in the night. Every glance hurtles out to distance itself, lands in the purple molars of the sparse, half-assed mountains, seals my lips and exhausts my desire to see at all.

My new man-on-the-ranch shtick aside, I nap, daydream about my Pulitzer, assign blame for Mary Beth and go for walks. I pass most of my waking hours in the shed. It has one drafty window, a built-in shelf for a desk, a brown metal folding chair, a leftover half-roll of pink fiberglass insulation and an old farm implement shaped like a wishbone that leans against the wall and takes up too much space. I keep my things in the shed. Aside from Dizzy, I'm the only one on the ranch with any privacy or property. I have a wallet, a laptop, some clothes, notebooks, a backpack, and a cell phone. But after Mary Beth drowned herself, I let the phone's battery run down and never recharged it. I may have hated Dizzy and the ranch, but there was no one I wanted to talk to back in the World, either.

To pass the time, I tried to get down all the everyday details I could about the daily workings of the ranch. That's what our readers want to know. *Where do astronauts poop?* That sort of thing.

Suicides aside, it's been a good year for the ranch. Its telemarketing business made it completely self-sufficient as of last year, so that Dizzy was able to skip his annual trip out on the lecture circuit. He held more audiences, and spent more time with the divine couriers. Dizzy wasn't trying to get rich off the ranch. He already was rich. The work kept the devotees busy, and the money shut out the World. Except for seasonal trips to town for supplies, and the impatient voices coming through their headsets during telemarketing hours, the World was just a dirty word on the ranch.

In my notes, I could see my reporter's reach for a labor-exploitation piece. But my heart wasn't in it anymore. The people here worked for Dizzy, and seemed content enough. The people in the World worked for money, which didn't track so neatly with contentment. The suicides were still the strongest angle.

But I knew that I'd have a hell of a story, as soon as those jackasses offed themselves. I would be the one to feed the gore and agony of a righteous slaughter to our salacious and sensation-starved readership. I'd be the one to get the lens right up against the religious death urge in the most powerful nation that man has ever seen.

But that meant waiting on the mass suicide, in my shed. It meant keeping on an even keel for two or so more months. Mo figured it would probably come ahead of Dizzy's deadline, so as to preempt any last-minute interventions by the devotees' families or law enforcement. If Dizzy gives the order to end it and they obey, that's a Pulitzer-winning cover story that revives a once-august newspaper's flagging reputation and puts my skinny, hound-dog face on TV. The deaths of seventy-seven people can help a career like that.

If it bleeds, it leads. And not much was bleeding but Mary Beth. And I couldn't stand to write about her, certainly not for our readers.

Looking for something, I went into my notebooks, to my first meeting with Dizzy, before I'd moved out to the ranch. In a folder, I found the transcript of that first interview. That day, I could tell he'd prepared for the interview. When he bowed hello, I could see my reflection in his freshly shaven head.

Dizzy was a lot to take in, jarring even. I'd seen photos, but they'd been photoshopped. And I'd seen videos of his lectures, first in a suit and tie, then open collar, then polo shirt, and finally formless, collarless linen shirt. In those, he was speaking to largely unfamiliar audiences, and so speaking more solicitously.

But I met Dizzy on his home turf, and imperious in his light-blue robe. I was caught off guard by his lazy eye, his painstakingly perfect teeth made strange by a single gold crown, and the fresh razor burn on his neck and the top of his head. He was a short but stout man, hairy enough that it seemed his shaving routine ended, somewhat arbitrarily, at the line of his collarbones.

Dizzy tried to pass as serene, but the effort was clear. And it came off as one more battle he was blithely and constantly fighting. Sitting still seemed to be his hardest-won ability and his most potent gesture.

That first interview was one-on-one, though later meetings would often include Jack or a lesser menace. In that first talk, Dizzy gave me his much-practiced introduction to himself and his religion. Most of it was a word-for-word recitation of the *About Us* section of his website. Once he dispensed with that, I asked about the ranch and its rules. He started with the part he figured, correctly, I'd be most interested in.

"So, sex," Dizzy said.

Then he paused, sat as still as he could manage and grinned, expecting me to squirm. I nodded, more bored than shocked at that point. But he let the pause hang another moment anyway, just to let me know I was on his schedule, and not the other way around.

"Just as with food or shelter, we don't forbid sex. But as with food and shelter, we do not embrace it or celebrate it. None of it has to have any bearing on our ultimate fate. Focusing more than necessary on food or sex or possessions will only keep us from our goal."

"So how do you handle sex, do people marry?" I asked.

"No. Just the opposite, in fact. Anyone can sleep with anyone. And everyone must submit to everyone else's advances, within reason," Dizzy explained.

"Really? Everyone?"

"I abstain, because I can. And it's not complete anarchy. It has to be within a person's sexual preference—hetero or homo. And, of course, the children are off-limits. Please be sure to include that in your story. There are other rules. When we work, we work. When we meditate, we meditate. When I teach, they listen. When they ask, I answer. There are times in the day when people can do what they wish, including sex with whomever they wish—within reason."

From the way Dizzy said it, it seemed like he'd had to say it hundreds of times before. It was probably the kind of thing he had to make very clear.

"Why do you do it this way?" I asked.

"The more you forbid sex or withhold sex, the more people become obsessed with it. Then you have to create more rules about sex, and that in turn, makes people into fetishists. People become as small as the objects that obsess them. Then their desire, instead of driving them, locks them away from enlightenment. So by minimizing the rules we have about sex, we free people from it, as best we can."

I could say from experience that Dizzy's plan worked, mostly. An open-bed policy sounded like utopia. But after a while, it was like a buffet in a hospital cafeteria: You can eat all you want, except you don't really want to anymore. I slept with more than half the women on the ranch, but Mary Beth was the only one I ever really thought much about. By the end, sex was just an excuse to spend time with Mary Beth.

"What about diseases?" I asked Dizzy.

"People can take precautions. We make prophylactics available. It's up to them. We've had, I believe, fourteen children born here on the ranch. We do not close the doors to souls who want to join us that way."

Dizzy smiled at his turn of phrase so that all meticulously straightened, filed and whitened teeth showed. He'd worn braces into his twenties, but had never gotten rid of the cheap-looking gold cap. It gave him the look of a casino pit boss, and made him good copy.

During that interview all those months ago, he still tried to be PR-savvy. But he still wouldn't lie to me when I asked him where he thought his church would be in ten years.

"We won't be doing magazine interviews, that's for sure. In ten years, we will be free of the future, free of the past, and free of the present. We'll be just where we need to be."

"Still in New Mexico?"

"I doubt it."
That's when I smiled.

4.

Three weeks after Mary Beth went under the lake, things became strange. I was sleeping on my stomach. The skinny alien was sitting on my back. I could tell what the alien looked like even though I couldn't see it. It was so close to me that it was almost like it didn't exist.

"You're hiding something," it said into my ear, its voice flat. "You're hiding it from the world and even from us. You're hiding it so well, just keeping it all the way down there."

I physically couldn't move. The alien stopped and sat so still that I thought it might have gone. But then it spoke again.

"Soon we will make ourselves apparent to you. All will be clearer than it is now. We are not what you think we are. We are you, but we are not."

There seemed to be more, but I couldn't remember it. It was more vivid than a dream. I could hear the alien's soft footsteps as it retreated across the dormitory floor. Then I could move again.

Even grownups get scared of what's under the bed sometimes. And there's nothing they can do about it.

The strangeness persisted past lunch, with aliens around the cafeteria. I was scared, but interested. I wished I was hiding something deep down. Because otherwise, I was a damn disappointment. Being shaky and preoccupied was a nice break from just being bored and sad and thinking of Mary Beth and death, death, death. Maybe some people go crazy because it's the best place to go.

The next night, my father visited. He looked like he did not long before he got himself killed. I was frozen in the same bed as he walked from the bathroom and pulled a chair up to my bedside. He lit one of his discount cigarettes, almost as pungent as pipe tobacco. He said he was sorry for what he did.

"A man needs a place to go and he needs to go there," he said, clearing up nothing.

It was emotional, so I don't have a lot of straight quotes. He said he was sorry he left Sandy behind. Sandy was a golden retriever puppy I bought him not long before he went out for cigarettes and came home with a bloody hole in his side. He was a hard man to read, but I sensed things were bad for him after Mom left. The dog was my way of trying to keep him above the waterline. That dog loved the hell out of him, at least for the months they were together. The damn thing wasn't cheap, either.

But Dad in the dormitory didn't say much, which was consistent with when he was alive. That night, he mostly just looked at me with pity, like it was my turn with the big fucking problem. He tried to console me, said soon it wouldn't matter at all, said terrible and wonderful things would happen. I'd have to tell the people the thing I least wanted to tell them, then all our problems would vanish in an enormous fire. It would all be even.

I should've asked him what he meant. But I had paralysis and more pressing questions for the taciturn bastard. I wanted to know about that day when he came home alone, acting like someone who hadn't just been gut shot while intervening in a convenience store robbery. I remember cleaning up the house and piecing it together. I found his keys and wallet in the bowl by the door, just like any other day. From where the body had fallen and what was around it, I could almost piece it all together. He'd lit a cigarette, picked up the remote control and tried to sit in his armchair. But by then the blood loss was bad, and he missed the seat. He slid onto the floor, unlit cigarette in his lips and remote in his hand. After he was down there almost a day, Sandy went a little crazy, barking and crying. When the police opened the door, she wouldn't let them near my father's body. The cops, to their credit, called animal control, who tranquilized her.

Sandy was probably somewhere else now, loving the hell out of someone else.

"Son, I have to go now. But I'll see you soon. Things will be better for everyone very soon," Dad said.

A pale, flickering blue glow, like a TV glow, rose behind him. He got up from the chair and walked off toward the bathroom. I didn't wake up so much as I suddenly regained motor control, spasming back from paralysis under my rough army blanket. I stifled a small shout, so as not to wake the dorm.

The whole thing scared me. I started seeing aliens loping out in the foothills and the brush. I feared Mary Beth would visit by my shed one afternoon with her own set of riddles. I wanted a drink. I wanted to replace the unfamiliar problem with a familiar one. It felt like something big was about to give way.

5.

As a refuge from psychosis, I started working again, asking more pointed questions of Dizzy's disciples about the coming apocalypse. And they all agreed: This old world is coming to an end, with wars and disasters on a scale scarcely imaginable to us.

"It'll be soon," Heather, a glassy-eyed hippie girl with curly red hair graying too early, said after a quick and unenthusiastic screw. She was pretty dry down there, given that it was her idea. What she didn't give was nourishing conversation. That was in short supply on the ranch. But she was mad for the end of the world. Everyone was, and everyone had a clear idea of how it would happen.

"It's the angelic warriors. They're gonna trick the nations into a nuclear war. Then they're going to clean up what's left of the bastards with their fiery swords. The streets will be sticky with boiled blood," Jack explained to me, seeming to relish the details. "After that, they're going to stir up the ocean and use huge tidal waves to wash the planet clean."

"Technology is going to turn on us," said Bob, a fat and unnervingly sweaty man who manages the telemarketing office. "Even simple tools, like pots and pans, will attack man while he sleeps."

"There will be a plague. It'll kill everyone except the chosen few. The very few who don't die will suffer unthinkable torments for generations. It will be a very dark time," said Laurie, who ran the websites for Dizzy's books and tapes. "I know I'm not supposed be afraid or to prefer one thing over the other. But I'm glad I'm going to miss that part."

"Zombies'll surge from the south and barbarians will sweep down from the north. It'll be the same for America as it is for Europe. And that'll be the end of both of them," said Tim, a telemarketer with his fingernails chewed down to just about nothing.

So much for having signs to watch for. It seemed like Dizzy had been dishing out a different Armageddon du jour to whoever asks.

At least the Gotterdammerung gang agrees on the reason the end is coming.

"Because the World has tried and failed us horribly. Or because we have failed it. Either way, the World has not taught us what we must know or shown us what we must do. So the World must be drastically transformed," said Sarah, speaking with the stilted cadence of a person reciting. She was a half-pretty, skeletal brunette with lopsided breasts who cleaned the dormitories and the kitchens. "Because so many have not learned, they, along with their souls, must be annihilated."

She smiled. It seemed like a funny time to smile. Her left eye twitched like she was about to wink but decided against it at the last minute.

"All of us?" I asked.

"In the end, only three percent of humanity will survive the calamity," she said, trying to keep her eyes in mine. "But far from being lucky, that three percent will suffer for twenty generations."

She gave me the twitchy-eye smile again, reached out and took my hand. And I was back at the dessert trough in the hospital buffet.

Twenty generations can pass in an instant if you know how to wait, Dizzy had said in one of his sermons. It was at one of the last sermons I'd attended, albeit without my tape recorder. Only after twenty generations of misery will we be shaken loose from this stopover in civilization. And, at last awakened from that long neurosis, we will begin to evolve again. Ten generations after the twenty of misery, humanity will become peaceful, genderless creatures who can breathe underwater, Dizzy explained. They will travel vast distances and repopulate the planet by the fortieth generation. The forty-first generation will no longer eat, but get all their nutrition through osmosis. They will be able to move effortlessly through time and space. Dizzy claimed that after three billion years of evolving into an increasingly specialized organism, human beings will become more like the most common stuff of the universe. The changes will speed up in each generation, so that soon human beings will exist without bodies, as the light of pure awareness.

"By becoming pure awareness, humanity and the whole physical world will be redeemed. The experiment will have succeeded, and all the suffering of life on this and other planets have been worth it," said Andrew, a tall, stooping Chinese guy with bad breath who sends off free copies of Dizzy's books to anyone who writes in asking for a copy, along with the $5 shipping and handling. "The fate of the whole planet and the meaning of all life on it, maybe of all the universe, lies in the balance. It depends on us making the right choices here and now."

"Sounds like great fun, being the pure light of awareness," Mary Beth said to me one afternoon.

She said it in that way of hers where you couldn't tell if she was kidding.

In an early interview, one of the first where Jack sat in, Dizzy explained how he'd learned the future from the divine couriers. They visited him on the first and the fifteenth of every month. Just like payday. Dizzy said sometimes they looked like angels, sometimes like aliens, sometimes like bike messengers. Sometimes they spoke to him, other times they delivered reams of blank printer paper that only he could read. They told him what to do.

"I am here to train their souls to survive," Dizzy said. Jack sat behind me at the back of the audience room. "This is the only chance they or any of us have of surviving what's to come."

"So, training their souls, how do you do that?" I asked.

"It begins with acknowledging the hopeless reality of our situation as I have described it to you."

"What then?"

"Then they need to overcome their traumas and, more importantly for some, their successes. They must first become nothing at all in order to become what they really are, to become something that might survive. They have to disown every experience and opinion they have. This is the part everyone hates, probably even more than the end of the world, especially smart guys like you," Dizzy said, cocking an eyebrow.

"I agree. Disowning my whole life isn't at the top of things I'd like to do with my weekends."

"That's not what I hear."

"Excuse me?"

Dizzy made a gesture like he was tipping back a drink, smiled mildly and sat very still.

"You heard that, huh?"

"You're not the only one who can do a little research."

"Well, I don't drink anymore. But thanks for bringing it up. So the training you do here—where do you go, where do they go, after that first step?"

"I can't tell you."

"Why not?"

"Because you haven't accepted the reality of your situation."

"But can't you tell me about the process, the theory?" I inquired.

"No. It's not for your purposes."

"Okay. But what are you training their souls to do?"

"They will be able to navigate through their own death and the death of the World and be born past the period of immense suffering, into the last eleven generations of humankind. From there, they will evolve into the pure light of wisdom that will redeem the entire universe."

"But what if the apocalypse doesn't come? What then?"

"It will come. It doesn't matter whether it comes in a week

or a century. We won't be here to face its horror. We will be waiting where it can not touch us."

He really spoke like that, without contractions. I looked at the open window of his bungalow, where the wind blew a blue curtain. I pretended I was trying to remember my next question. But I wasn't allowed a notebook in the interview, and I was trying to memorize his answer.

6.

To get away from the ranch, all of which reminded me of Mary Beth, I went with some of the guys on the seasonal supply run. They loaded up on rice and gasoline and the like, picking up mechanical parts from the PO Box and buying fresh ammo.

With some time to kill, I went off to the bookstore in town, a huge place, like a warehouse. I didn't want to be caught with a lot of trashy fiction, so I went to the philosophy and religion sections first. So I really have no one else to blame for what happened next.

A headache is the symptom. But the disease is deeper. The books in the bookstore, juxtaposed on shelves and tables told their terrible and pointless story: You argue against everything. You undermine and outsmart yourself at every turn, one idea at a time. You go through the whole circuit, from medieval Christianity to postmodern socialism to Mahayana Buddhism to occult fascism, to a pleading, mealy-mouthed humanism, to free-market utopianism and back again. In your fight, you take a turn as every idea's worst accuser and its grandest champion. And after all that fuss, you come back to the place you started, having been failed equally by both God and godlessness, betrayed by civility and barbarism alike, thrown out of the bank and the gutter, expelled from the temples of this world and those of the next. And there you are, an orphan, naked except for the ill-fitting garment of your own caustic personality. You're the one restless mind of mankind. And what the hell do you do now, when you're out of things to cover yourself with or to attack?

It wasn't a good feeling, especially for a smart guy, like I think I am. I never knew what to do when I got those bookstore blues. I just went back to the truck and waited until Jack and the other guys had all the supplies.

That sleepless night, Mary Beth came and sat by my bed. She was in the same spectral folding chair, wearing a sheet, her legs crossed at the thigh and her foot wagging up and down restlessly. She didn't say anything. She didn't even look down at my paralyzed form more than occasionally. But it smelled like her and it felt like it felt to be near her. She was clearly and vividly there, not acknowledging my paralyzed form.

And that decided it. I had to leave the ranch.

Spasming back to proper reality, I decided I could wait out the suicides in a newsroom or a hotel room. I had enough material.

I'd jump the fence, where sandbags were piled against it, by the rifle range. I replayed the way to the highway from the trip to town. I decided I could hitchhike out to Las Cruces or El Paso and rejoin the regularly scheduled World. I could write up most of the piece with what I had, and then hit our readers with a hell of a story before every toe was tagged.

7.

But before I went, I wanted one more talk with the bossman. Despite my skepticism, maybe he could help with the visitations, or whatever they were. Also, there was a big question I hadn't answered yet: Is Dizzy a total fraud? I could write a magazine article agnostic, and even a book. But it would be nice to know.

So far, Dizzy had given me a lot of New-Agey apocalyptic vagaries, along with the metaphysical justifications for telemarketing from him. But every now and then, he'd seem inspired. Those were moments I really couldn't tell where he was getting his stuff from. He could say things that made it easier to live in your skin, even as he led you down a path that ended with a police shootout and a well-rehearsed suicide.

I asked for an audience in the morning and had one before dinner. It was the first time I'd met him without Jack or someone else in the room since those first interviews, a lifetime ago.

"Maybe it's just constipation, the dreams. You been eating your greens?" was Dizzy's first response to my paralytic visions.

"All right, I already told you that what I'm after is an audience, not an interview. This is all off the record. Really," I said.

"So you want my help?"

"Yeah. Like I said. I didn't know who else to bring this to."

"You don't have a therapist back in Manhattan who can FedEx you some pills to smooth all this out?"

"Hey, if you don't want to do this, just say so. But look, I didn't even bring a pen."

"So this is off the record completely? You promise?"

Dizzy was wearing a dark blue robe. It was about two days since his latest meeting with the divine couriers, and a month since Mary Beth drowned herself. Over the course of the next thirteen days, his robes would become lighter and lighter. By his next meeting with the divine couriers, he would be wearing a white robe again.

The robes were slimming, giving Dizzy's fat a kind of stateliness—a fact I doubted was lost on him.

"Totally off the record. Not on background. Not not-for-attribution. Completely off the record. I'm here about these dreams. It's personal. Just for me, I mean," I assured him, leaking a little desperate alto into my voice.

"Okay. I guess by the time your promise doesn't matter to you, it won't matter to me either."

Dizzy loved to talk like that. Playing pricktease to vultures like me. I didn't take the bait this time, and simply told him about the visits, all their sad and scary details.

"So you have aliens and you have ghosts and you have you. The ghosts and the aliens both have something to say to you."

I nodded.

"The ghosts can't escape what they have been. They are done becoming, buried up to their eyeballs in what they are. They can't move forward, but only reach backwards. And they want something from you. But they don't know what it is, because nothing will help them. So they grab at you in useless, confusing ways. And the aliens are so close to becoming pure light that they can do no wrong. They can go wherever they please and do as they please. Nothing can harm them. They don't want anything from you, and so they make no sense when they speak."

"So why do the aliens bother talking to me at all?" I asked.

"The aliens are reaching out to the ghosts to redeem them. And you're the uneasy intermediary, the uncertain link in a questionable chain. For you, the doomed state of the jealous ghost and the disinterested omnipotence of the alien are both possibilities. Absolute uncertainty is the thing you have that neither of them does. That's why they're attracted to you. You still hold all possibilities."

"I do?"

"It should be obvious. Just look at yourself. Even calm, you quiver, and waver. Even asleep, you change. No drink or pill will stop it. No smartass smirk will cover it up or undo it. More than anything else, you are uncertain. That is the state of our World. It is an uneasy passage through very real perils. But still, the gods above us and the animals below envy us our uncertainty. The ghosts behind us and the aliens ahead can't help but want a piece of the action. Everything is, as the bankers say, 'in play,' for us. It can go better for us than any creature in the universe. But it can also go far worse."

I had read something like this in one of his books. But he was on a roll, so it had a good ring to it.

"You think there's a hell for the cats and dogs?" he asked and paused. I was getting the full show. "No. And the gods might stop in and give hell a whirl, but only for fun, and never a hell they couldn't get out of. We are the only ones who could push a real, real world into utter destruction, like we are about to do. We are the only ones who could turn such quivering fullness into utter despair and oblivion."

I blinked and his spiel lost its appeal. He wasn't answering my question anymore, just unwinding his cosmic formula. But like a true salesman, he could see my disappointment before I said a word. So he changed gears and went on the offensive.

"But the dreams aren't what's really troubling you. It's Mary Beth, isn't it?" Dizzy said, locking on my gaze with his good eye.

"That's not why I wanted to talk to you. But, yeah, I guess it does bother me."

"Unfortunately, this is still the World that we are in. This is simply the best we can do here, inside of it. And some of the people here are so hungry for something better, so hungry for what's to come, they can't wait for it. We don't condone suicide. But we also don't fetishize it into the dark, romantic tragedy you're accustomed to thinking of it as."

This was the sort of stuff I was assigned to report dispassionately for our readers to shake their heads about over breakfast, to joke about with coworkers in the afternoon and warn their children about over dinner. I reflexively asked their questions.

"So you don't feel any responsibility?"

"You're missing the point," he snapped.

"Helping people isn't part of the point?"

Dizzy became calmer, more deliberate in his annunciation. This was one of the questions he had obviously prepared to answer calmly for the nonbelievers.

"I can tell you are angry. But death, whether by suicide or by another path, means much less than you can comprehend at this point. *You* use death to sell newspapers and the newspapers use death to sell cars and shoes and watches. Beneath all your shallow protests about 'helping people,' or 'saving people,' death is just a currency to buy people's attention. And so you want to protect the currency, like any businessman would. But the currency will lose its value. The World will soon evaporate, and not gently. Mary Beth may have missed out on ten weeks or ten years of life. It was hasty, unplanned, and premature of her. But she was better prepared for what is to come than most."

"Is that why you've prepared plans for everyone here to kill themselves when the time comes?" I asked for good measure.

"That's a blatant lie. You should know better than to believe it. Who told you that?"

"It was not-for-attribution. And I protect my sources. But more than one person told me," I said.

It was a bluff. I'd heard it all from Mary Beth. And she'd heard it from Jack. Supposedly, Dizzy had the whole mass suicide well-rehearsed and ready to roll. It included speeches, toxic cocktails, hunting down stragglers with rifles, group meditation as the lights dimmed, even a good-bye toast for the inner circle after the unwilling were murdered. It sounded like a cross between a fire drill and a high school graduation. They had one version that took four hours and one that took forty minutes, she said, and both versions left everyone dead.

"I will tell you now, on the record and for attribution, that there are no suicides planned whatsoever. I don't encourage it and I don't condone it. Tell your readers that came from my own lips," Dizzy said, remembering there was a reporter in the room.

"Like I said, I didn't bring a pen. And you just said that Mary Beth killing herself wasn't all that bad of a thing."

"That was off the record."

"I know. I'm just trying to understand."

"On background, we know that we are trying to achieve and maintain certain highly spiritual goals in an extraordinarily violent and perverse place. And we know that the World is not indifferent to us. It is strongly inimical to the spiritual achievements that are at the center of our lives. That being the case, we are not entirely averse to 'willed departures,' if the only other option is to be swallowed up again by the World. But these are not 'suicides' as you know them. They are a form of spiritual self-defense."

"So how do the 'willed departures' fit into your plans?" I asked.

"The Redeemer loves his own like a father. He doesn't want us confused or chewed up by the World, or by the machinery of his wrath. 'That which is damaged will not abide the passage.' I have heard that directly. He wants us to remain whole. Otherwise we won't spiritually be able to rejoin the survivors, the evolvers."

"So when will it begin?"

"When will what begin?"

"The end."

"Sooner than you think. The World is worsening by the day. There was a time, not even that long ago, when doctors, lawyers, bankers, entertainers, and inventors made the World better with what they did. They helped humanity progress. And I don't know exactly when everything changed, but it did. It reversed. Now every new development in the sciences, the arts, and the law only makes humanity a little worse. It's too late. Things can no longer improve."

Cosmology aside, he sounded like a lot of cocksure men who've passed middle age and have decided that the world's going to pot. But I kept that to myself.

"Really?"

"Even here, we are worsening, slowly, but we are worsening. So, to answer your question: I wouldn't bother paying off my credit cards, if I were you."

"Thanks for the advice."

I hadn't meant the audience thing entirely as a ruse. But as a ruse, it worked. Maybe I hadn't gotten much help with my dreams, but I did get more candid answers that afternoon than in the months I'd been there.

Then it was Dizzy's turn to ask questions.

"On another subject, though. I am curious—how is the story coming? What will you write about me, about this place, about what we are trying to do?"

"I don't know. I guess I'll stick around a little longer, soak things in a little more ..."

"Until we go ring the Armageddon bell and drink the Kool-Aid?"

"Not exactly, um, I was thinking that I'd stay another month or two, if that's okay, then go back and mull it all over, and then write something up. I don't really have an angle just yet."

"You seem uncomfortable. It can't be easy being the first vulture to the party," Dizzy said, fixing me with his one good eye. The lazy eye was looking out an open window behind me, at something that did not stir it.

"It's not necessarily going to be a bloody story at all. From what I've seen, it could be innocuous enough to get me fired. 'Celebrity Leads New Life in the Desert'—something like that. I really don't know where the story is going. Do you?"

He didn't raise his voice, but suddenly Dizzy was angry.

"I'll tell you what I think. I think your view of this place has been unduly colored by what happened to Mary Beth … by what she did to herself. I'm afraid you won't tell people what we're trying to do here. I think you have your little bit of carrion and you're ready to cut your losses. You liked Mary Beth, maybe you *really* liked her. But still, she's just grist for your mill, a suicide to anchor your story. That should be gory and grim enough to make your editors happy and to reinforce the cow-brained notion that we are some kind of dangerous death-and-sex cult. You want an all-access crucifixion. And you don't care who hammers the nails. That's what I think."

There was a long pause while I thought about the situation from his point of view, in which I was as the agent the World had sent to gather the evidence it needed to mock and discredit him. I'd already begun rehearsing the sober, close-cropped sentences and pop culture references I'd use to express my phony anguish and righteous indignation over Dizzy's Depraved Death Cult.

I guess Dizzy was better at my job than I was. He was right, the story already had the legs it needed. Thank you, Mary Beth.

I thought of running that story. On a slow week, even without a mass suicide, the story *could* score a front page. Then there would be the predictable outcry. The police would start asking about the suicides. Social Services would start poking around about the kids. The ATF would want to check out the rifle range. The IRS would find problems in a tax return. Sound familiar? It did to Dizzy.

As a reporter, you can make a difference, just not always a good difference. Thinking about my role in the whole process made me wonder who I liked less, Dizzy or the World.

"It's really like I said. I'll have to get my notes together, my interviews, along with your books, pamphlets, Xeroxes and the other stuff you gave me. I won't know what the story will be until then."

That was a lie. I did want blood. I did want a massive, livid outrage from the cow-brain of our great nation. *Just fucking kill yourself. Just fucking do it, you bloated megalomaniac*, I thought to myself, focusing hard on the bridge of his nose so as to keep my gaze from jumping uncomfortably from his lazy eye to his good one.

"I knew what I was getting into, letting a reporter in here. But I realize now that *I* haven't been going about it right," Dizzy said, breaking out his most solicitous tone. "To avoid disrupting the routines of my disciples, I've been keeping *too* much from you. I want you to start to see the real workings of this place, to see what goes on here. From now on, nothing will be off-limits to you. You are welcome at *all* the audiences, *all* the teachings, and *all* the meditations. You're even welcome to work in the telesales office alongside everyone else if you would like."

"That would probably be good. I'd like that."

"Great. It starts tomorrow. And I realize I haven't given you any instruction, any real perspective on how beautiful and important everything we are doing here truly is. I know these last few weeks have been a trial for you. And I can tell that you are unhappy. You have been unhappy for a very long time, going back to before you were born."

This was Dizzy's holy hard sell, I could tell. I nodded to draw him out further.

"I want you to try to trust me just a little bit in the next couple weeks. I know you won't give up the skepticism that's so central to your trade. But I want to show you why we are *really* here. I want you to give yourself the oppor*tunity* to understand the *reason* we are all here, living like this. We aren't just some arbitrary monstrosity of mental illness off Interstate 10. I want you to *try* to learn our reasons for yourself. If nothing else, it will add a counterpoise to whatever else you are ready to write. Does that sound okay?"

"Okay. That sounds good," I bleated.

Dizzy was offering me more access, and more Dizzy, for my story. I should have been excited. But it only made me want to jump the rifle-range fence that much more.

8.

When you can't keep calm is usually when you need to most. And it wasn't easy. But I managed my best impersonation of somber reflection as I walked back from Dizzy's bungalow.

In the shed, I put the folding chair against the door. It wouldn't hold long, but it would slow someone down. I stooped over the shelf desk and wrote down all I could recall from my conversation with Dizzy. I couldn't wait for my laptop to start up. I had to get as much down as I could before I forgot. I tried to focus on the willed-departure stuff. Death was my dollar, all right, and I was hoarding as much of it as I could. Before I stopped to take a breath or scratch my head, someone knocked at the door. Three quick, impatient knocks. I folded my legal pad shut and shoved it under my backpack. Three more knocks. I pulled the chair out of the way and answered the door. It was Jack, who had never visited the shed before.

"Hey, Jack, how are you?"

"What are you doing in here?"

"Just organizing some notes I took, just working."

"Oh. You're working now?" Jack said, flaring his nostrils.

"Yeah. I'm always working."

"How'd your little chat with Dizzy go?"

"It went fine," I said as flatly as I could manage.

"What did you talk about?"

Jack was standing about a foot inside the doorway, not moving, flexing his back muscles to seem wider and standing too close.

"It was a private talk."

"You get anything good to use in your story? Any good quotes?"

"I didn't get anything. It was all off the record."

"So when's the story coming out?"

"I'm not sure. I have to talk to my boss, my editor, about that."

"Yeah? So what are you going to say about Dizzy and us, in your *story*?"

"I don't know yet. I still have to go over my notes, talk to more people, like you, and do more things like that."

"Does it really take this long for you to tell people there's a bunch of dangerous religious wackos out in the desert?"

"I beg your pardon?"

"Because that's what you're going to write."

"No. In fact, that's exactly what I'm trying to avoid do ..."

"Don't give me your horseshit. I knew guys like you in college, little goddamn dickless wonders. Couldn't get laid so you walked around acting like you're smarter than everyone. You go around commenting on what everyone else is doing, trying to make their lives as shitty as yours. I always wondered, if you're so much smarter than we are, then how come you're such a miserable little asshole? Why the fuck are you wasting your time walking around and judging the only people who will ever be happy again? I used to think guys like you were just losers. But really, you're dumbasses. The fucking dumbest."

"Sorry you feel that way. Are you done?"

"Maybe I'm just getting started."

He stepped closer. I could smell the spearmint gum on his breath. Where the hell did he get the gum? No one had gum on the ranch. The thought distracted me from the supplication I apparently owed the bully.

"Jack, come on. I don't want any trouble."

"That's right you don't. Just remember that."

Jack spat on the slab floor of my shed, smiled and walked off, daring me to close the door hard.

So that was the plan: Dizzy the good cop and Jack the bad. If I was the next suicide it wouldn't really surprise anyone, I suppose. All-access wouldn't come so easily after all. One thing worth knowing about Dizzy was that he made his wife and children sign lengthy ad punitive nondisclosure agreements before leaving them to go to the desert. I learned that from his lawyer after repeated phone calls to his family's many homes failed to land me so much as a "no comment."

Digging through my backpack, I pulled out the back story I wrote up prior to coming out here. Just a quick 650 words. It's meant to work as a cut-and-paste background for a feature piece, an obituary, or a massacre story. I needed it to remind myself that Dizzy wasn't the whole world, and to remind myself of the larger World to which I belonged. My courage needed perspective. So here's the rest of what I thought my readers should know about Dizzy.

"John Howard Sheehan first distinguished himself in the late '80s at investment bank Kennel & Canisch, where he rose through the ranks of its fixed-income division. It was at Kennel that his lazy eye and feverish energy earned him the nickname 'Dizzy.' In the early '90s, Sheehan was one of the driving forces behind the string of leveraged buyouts and hostile takeovers that catapulted Kennel to prominence. His crowning achievement came in 1997 with the mega-buyout of Gaol Industries by Sepisid International.

"After losing a succession battle to Edward R. 'Ned' Kennel III in 1999, he left the firm to 'spend more time with his family.' That's when Sheehan sat down in his sprawling Saddle River, New Jersey, home and wrote his first best-seller, *Millionaire Consciousness*. The book spurred an avalanche of imitators and made Sheehan a celebrity. He quickly became a favorite guest of Oprah's. His second book, *Billionaire Consciousness*, outsold the original. Sheehan capitalized on the book with weekend seminar retreats that drew thousands of paying acolytes.

"By 2004, Sheehan was a fixture on morning daytime talk shows. But his attempts to get his own TV show faltered, reportedly because it consisted mostly of him talking to a studio audience, as opposed to a more traditional talk-show format. But Sheehan '… would never be a mindless talk-show cipher with no talent except for nodding, condemning, clapping, and stating the obvious,' Sheehan inadvisably said in a 2007 *Variety* interview. He later claimed that the quote was taken out of context and sued *Variety,* unsuccessfully. But the damage was done. That quote was the end of his relationship with Oprah, and the beginning of the end of his career as a TV personality.

"Around this time, his seminars began to change. Attendees started complaining that Sheehan's message of leading happier, more energized, and more prosperous lives had given way to lengthy sermonizing on the development of the immortal soul, and the dangers it faced in a materialistic world.

"Sheehan did not title his next book *Trillionaire Consciousness.* And it did not do well at all. His publisher, Monocle, Oriole & Underall, reluctantly did an initial print run of 100,000 for *Beyond Millionaire Consciousness* after being threatened with a lawsuit from Sheehan, according to sources familiar with the matter. Critics blasted the long and rambling discussion of the soul that ended with thirty pages of poems, called 'meditations,' which Sheehan had written.

"In 2008, Dizzy Sheehan Enterprises folded and Sheehan gave up the lecture circuit, so that he could, as the press release again said 'spend more time with his family.' From Saddle River, he began to cultivate a group of true believers and wrote *The Final Revelation of Our Terminal Age*, in which he first claimed that all life on earth would soon be terminated. It was Sheehan's coming-out party as a new-age messianic figure.

"In 2010, he bought a disused cattle ranch in the Southern New Mexico desert and had dormitories, kitchens, bungalows, and showers built on it. He would quietly and expensively divorce his wife, leave his children, and move to the ranch, along with fifty followers. By the end of 2011, the ranch's headcount had reportedly grown to more than eighty. In early 2012, several disciples, speaking anonymously, claimed to have escaped the ranch. They told a *Los Angeles Times* reporter that Sheehan said he would kill everyone on the ranch to protect them from the evil of the world. He'd repeatedly promised the whole congregation a straight route to paradise by abruptly departing from the world, according to the former disciples.

"Sheehan issued a quick press release calling the story a 'complete fabrication.' None of the disciples had left the ranch since it was founded, the release said. And he sued the *Times.*

"To this day, Sheehan remains a canny businessman. Roughly half of the disciples comprise a formidable telemarketing army-for-hire. The income from telemarketing, along with the sales of his books, tapes, and trinkets helps support the ranch financially."

That's what I had down when I left New York for the ranch. It reminds me of why I came here: To spy. Not for the government or the military. I've come to spy for my nosy neighbors, desperate to hear about something new, if only to disapprove of it. It makes me eager to return to its matrix of simple prejudices. If I stay, I'm afraid that I'll lose even that shabby sanity.

9.

Jack gone and my notes written, I started getting my things together.

In those last free hours of captivity, I replayed Mary Beth's bob under the water. And I decided that it didn't have much to do with me, Jack, Dizzy, a loss of faith, or anything in particular.

Sometimes a streak of bad luck and bad decisions will persist mercilessly for years at a stretch. After a while, it all kind of bounces off you. It still hurts, but you don't mind it. And you become so uninvested that you don't even blink when things fall to pieces.

But the truth is you're never really immune to even the tiniest turd of it. None of it ever really goes away. It stays close and it waits, for one moment of weakness. And one cold morning, you stub your toe on a dresser and you scream and moan more than the pain is worth, and suddenly you're ready to hang yourself. Not because of the toe, but because all it takes is one crack to suck all the cabin pressure out of your heart. I think that afternoon was Mary Beth's crack.

My own crack feels closer. You can never be sure with these things, but if it does come, I want it to happen anywhere but here.

When Mary Beth went down under the surface of the lake, it felt like she was taking me with her, like she was dragging the whole World with all of us, all the great books and the good times and big highways down with her. It was her impersonation of the apocalypse.

It was convincing.

10.

Most nights, the disciples on patrol just watch the dirt road that runs from the I-10 to the ranch. There are other nights, though, when Dizzy has a bad revelation or Jack suspects that someone will try to escape. I've seen about a dozen nights like that, when all the lights stay on through the night, and Dizzy stations devotees around the fence, at the doors of the dormitory buildings, and along the road from the ranch to the Interstate.

But this was a regular night.

I counted an hour after the humping in the dorm ended and crept out. I grabbed my backpack from the shed. The grounds were so empty after curfew that I didn't even take the trouble to run. I just hugged the shadows where I could. I climbed the sandbags and jumped the fence behind the rifle range. I walked out into the desert, out of view of the ranch buildings. It was pretty easy going, all low scrub brush, sparse grass and hard dust. I kept going in the direction I figured was west.

There was no moon out, but the stars in the desert were bright enough to lay a pale blue light on everything. I kept my distance from the road, but also kept in view its telephone poles, like a succession of unoccupied crucifixes. Otherwise, it was just me, the scrub, the mountains, and the starlight. Even on a summer evening, after a hot day, it was cold at night.

Walking in the chill, I looked up at the sky for the first time in a while. The band of the Milky Way spanned the whole sky. And the stars seemed to look down at me. The stars and I were like two strange animals deciding after a startling moment to have nothing to do with each other. The moment made the whole situation seem funny—Dizzy, his apocalypse, Mary Beth, my feelings for her, and now, this mediocre escape.

Cresting a low hill, I looked back at the ranch. There were a few light bulbs burning. But no activity or commotion. Seen from the desert, it was small and a little funny. I kept my chin skyward and tried to drink in more of the comedy the sky mirrored down onto me, until I turned my ankle in a snake hole and took a tumble. I kept my eyes on the ground from then on.

And after a long limp through empty land, I turned left and I saw the 10—an old friend keeping an even older promise. That artery of the World was dark and quiet, no orange streetlights out here. I was so glad to see the bold, clean line of asphalt that I ran to it.

I was out on the 10 for about two hours before some Mexicans in an old pickup stopped and drove me to Las Cruces. Motel is the same in English as it is in Spanish.

You want something to prevent you from remembering this for a very long time, but no matter how long you stay asleep you keep coming back to this and it's as if you were never gone.

—E.J. Gold, *American Book of the Dead*

11.

Las Cruces, NM—I got to the motel just before dawn, wild-eyed, dirty, and scraped up. I fell down on the bed and got up, turned the TV on, off. I was seized with a mania that whatever I was going to do, it should be something significant, expressive, and meaningful. But I had no idea what to do with my freedom.

I wanted to watch TV. I wanted a big, greasy meal. I wanted to put the "Do Not Disturb" sign on the doorknob and sleep under clean sheets and heavy blankets for a few days. I wanted to flirt with a waitress. I wanted a drink. Alcoholism, schmalcoholism. I wanted to read a great book. I wanted to write a great book. I wanted a rail of coke. I wanted a jukebox. I wanted to stop wasting my life (whatever that means). I wanted to waste the rest of my life so I could stop worrying about.

It reminded me of something Mary Beth had said. "... this kind of thing is no good for me. I've been through it a dozen million times and it never ends well ..."

And free at last, in a land of boundless opportunity, of legendary freedom, in my brown motel room, it hadn't ever worked out well for me. And I did not know what to do about it. My excitement turned to dread—the official feeling of this kind of thing not working out so well.

So I turned on the TV and jerked off to a music video.

Calmer, I took a shower and went to sleep. I woke around eleven, only to be swept up again in a fresh wave of excitement and dread. Mo could wait. I needed to get my head straight and before I went back to work. I told myself I could take a little vacation and still have the story ready to go once the first gory dispatches started coming in from Rancho Revelation.

I took a cab downtown to the ATM. Then I got some delivery menus from the front desk and ordered in. That was all I did the first two days. I knew bad things could happen to me such a short drive from the ranch. But I can be lazy, lazy to the core. I resent the impositions of the World. The act of tying my shoes saps my will to live most days. It's all uphill—the snooze alarms, pulling on my socks, buttoning my shirts, waiting in the elevator, buckling my seatbelt.

And now laziness covers a massive raw nerve that wants to do everything, but despairs of everything that can be done. It may get me fired and it may get me killed, but laziness is the only thing that's doing me any good now. Like when they turn on the artificial gravity in a space movie, it holds me down.

Falling asleep, it calms me to think of a gun to my head, knowing a bullet's about to tear my brains to rubbish.

Two more days. I went out and rented a car. Not even a week yet and I'd had too much time alone. My dreams didn't end entirely when I woke up. I could still see Mary Beth with bright pearly eyes shrugging her shoulders and coughing up water in one of her dark little chuckles as if to say, "What did you expect, anyway?"

I drove into town and bought a three-pack of dirty magazines in a plastic sleeve. I couldn't stand the thought of the internet. There'd be a few months of e-mails and more news than I needed.

I also picked up a twelve-pack of beer, two packages of underwear, and three packages of socks. They calmed me almost as the beer. I kept the lights off in my room, ordered pizza, and tried to sneak my way back to normal under the cover of the flickering TV light. I tried not to, but I wondered about my safety. If Dizzy was willing to have Jack intimidate me, would he go much farther? When the end is nigh, it all comes out in the wash anyway, doesn't it?

But I couldn't stand the thought of making a decision. Mo kept his end of the bargain. After months of not producing a word of journalism, the paper still deposited paychecks in my account. There was a lot in there, maybe enough to hide out in a motel for a whole year.

For all my talk about winning a Pulitzer, I never really was that ambitious. Ambition was just a storyline I held on to because it let me ignore everything else. I put off the story along with everything else.

Scraped up and buzzed on light domestic beer, I listened for threats beyond the tings, clanks, and small thuds of the room's air conditioner/heater, and waited in the desert for another man's apocalypse, to make my little souvenir out of it.

12.

The guns at the sporting goods store scared me, to be honest. All I could see was myself shooting my foot off.

The guy at the store, a stoic Okie, didn't seem too alarmed or disappointed when I opted for a few big hunting knives instead. I bought four, with leather sheaths and different colored handles. They looked scary enough for me.

It was a clear desert afternoon, with wisps of cloud around the stubbled mountains. I set the car radio on some Mexican guitar music—love songs, from the sound of it—and drove around inventing errands to run.

I returned the rental and bought a used Pontiac that a Mexican guy was selling in his yard for $800. I paid cash and gave him an extra $100 to leave the plates on. Then I got some lunch at a little tacqueria and hit the local stores for more socks and underwear, probably more than I needed. But the feel of the cotton under the plastic calmed me. That's what money is for anyway—to calm you down, right?

Then I bought a new pair of shoes, new shirts and pants. I stocked up on toothpaste and shaving cream and good metal razors with expensive razor-blade cartridges. I went to the supermarket and bought beer, chips and dip, cups and plates.

People generally have good instincts about how dangerous or damaged the person across from them really is. So I watched the cashiers to see how they responded to me. An old white woman, a fat Indian girl, a mouth-breathing young man with a sunburn and pimples were the barometer I had of how badly my personality had disintegrated. Did they avoid my eyes? Were they unnerved? You always think you know how you're doing. But a second opinion is probably a good idea. Because experience has taught me that sometimes you have no idea how you're doing.

I hardly reflected at all in the cashiers' eyes. The Okie at the gun store was the only one I really spoke to. And he didn't seem to see me as anything worse than a little skittish.

My plan for the evening was to shave off the thin beard I'd grown, brush my teeth until my gums bled, and shower for at least an hour. Then I'd watch TV, swaddled in my brand new clothes, drink beer, and eat chips under the covers.

I would fall asleep and wake up as a new man. He would be clean and responsible. He would not remember his dreams or see things that aren't there. He would get started on his Pulitzer-winning article, and his generally bright future.

13.

I tried to clean up the mess, like any good murderer would.

I wiped some of his blood around the floor with my new underwear. That didn't do much of anything but spread the blood around. I made a few big ovals of the stuff on the rug. There was too much blood. And the blood was still coming out of him.

It was too much work and I wasn't really into it. So I gave up. I never signed on for a goddamn life of crime.

I changed my clothes and washed the blood off my arms and my hands and my face. I grabbed some underwear, socks, knives, my wallet, keys, and backpack. I had to jump over Jack's body to get to the door.

When you leave a corpse, a pistol, and a big hunting knife buried way up in a corpse in a motel room that's registered in your name, well, that must make a detective's day. It wouldn't take them too long to start looking for me. The door to my room wouldn't even shut right after how Jack kicked it. And, driving away, it dawned on me that I must have left some bloody shoeprints outside the door. The search wouldn't even have to wait until the maid service in the morning.

I know what you're thinking. And you're not wrong. I could have done a dozen other things right here that would have come a lot closer to doing "the right thing" than what I did. I could have called the cops. I could have made more of an effort to cover my tracks. But I just ran.

A ring of blood clung near my elbow, where I'd lost interest in washing my hands. I was shaky and just wanted some air. I hit up the little ATM at the first gas station I saw for $500, the maximum. I didn't bother to hide my face from the ATM camera when I did. Then I went west on the I-10, officially on the lam.

I got the revolution blues, I see bloody fountains
And ten million dune buggies comin' down the mountains
Well, I hear that laurel canyon is full of famous stars
But I hate them worse than lepers
And I'll kill them in their cars
—Neil Young, *Revolution Blues*

I'm never gonna know you now, but I'm gonna love you anyhow
—Elliott Smith, *Waltz #2*

14.

Interstate 10, NM, Ariz., Calif.—I didn't have the slightest clue where to hide. And my brain just wouldn't play along. I guess I can't blame it. I raised it for better things.

Dread pursued me out of Las Cruces. I bought a McMuffin I couldn't eat by an overpass in Deming, then crossed into Arizona. The long shimmering road through the desert felt like it would fall from beneath me at any moment like the trapdoor of a gallows giving way.

I obsessed fruitlessly over how many bloody fingerprints I'd left in the room. I pondered whether the act of cleaning up, no matter how half-assed, would speak to scienter at trial. Bloody handprints, shoeprints, and twenty pairs of new underwear left at the scene. I'll be lucky if they don't book me with a sex crime.

I hoped that buying the Pontiac with cash would give me a day or so. I was going to lose this game sooner or later. And I conceded as much, I just wanted to enjoy the drive. I had to get out of New Mexico and had already thoughtlessly started west. And I, the killer, didn't like my chances in Arizona. That meant

California.

And I was never crazy about California, especially Southern California. In the months I'd spent there, it seemed a place where all the scales and mechanisms that give meaning and form to success and failure, love and hate, life and death have been washed out by the sun. It promises to take whoever or whatever bothers you most mostly off your case. And it delivers on that promise. But that terrible thing that judged you was always your best and, in a way, your only real friend. But I wasn't on speaking terms with that terrible friend at that point. As a killer, the sunny void of Southern California suited me.

The sun was up behind me after an hour or two, hot and bitter. There was so much light and so little in the desert to absorb it. My eyes hungered for color and started hallucinating an aura over the landscape. I could almost hear the desert waxing nostalgic about the days before the Interstate, when it would have killed a guy like me in a day or two, no problem.

It's hard to describe nothing. But that's what was out here, barren mountains to barren dust and back again. There were occasional trucks, occasional places to eat. In the Pontiac, something hissed through the radio. Aliens changed the words to the classic rock songs. Ghosts whispered in the Mexican horns, saying worrisome things.

There's a harsher eye than yours that watches, they say. *And you didn't keep your receipts for when it comes looking for you. You were crossing your fingers for a very long time. But now the mountains will shrug their shoulders and a big murder will come down from the clouds.*

It was just a question of the mental hospital or the penitentiary at that point.

When night threatened, I parked in a big gas-station complex for truckers, and got whiskey drunk in my car under big lit signs for four-dollar dinners, three-dollar showers, and cheap gas.

Looking for a happy thought, all I came up with was Mary Beth. We got it on a few times, maybe more than a few. And she extended me the courtesy of restraining her overpowering apathy. I mostly missed talking to her. She was honest and cruel in a way that obeyed none of the conventions of self-protection. The week before she went under the waves, drunk on postcoital optimism, I made a sort of pass at her.

"You going to put me in your story?" she asked, rolling over to face me and smiling. We were on a scratchy blanket in my shed in the precarious and precious two hours of free time Dizzy allowed the disciples every day.

"I don't know. It depends. Probably. You say some funny stuff. You're what we reporters call a good quote."

"A good quote? What's that? A nice way of calling me a bad lay?"

She gave a smile, which, like her laugh, seemed to conceal as much as it revealed.

"Don't worry about that. You'll get high marks in my story for that too."

"You're not really going to write about this part, are you?" she asked, grabbing my softening dick and shaking it.

"I don't know. Probably not. Reporters are supposed to be like those guys who film nature shows. We're not supposed to get involved in the action. We're *definitely* not supposed to screw the animals."

"You're an asshole, you know that?" she chuckled, brushing her hair away from her face.

"I know. I'm just trying to get some of my objective distance back. With reporters, this kind of hot, sweaty, jungle sex can skew our perspective."

"Jungle sex?" she laughed.

"Yeah, jungle sex. I mean, I couldn't be expected to be objective if I was doing it with someone I was supposed to be covering."

"So what does this make you?"

"A bad reporter, I guess. Not that anybody is *really* objective. I'm getting paid to do this story. I have my own agenda back in the World, and so does my boss and his boss, and so on."

"So much for objectivity," Mary Beth smiled.

"Yeah. The only trick is to conceal exactly what your agenda is, to hide what you really want."

"I know all about that," she said.

I remember how she would absentmindedly chew on her index finger. I imagine her doing it then, in a distracted sort of way. You could tell she wanted a cigarette. But Camp Salvation was a non-smoking facility. She took her hand off my dick and rested it on my stomach a moment. I thought she was going to get up and get dressed again, which panicked me.

"It's funny, us meeting like this," I said, to keep her attention.

"What do you mean?"

"You and me, meeting here. Me, a reporter, and you, someone I'm reporting on, here, on the ranch and all. I mean, it's just a nice coincidence, you know?"

"I'm not sure I do."

But she knew what was coming.

"Well, we seem to get along, I mean, we have good conversations, and the sex is good, and ..."

"Oh geez. Listen, lover boy, don't go all goo goo on me now. You know I can't go steady with you, or with anyone. You know the rules."

"Yeah. I know. I just thought ..."

"I know what you thought. We have fun. Fucking in your little shack. I like talking to you, too. But I'm not about the conversation anymore. And the fucking is just to take the edge off. What I want you can't give me. I'm here to overcome the World. I'm serious. This isn't a hobby or a fad or a fucking joke, like you think it is. I want out. You can make me laugh and make me come. But you can't give me that. You can't get me out of this World."

"Jesus, Mary Beth, I'm just saying, don't you think there's another way to be happy? That maybe the World isn't such a curse?"

"I'm not going to argue with you. You have your agenda and I have mine. But I've made my decision. Hey, I like you. I do, really. But this kind of thing is no good for me, and it wouldn't be any good for you. I've been through it a million times and it never ends well. Ever. Any other time, I'd be happy to run away with you and ruin both of our lives for a while. But I just don't have it in me anymore."

"I know it's scary and I know you've been through some bad stuff. But we could *try*, I mean really fucking try to make it work. We've both fucked up a lot on our way here. But we can learn. We can change. We can do better. You just have to want to try."

I was pleading. But it didn't matter.

"Hey, I'm sorry. But I'm not like you. I don't even want to try anymore, not for that. It's not you. Just bad timing, I guess. I think you should go with other girls for a while. I'm going to go with some other guys. Let's just not do it with each other for a while. I really need to focus on my meditation. I can't afford this kind of distraction. It's hard for me. And I need ..."

"Maybe you just need to learn how to *live*, instead of trying to escape. It's really cowardly. It's cowardly and childish. I mean, I really like you. I want to leave here with you. I mean, life can get better. It's not just the crap that Dizzy says it is."

"What are you going to do, *save* me? You save me—that's a laugh. And me saving you—that's a death sentence. And all your snide journalistic bullshit aside, that's what I think you're really after here. You try not to let on, but I can tell you're not exactly a picnic either. I don't know what kind of shit you're keeping to yourself. But I can tell it's bad. Probably as bad as my sad story."

"What makes you say that? I mean, if you think that ..."

"Why bother bullshitting? How can I tell? How could I not?"

"But I don't drink anymore. I stopped, and I have a job, and ..."

"Listen, sweetie, I know you stopped. I know you can pass muster and pay your taxes. But you're not redeemed. And I can tell there's a whole horror movie playing inside you. And I want to know what it is. I really do. I've always been that kind of girl. But I can't be that anymore, I can't want that anymore. I have to go all the way with this here. I've followed too many fucked-up men to too many fucked-up places. I just can't do it again. This is my last chance."

"It doesn't have to be that way. It doesn't have to be bad. It's up to us," I argued, not convincingly.

"That's exactly the problem: It's up to us. I know enough to know that with the two of us steering the ship, it can't wind up anywhere good."

And with that, she got up, dressed, and left. It was one of those times I was glad I would have to hitchhike through thirty miles of desert to get a drink. We didn't talk again after that.

In the truck stop parking lot, I finished my bottle with a big swig and reclined my seat all the way. I was tired as hell and fell asleep quickly. The big lit signs for four-dollar dinners, three-dollar showers, and cheap gas flashed through my eyelids all night.

Yes I know: I am that asshole criminal you hear about who's just waiting to get caught. I was just waiting. I would've turned myself in, but it seemed un-American not to at least play fugitive. I'd be letting the cops down, and giving up all hope that the World holds something decent for me.

I never claimed to be John Dillinger. I'm just a screwed-up kid from the suburbs who grew up. My dad's a possible-hero/possible-suicide and my mom's a reborn Canadian who's more screwed-up than Dad, respiration notwithstanding. I went to college and got my little job writing news stories. I never planned to do much damage beyond a harsh editorial and a busted marriage or two. I don't know what I did to wind up so alone, rotted-out and goddamn lost out here. I wanted to be forgiven, but I couldn't even begin to guess who to ask about that.

The next morning I pulled another $500 from the truck stop ATM. I didn't think it'd let me. The cops or whoever should've cut off my money by now. Oh well. I had the lumberjack breakfast at the truck stop and left a big tip.

Come and get me, piggies. I'm ready to confess.

15.

Speeding past the thousand numbered, empty blocks of Phoenix, it came through on the radio: Dizzy and the rest of them finally did it. I slammed my hands on the hard plastic steering wheel, furious, thrilled and sick all at once.

Outside Phoenix I stopped and got a motel room, just so I could watch CNN and get what gory details I could: They were all dead, seventy-six of them, including the children. But details, the pretty mestizo woman from the El Paso affiliate told the camera, were still sketchy. In that first hour, the TV cycled through the same five or so basic facts a dozen times. From what I can make out of that, the cops had gone to Dizzy's ranch to see him about something. The police weren't saying why just yet. But I know. The cops went to tell him about Jack.

Exactly what happened when the cops got there, no one knows, or will know, unless Barbara Walters does interviews in hell. Maybe Dizzy thought Jack had snitched on him. Maybe he thought the police were coming to get him for my murder. It could be that the group watching the road to Camp Utopia just saw the riders of the apocalypse in the cop cars coming up the road, and started shooting.

Whatever the reason, the apostles at the gate opened up something fierce on the first police cruisers to come up the road. The first gunfight was short and decisive in the disciples' favor. The screen flashed the dull, earnest faces of the three dead desert cops. The actual police siege lasted just a few hours, during which the disciples held the perimeter, killing one more cop and wounding four others. The police sent for a negotiator, who was choppered in from El Paso.

That was all the time Dizzy needed to hold his graduation ceremony/fire drill. I guess he did what he promised: He protected the men, women, and children on the ranch from the World. By morning, when the SWAT team raided the ranch, Dizzy and the seventy-five men, women, and children who followed him were all dead by pistol or poison, and most of the buildings were well ablaze.

There goes my scoop. That was my first thought.

The next day, the story would make page one, above the fold, at least in *USA Today* and the *Arizona Republic*, and everywhere. They broke out the **BIG CAPITAL LETTERS**. Mo and I were right, it *was* a great story. Angles galore. It was everything Mo said it would be: Faith Run Amok. A Grim Step by Those Too Good to Live. God Caught in the Act!

Even in flat AP-style reporting, the story raised the terrible questions every suicide did. Questions like: *Could they have possibly been right to do what they did? Are we just kidding ourselves by keeping alive and well?* The story picked at some big, ever-itchy scabs.

But even without the scoop, I still had everything I needed to really nail the story. I had the sources, the quotes, the background that no one had. The story could run in installments for weeks, for a national audience and for the Pulitzer Prize committee.

Seventy-six dead, plus four cops and one in intensive care. Let's say he dies and call it eighty-two bodies, counting Jack. That's a book deal for sure, probably a movie deal too. I'd be asked to be on the cable TV shows as an expert for decades to come, my face right next to Vince Bugliosi. The doors were opening.

I was the only one who could write definitively about Dizzy's ranch. I was the only one there who lived to tell about it. And I was there up until the end. I actually kind of caused ...

Oh shit.

My thoughts jumped the police tape cordoning off the crime scene at the motel. My ambitious rant tapered. And I was back where I started, not knowing what the fuck to do. After a few minutes, my inner fugitive spoke up, said I could let them think I'm dead, too. Some bodies had to be lost or disfigured in the fire. And that would, at the very least, buy me some time.

It was my turn at bat. But there was nothing I wanted to do less than cross the police tape into that county of my mind. For now, I couldn't afford to let the details become less sketchy.

I left the motel after a few hours of TV and kept driving west.

*Every time you've committed suicide,
you ended up here anyway.*
—E. J. Gold, *American Book of the Dead*

*I'm an accident
I was driving way too fast
Couldn't stop though
So I let the moment last*
—Neil Young, *I'm The Ocean*

16.

Redlands, Calif.—Arizona ended as the sun began its long crash into the desert mountains. Driving through the spooky deserts of Eastern California, a fingernail of moon rose after a few hours. At Palm Springs I finally gave a thought as to where the hell I was headed. Los Angeles was at the end of the road. I knew I wasn't ready for that. And I'd had enough desert.

At dawn, I crossed over some mountains, and thick smog filled the fruited valley below. It made the scenery a bright nothing. I pulled off the I-10 in a town called Redlands and drove around. It looked like a nice enough, sleepy little town—orange groves where the desert turns to suburbs. The radio said the towns here are called the Inland Empire.

The Good Nite Inn by the Interstate did weekly rates. It was clean enough for me and dirty enough that they didn't seem to pay attention to people's comings and goings. I was so tired that I paid a week up front.

The first week of hiding was a good one. Redlands wasn't so big that anyone would think to look for me there, but not so small that I would stick out. It was shielded from the world's interest by the larger and more frightening obscurity of poor San Bernardino to the west, the golfing banality of Palm Springs to the east, and by the empty deserts and orange groves on the other sides.

I could see the I-10 from the porch-walkway in front of my room. It was a talisman and an escape route all in one. It calmed me.

My first empty days in Redlands were busy. Pushing Dizzy and Jack and Mary Beth and all my dear, dead friends farther under the dirt was hard work. I went shopping at a dying mall downtown. I stocked up beyond reason on socks and underwear, new clothes and snacks. I even bought pajamas.

I blew around $200 in the pharmacy. I don't really get headaches, diarrhea, motion sickness, sinus blockage, nail fungus, constipation, or dry, flaky skin. But I couldn't help myself. Each new purchase calmed me down a little more. And I figured they would save me a trip out of my room if those ever did become my problems.

There's the breadcrumb trail, the ATM withdrawals and the motel room in my name. But the cops have left me alone here so far. I can just imagine Mo yelling at the Feds to sort through the corpses to find out if I was among the dead, demanding they dig through the burning rubble for my notes and fax them over before he called the ACLU.

17.

The cops weren't the only danger, though.

Leave a lapsed alcoholic alone with no obligations, no one to talk to, and a bank account full of money and you get what comes next. I know I'm not supposed to drink. But I'm also not supposed to kill people.

It was my first binge since New York, three years ago, when I swung from bar to bar like Tarzan. Or at least I smelled like him. Neither puke nor the threats of strangers nor the disappointment of whoever was dumb enough to care about me nor the disdain of my colleagues could dissuade me. I was 86'd from as just many bars as endured me. By the end, I slept on a pile of blankets and cardboard I'd lugged back to my apartment—one more reason not to go home at night. I would wake shaky and worthless, but still angry and thirsty.

And drinking in New York, you will likely run out of money.

I made rent, but missed gas and electric. I ate hot dogs and eggs a lot. Pasta, beans. I made it to work, but not well. I'd been drinking hard and getting my stories in for a few years by then. But this was another sort of drinking. My boss, my colleagues, the janitorial staff all knew what I was up to. My stained clothes, yellow and bloodshot eyes, sweet rotten breath, sudden mood shifts, and increasing incompetence gave me away. I should have been fired and left to my sidewalk-and-malt-liquor fate.

But the newspaper that employs me is part of a big corporation. Its reporters are in a union. And alcoholism is a disease nowadays, not the moral and personal failure that it had so long been regarded. So I had a disability. And I had it most nights. Anyway, it's awfully gauche to fire someone for a disability. You can even get sued for it. So in my case, Lady Justice dropped her sword, shield, and scales, and just shrugged.

Mo took me out of the newsroom one afternoon. I remember him shaking his head in impatience or disappointment, brandishing his ability to hold eye contact like the weapon that it was. He'd had enough of my shit and it was time for me to get some help, he said. He passed me over to Human Resources, and they sent me off to a beach resort for dipsomaniacs in Eastern Long Island. It was either that or be fired.

In my own defense, I would like to put forth the notion that, for certain people and in certain times, self-control is a luxury, not a virtue. And I have never been rich enough to afford it consistently.

On Long Island, once the DTs subsided, I enjoyed the beach a little. And for whatever reason, it worked. I've been a club-soda-with-lime guy ever since. I don't think I was cured. I don't really know what happened and I don't ask why. Introspection makes me want to drink.

I was doing all right for a while. But there were those beers in Las Cruces. And in Redlands, the dam broke.

A lot of things happened in those first weeks in Redlands. None of them will get me elected mayor. There was the squalor, vomit, and shaking, waste misplaced, lost evenings, mornings, afternoons. Beyond that I have two kinds of memories: vivid ones and vague ones. The latter I think really happened. The former I suspect didn't.

Let me show you what I mean.

Vivid: One night, the people from the ranch visited my bedside. It began with flecks and splotches of light moving around my room. Most of the strange stuff starts this way.

Then Dizzy, Mary Beth, the men I never befriended, the unwashed children, Jack, the always-available women with meaningless smiles, all came to my bedside in the motel. I couldn't find the remote and I couldn't move, so the busy blue television light danced behind them. They looked sane and sad, well-scrubbed and dressed in dark, formal clothes. They each took their turn by my motel bed. Some crossed themselves as they moved on. Some of the women gave me flowers. Then they went to the other end of the motel room by the window and talked quietly.

The men in the crowd were uncomfortable. They kept taking their hands out of their pants pockets and then putting them back in. The women held their wine glasses in front of themselves, with two hands, and hardly drank at all.

On the other hand, the things I remember hazily seem more plausible.

Vague: Driving away from an accident in the parking lot of the Stater Brothers Supermarket one morning. It was early. Kids were on their way to school.

I'd been drinking through the night and wanted more. I was one of the supermarket's first customers, a zombie lost in the cereal aisle, carrying big bottles with handles on them to the cash register.

Backing up, I hit a parked car. The impact of the crash whipped my head back and yanked me up to sobriety so fast I nearly got the bends. The impact rocked the wobbly edifice of my life, built as it was on broken promises, recidivist alcoholism, and one dark and shining murder. My face curled into a hot screaming ball and I took some quick, desperate breaths to keep from breaking down completely. I peeled out of the parking lot, knocking into an empty shopping cart.

Tears blurred my drunken, desperate vision as I took slow, wide turns on the empty streets of morning.

Also Vague: The Flamingo, a cheap and dirty bar in town—a place to hide within a place to hide. There were women there, pretty but flawed, ugly but compelling, at least to a drunk. Women whose best virtue is their proximity. I remember fleeing or being smacked to the ground by wrathful boyfriends who muscled their way into my unpersuasive blur.

And I remember succeeding in hot, breathless humping one night. That was actually the worst thing that could happen. Moonfaced and pretty as she slept, the nameless woman terrified me. She seemed impossibly young and innocent to me. She probably wasn't spiritually destroyed by having to tie her shoes every morning. But who knows? I certainly couldn't recall what truths or lies I may have told her.

I left without waking her. I ran. Like many in my situation, I took to muttering. My parting mutter for the girl I left in her apartment that morning went a little something like this:

"Lady, I'm not even allowed to look behind the curtain. And it's *my* soul in there, being worked on by the aliens and the hungry ghosts. And I don't really know if it's surgery or revenge that they're up to."

My attempts to lustily regain the outer rings of normalcy were dispiritingly thwarted. I guess that's what you get for acting like you belong.

Vague: A lot at the Flamingo, actually. I remember puking into my beer and drinking it and getting thrown out for that. I remember sleeping next to my car in the parking lot after the bartender took my car keys. I remember running behind the bar while the bartender took a cigarette break, grabbing the first bottle I could and pouring it into my mouth. Fucking banana liqueur. They made me pay for it, but that was all. I have to hand it to the Flamingo. I may have spent a lot of money there, but they were still a pretty forgiving bunch.

Vivid: A beach town, like Cape Cod or Montauk. Mostly boring episodes about painting my summer house, driving to the beach, renting a video, cooking dinner for friends, going out to eat with people who seem familiar, but who I can't quite identify. It was a very clear dream or fantasy, clearer than Redlands at that point.

One night, cracking open the seal on a plastic handle of supermarket vodka and absentmindedly regarding the strip of parking-lot light that broke through the curtains of my room, a familiar voice spoke from the darkness.

"You only dream of that beach town every night because you can't face what they're doing with you while you sleep."

I opened my eyes. At least I think I did, and I saw the face of an alien, right up against mine, winning a blinking contest with me by about a million to none. It seemed to last forever. And when I could move again, I walked a few laps around my room with all the lights on.

Vague: Telling a bartender at the Flamingo that I'd killed a man. To his credit and my benefit, he mostly ignored me. We all have to cope.

But I wouldn't shut up. I told him everything except who it was I killed and why he was breaking into my hotel room with a gun in the first place. *One stab, one shove*, I kept saying, *right up in the guts*.

I made sure the bartender knew that *He kept pushing his way into the room, and into the knife. He kept pushing into the room and I kept shoving the knife up into him. I was so afraid to pull it out, so afraid of what he would do to me. The knife and then my hand and wrist pushed up into the guy's body. Like all the way up. It was warm and juicy like a vagina in there, more than any pussy I ever had*, I told him. My educated guess is that I wasn't afraid to let the whole bar in on this.

The bartender told me to finish my drink and leave. Then he walked away to talk to some other patrons, probably ones who weren't loudly confessing murder. But I kept on. *The blood poured out and I pushed the knife farther up. And this guy played college ball at Michigan State! He was a fucking strong safety, a tough guy*, I remember boasting.

Now I had gone from being a crazy liar, straight through being disturbing, to something even worse. *When he finally started to fall down, still toward me, I almost lifted him off the ground*, I said, *from the inside.*

The bartender took my drink away and told me to get out. But he was a little afraid now. You can always tell. So I kept on talking, even louder, making the bar flies and respectable regulars uncomfortable. *And this murdering bastard kept pushing into me. I could feel his lousy heart shudder and stop and then he pissed himself and dropped the gun*, I announced. *And it didn't even feel that bad. It felt like cooking dinner or painting a house*, I said. *I could do it again—easy—for no reason at all*, I let them know.

The bartender said he was going to call the cops. So I left, bowing to the mostly disinterested crowd on my way out.

I woke the next day with the feeling that I had done something worse than simply drink myself through humiliation to the edge of brain damage. Only when I was driving over to the Flamingo the next night did I remember what it was I had said. I turned around and went to the supermarket instead. Albertsons this time, not Stater Brothers.

The worst part is that I don't even remember which bartender I'd confessed to. So much for the Flamingo.

After that night, I started waiting a few hours to really start drinking, trying to spend two or three of what I call "healthy hours" walking around town. And parts of downtown Redlands are gorgeous, especially the library, the Victorian houses downtown, and the outdoor theater. Then there are parts that look like the towns built just to see how towns would hold up if they were hit by a nuclear bomb. Spare and hurried, cinderblocks and stucco, like they'd been built for a blind community.

The desert is close, and I can feel how it despises us, as impotently as God seems to. It mocks the town, dropping dust on its palm fronds and sprinkler heads. The hot days and cold nights take no aspect of human comfort into account. Even the orange trees need heaters.

In my healthy hours, I look into the yellow smoggy distance, and get a bitter taste way down inside me. The land seems to say, "You can have your town for now, if you really want it that bad. But someday, you are going to have to take it all down, your Interstate 10 and everything."

And I can't think of a better place to hide out.

18.

Sobering up the last two weeks. Not sure why I couldn't ride the bottle all the way out of this situation. One morning after a few healthy hours that felt anything but healthy, I crept back into the Flamingo. I ordered a beer, but I couldn't choke it down.

So much for that solution.

With nothing to alleviate the evenings, mollify the mornings, or obviate the afternoons, I tried to mimic the rhythms of normalcy at the Redlands Family Restaurant. But I still wasn't ready to call Mo. I wasn't even ready to start watching the news again. I went around not knowing who we were at war with or who was famous.

I drove a lot, as a way to almost think about things. Gas was up over five dollars a gallon, but still cheaper than whiskey.

I'd almost think about what the alien said while the DTs were shaking me nearly blind the day before. Tall, thin, and beige, with big black eyes, it seemed like it was just killing time. We had a long conversation over a cold Domino's pizza. I offered him some.

"Maybe in my dreams. But if I ate that, it would probably kill me," the alien said.

"Really? Just one slice?"

"The smell is more than enough for me. Bad stomach," it said, nodding down to itself. "You should see the shit we have to eat."

"I thought you guys lived on photosynthesis and osmosis and whatnot," I said.

"Don't believe everything you hear."

"It's funny to hear that from you."

"I'll bet."

We chatted for a while. Then it started telling me about the universe. It spoke without words, but every word it said relieved me. Its whole sad story just made me so damn happy, even if it was the bad happy—half-hysterical and out of control. Blinking its big eyes but not its little mouth, it told me about the broken, blind planets, the hungry, fading suns, and the limitless reservoir of failure that awaited the rare planet to emerge from the boundless unthinking oblivion. It said life and hope are outnumbered about a trillion to one. All the great efforts at sustaining wakefulness will fail, at least from what it had seen. Physics, chemistry, and biology are all working against us, it said. And they're not the only enemies.

It was very friendly about the whole thing. And at least it wasn't trying to pin the whole mess on me.

Every shred of comfort, every habit that ever made the pain go away for a moment—will rise against us the moment we admit what we are really after, it told me. And if that wasn't enough, even *we* are not entirely on our own side, it said. I bit into a slice of cold pizza and wiped the sauce off my mouth with the bed sheets. Then it asked me some questions that were, surprisingly, not rhetorical.

Should we keep searching even if we keep finding the same disappointments all over the universe? I guess so, if you're able. You have to do something.

Are we helping you? Not really. I think I'm losing my mind. And that's a little frightening. You make me want to go back to my job and get married and keep busy until my world doesn't include things like you. If that's the idea, then I guess you're helping.

Do you believe that we are real? No offense, but no. Between getting sober and my murder rap, I just can't be having aliens over for lunch.

This world—do you like it? That was the hardest question of all. I hemmed and hawed. I left a pile of unfinished sentences hanging in the air. Then I asked it to ask me another question. Its little mouth frowned in a way I could almost sympathize with— like I was confirming its worst suspicions.

It had more questions and more sad insights into the universe beyond the blue yonder. But you get the idea. It was a sad and likable companion for the afternoon, though.

The way I figured it, if the aliens and the late-onset schizophrenic whispers were on my case, at least it wasn't the cops. They grabbed the guy in the room next to me yesterday. It was drugs, I think.

The woman at the front desk apologized to me for the ruckus when I went to pay that week's rent. Her apology threw me for a loop even more than the aliens, probably more than it should have.

Sometimes I'd drive as far west as Covena, so I won't think of what comes next. Drive out to another nowhere to hide a while longer? Call Mo? The paychecks kept going into my account, so at least Accounting believed I was alive. My livelihood was, after all, a rounding error of a rounding error (of a rounding error) to the parent company. But I still couldn't think in headlines—

Rabid Rummy Reporter on the Run Pizza for the Killer Newsman

Cult Killer in Drink-Binge Disgrace

Messy End for Stab-Crazy Journo

—at least none that would work. And, crappy fugitive I am, I kept forgetting the most important reason I couldn't simply waltz back to my cubicle: I was still on the lam, at least I thought I was. Who could I even ask about this? The ambiguities of my situation were immense.

I felt like the remora swimming under a shark's belly—I know it's hungry and I know it's able to eat me. So why doesn't it? It knows I'm here, right under its mouth. Is it some private joke that's keeping me alive?

Sometimes I'd drive south to the desert and the cattle ranches, the hilly, empty roads through towns like Elsinore, so I won't think of Long Island and my parents.

Dad's funeral was about as bad as it could be. No one knew what to say. That's largely because no one knew what he did, or why he did it. The details never got any less sketchy. He was buying his tax-free, discount cigarettes on an Indian reservation out on the island. And there was a robbery. That's when my father, a shy post office lifer who deferred to my mother, or whoever else was nearby, in all things, intervened. He raised his voice and raised his hand to a skittish teenager with a gun. The kid shot him in the side, panicked, and ran. My father insisted he was okay, got into his car, drove home, and died. This was three months after Mom left.

Mom got me alone afterward and wanted to talk to me. She had showed up to the funeral with her Canadian. I can't blame Mom for leaving after almost thirty years of his stoic, deadening presence. But the last thing I really wanted to hear at that point was her covering her own ass after whatever it was that Dad did. Still, she kept after me until I grabbed her and said I'd hit her if she didn't leave me alone. It was a big dramatic moment. Eugene O'Neill or one of those other miserable bastards would have been jealous.

I told her she should just pay her end of the funeral and get her ass back to Canada. She pulled out the heavy weeping, saying her life was a mess, that the Canadian doesn't understand, and now her own son hates her. I just walked away.

Sometimes I'd just drift from freeway to freeway, taking the ones that appeal to me and drive around a town with a good name, like Fontana, Ojai, or Azusa. On the summer nights, the kids rode bikes or skateboards, teenagers waited by a convenience store for something to happen. But most people seemed to stay very still in their blue-flashing living rooms, looking for something or hiding from something. And maybe they were right to do so.

I've seen desperate women and men forsake their own lives and worship with full hearts the every careless and deadly utterance of a fat millionaire. And I've seen the traffic run to the store and back, to work and back, gathering up money and entertainment and supplies to fill the void called home. And all I've learned is that it really doesn't matter if the flame the moth chases is real.

At rush hour, the highways filled with cars and the radio with advertisements, telling a single story: They gave us everything we could want, just to show how badly that would turn out. And we would discard this entire world that we have made for something that would pierce our cynicism and make us human again.

Or maybe that's just me.

And when I got back to my own void called home at the Good Nite Inn, with its blue-flashing screen and its orange strip of light coming through the curtains, catastrophe was the only thing that calmed me.

The sober days blended. On the highways, beauty became ugliness and ugliness returned to beauty. In the towns, money became everything, and everything became money again. There may not be a heaven and there may not be a hell. But there is a limbo. I walked into it every damn day.

On one of my drives out in the desert to the north, on some empty road out by Hesperia, I started seeing splotches and flecks of light swirling around the car. Before the strangeness got too thick, I tried to pull over. But it was no dice.

One alien rode shotgun, another in the back seat. They seemed sad as always, and not as friendly as before.

"Hey guys. It's nice to see you and everything. But like I said, I'm trying to find my seat back in reality. And you're really not helping," I said.

"Reality. This thing you call reality is just six billion completely insane people fucking each other with differing degrees of consent. And you really want back in?" asked the one beside me.

"They're not all crazy."

"Look at the men in charge—they're all wearing ties. But not a single one of them knows why," the one in the back said.

"You remind me of my editor. Where are we going?"

"Same place you were headed."

They said a lot, but I forgot more this time. They asked me about Dizzy and Mo, but I forget what I said about them. All I remember is the end of the conversation.

"You warriors of selfishness, where will you go when the real war begins?" the alien riding shotgun asked me.

When I was regained control of my Pontiac, I steered it into the In-N-Out Burger and ate until my psychosis succumbed to drowsiness.

19.

A new guy, actually named Guy, moved into the room the cops raided a few weeks back.

He hauled duffel bags, a guitar, and a trunk up to the room. Most people tend to leave heavy stuff in the car when they go to a motel for the night. Must be a weekly resident, like me. He's unshaven, with a lot of tattoos on his arms, getting on to a paunchy thirty.

I guess sobriety has made a nosy neighbor out of me.

Yesterday I said hello, like any normal neighbor whose senses haven't been amplified beyond the bearable frequencies by weeks of drinkless solitude.

Most guys I've met named Guy pronounce it so it sounds like "Gee," with a hard *G*. I think it's supposed to be French. But he said it like you would say an ordinary guy. Way to go, America.

The next night, I was watching TV and eating crackers in bed when Guy knocked. It was around eight. My grand plan was to sleep as long as I could. Guy invited me out for a beer. And I said yeah before he finished asking.

I deliberately didn't mention the Flamingo, and so we went to a dippy British-themed place by the mall called the Royal Falconer. It felt good to talk to someone I was mostly sure existed for a change. After a few rounds, we walked around the mostly shuttered downtown a little, then picked up a couple cases of beer from the supermarket.

We put our motel chairs out on the balcony and drank the beer, smoked his cigarettes, ate his Pringles. He had those goddamn Pringles cans all over his room. We talked and just stared off over the motel parking lot and the 10. The desert night was cool. It was good to be outside, not going anywhere.

Though I was excited to talk, I left out the aliens, ghosts, Dizzy, and the murder, and made do with what scraps I could contribute. Thankfully, Guy took over a lot of the conversation. The truth can usually wait.

"Man, this town is dead," Guy said. "If that Falconer place is the best we can find, this is going to be a long few weeks."

"You ever been here before?"

"No, just passed through. I'm only in town a little while, meeting people for business and stuff."

The way he said it indicated he'd consider it a courtesy if I didn't inquire further. I obliged.

"Yeah. It's pretty dead. There's a farmers' market on Thursdays and the library's nice. Not much else to speak of, though."

"Fuckin' great—a town with a nice library. Don't get me wrong, I like to read a good book, when I can. It's just, if the library's the highlight … I dunno, that kind of sucks."

"I hear you," I said lamely, feeling bad for betraying the library, just for a little company.

I got a look at the tattoos on his arms and shoulders while we talked. There were pistols, dragons, religious symbols, a skull, a woman's weeping face, a pair of carp, the word PEACE embroidered with barbed wire, and two women's names next to each other. Some of them were the blurry amateur jobs, done with India ink and a sewing needle just to kill the time. Others were professional, full of color and detail.

"So what brings you out here?" he asked me.

"Uh, I'm a professor. This is my sabbatical. I get a year off of teaching classes every seven years to do some independent research."

The lie came out smoothly enough.

"Fuckuva place to do your research. Wasn't there anything interesting to research in Hawaii?"

"I wish. But I'm actually researching Western suburban backwaters like this town, to chart how these places develop, how they survive, how people wind up here, what they do for a living, how long they stay, things like that. It's modern anthropology."

Not bad. I was even prepared to make up a methodology and a thesis. I'd been quietly preparing for a life of interrogation before I left Las Cruces. Guy either wasn't interested, or he could tell I was lying and didn't want to push me.

"Oh. That's cool. I mean, it sounds like a good job, going around and researching. As far as teaching goes, I don't know if I could handle it, with all those girls like nineteen, twenty. Do they have rules about that?"

"Yeah. Some professors still do it. But they have to be discreet. There aren't strict rules. But if it gets out of hand, you can get fired pretty easily. It's tricky."

"I was never much into school myself. I like to read, but I stopped school after high school."

"So how did you wind up in the line of work you're in?" I asked, just to get the focus off my bogus life story.

"I was working the ports in East Bay. Then the Feds turned the whole container-shipping business into a police state, so I couldn't get work on as many docks as before because of my record. Then I drove trucks in LA and up in Fresno. In Fresno, I hooked up with one of the guys I knew from the East Bay. I started working for him, shipping antiques and collectibles all over the West Coast."

"That's your business?"

"It is for now. It's fun, but it's real feast-or-famine type of work. And I'm getting older. I have obligations, an ex-wife and two little girls, Natalie and Chloe, to support."

"They up in Fresno?"

"Nah, she moved back to her parents' in Vermont and took the girls with her. That really sucked. How about you?"

"How about me what?"

"You have any kids?"

"No. I'm not really a family type."

"I used to think that, too. But you should have kids. It changes you. Parts of yourself you didn't even know were there, feelings and stuff, you suddenly have. There's nothing I care about in the world more than those two girls. I'd do fucking anything for them. Once I get some things straightened out on this end, and get some money together, I'm going out to Vermont. I'd even get back together with my ex to do it."

"How long have you two been separated for?"

"About two years now. I met her, I guess, five years ago when I was in LA. She was a hot little hippie chick back then. We had some fun. But things got complicated. Some bad shit happened, you know how it is. Anyway, one night, we're fighting and the cunt called the cops. Truth be told, I *may* have gotten out of hand. I don't really know. But she starts telling the cops, just lying about all sorts of things. Bitch almost got me sent back to jail. The next day she sobered up and didn't press charges, thank God. But that was it. I called my PO and said I was going up to Fresno. I gave her half of all the money I had— two thousand dollars—and I just trucked it up to Fresno. Not that she was happy with two Gs."

"Jeez."

"Jeez is right. I'll get it together and take care of those kids, though. I swear. I'm thinking that after this I'll try and go into construction. I have an uncle who's big into that in Phoenix. That's where I'm from. He says he has a job for me whenever I want it." He looked at his beer and off into the distance.

"So how long are you in Redlands for?" I inquired.

"Shit, a week, maybe two. Hopefully not too much longer

than that. My boss up in Fresno is setting up the meetings from there and then he's coming down to help negotiate on some of them. How about you?"

"I'm not sure. It all depends on how the research goes. I still have to do a lot of reading through the stuff I've compiled, then analysis and so on. I was thinking of maybe moving on to Oxnard after this. You ever been there?"

"Maybe to stop for gas. That's all though. I used to drive an art truck through it on the PCH."

"What's an art truck?"

"It's just a truck with art in it. Before I met my boss now, I had a job driving art, like paintings and statues and stuff, up from LA to people's houses in Santa Barbara and Montecito. They prefer that you use small trucks for art. That's fine by me because you don't need a big-truck license to drive them, plus you get to charge for more trips. I would drive their art in these little trucks from their huge houses in LA to their other huge houses."

"Sounds like an okay job."

"It wasn't, really. Insurance company made more money than the driver on most of the drives. I mean, it paid okay, but I was in a bad place. One time, I got to drive a bunch of Picassos. My boss said they were famous paintings, worth millions. That was sort of cool, I guess. But by then it was too much time on the road, too much time to miss people and regret things. You get crazy. You spend all that time on the PCH, watching the waves crash, with millions worth of art in the back, and you start thinking that one turn of the wheel will get you in the newspaper."

"I hear you. I've been doing a lot of driving lately. Too much. It calmed me down at first. But it's starting to drive me a little batty."

"Is that part of your research, driving around?"

"Yeah. That's part of it."

We called it quits around three, more happy than drunk. We were at least partially relieved of our burdens, even if neither of us got around to saying what we were really doing as semipermanent residents of the Redlands Good Nite Inn in this year of our Lord 2012.

It was my first good night since Mary Beth went under the pontoon boat.

20.

As a hard-bitten murderer, negligent fugitive, and a motel hermit, it was damn nice to have a friend. There were about three good weeks when Guy and I were on the same page; sleeping in, keeping a low profile, and killing time. Some nights, we'd hit what there is of the town. Thursdays would be tri-tip tacos at the farmers' market, and more drinks at the Royal Falconer by the mall. Other nights, it was just drinking beer on the motel's balcony/walkway and telling each other whitewashed stories.

He wanted to go to the Flamingo the one night, but I told him I was blind drunk one night and ran out on a big bar tab there. I said I'd get arrested if I went in.

Some nights we'd drive to San Manuel, a big Indian casino out past Highland that services most of the San Bernardino-area gaming public. I didn't need another burden on my nerves, so I just played the poker slots or a few $5 blackjack hands. I didn't win much, but I didn't lose much either.

Guy was big into craps. He won a lot the first night—more than a thousand bucks. We left the casino around 3:00 a.m., flushed and excited. He was going to buy us a big dinner, he said. So we drove around San Bernardino looking for somewhere to eat. This was the beginning, Guy said. Things would start turning around. With that money, he'd get ahead of his child support payments. Then he'd finish up his deal here in style, and then go work construction for his uncle in Phoenix, like he should have done a long time ago. *No more dangerous bullshit, it's over after this*, he said, more to himself than to me. *This is the night it all turns around.*

There wasn't much doing in San Berdu at three a.m. Nothing was open but a few burrito places, an International House of

Pancakes, and Denny's. We went to Denny's and did it up as big as we could—dinner with appetizers. I drank a lot of Sprite. Guy got the quesadillas and the chicken-fried steak. I went for the mozzarella sticks and a bacon cheeseburger. Guy paid and tipped the waitress a ten dollar bill. It was the only high-roller thing he could do. There was no booze to be had at Denny's or anywhere at that hour. So we picked up a couple six-packs at an all-night CVS.

Guy was clearly deflated at having all that money and nowhere to spend it. Our disappointment congealed with the greasy food on the drive back to the Good Nite Inn. We didn't even finish the six-packs. That was the night that winning lost the pennant.

We went back to San Manuel a few days later. That time, we were there for a long time. Guy lost the money he won last time. I came out about $20 richer on the poker slots. So I bought dinner at the IHOP.

On the ride back out to San Manuel two nights later, Guy was quiet and pissed off. We parted at the door and stayed apart for a long time. I dropped $40 at the blackjack table, then lingered on the quarter slots, where I won a few bucks, waiting more than playing. The casino had lost its charm. After I don't know how long, Guy finally tapped me on the shoulder and gestured with his chin that we should go. He was silent and inconsolable in the car. I don't know how much he lost exactly. But it was a lot. I bought us some dinner at Denny's, and he threw it up in the bathroom.

Then he told me the story of how he lost his money. But all gambling stories are pretty much the same to me. The drama doesn't translate to me. I could give a shit about some drama involving a hard four and playing the field. Anyway, the point of his story was simple: He lost his money. And so he couldn't afford to go out anymore. He wouldn't make this month's child support. My poor friend had fucked himself.

From then on, we kept a lower profile, staying up late, drinking and talking on the balcony or in one of our rooms until dawn broke over the bearded palms and the I-10. Drinks were on me.

Sometimes Guy would break out his guitar and we'd screw around, making up songs. We'd talk about moving out to Oxnard and starting a band and only playing our songs in crappy little towns until we get really good. We both knew it was a lie. But we didn't care. It beat telling the truth.

I didn't mind buying the drinks. Having a friend made me a little more human. And we all need help on that one. And despite the drinking, the madness where the aliens and dead friends beckon receded.

21.

It was about two months since I killed Jack when my run in Redlands began to end. That afternoon, Guy came by for a beer. He was jumpy, and a little scared. I offered a beer and suggested we sit out on the walkway. But he said no, and pulled up a chair.

"You know, you know people and you think you can trust them and talk to them. You think you're on the same wavelength and that both of you will try and do what you think is right. You think you can depend on them, you know, trust them not to dick you over. I mean, they're supposed to be your *friends*, right? And then they just *flake* the fuck out. They get on some paranoid trip and just flake and leave you completely fucked, just flapping-in-the-breeze fucked. I'm done with people altogether. Really. No offense."

"None taken. Something happen?" I asked.

"My buddy, Buddy. That's actually his name. Well, it's what he goes by, you know?"

"Got it."

"So he's also my boss that I was telling you about, up in Fresno. Anyway, Buddy was supposed to meet me down here and introduce me to some people he knows out in Yucaipa and San Berdu. That was like two weeks ago he was supposed to be down here. These are these people that I need to meet for me, for me and Buddy, to get our business done. That's all I want—to get this done. So after four weeks, Buddy's still up in fucking

Fresno, fucking around. I mean, he's a good guy. And he said it might be a while before we could get this one together. But four weeks? I'm running out of money and I need to get this thing *done*. So I called him to see what's up. If he can't come down, he can find another way to make the introduction, or at least front me some money until he does, you know?"

"Yeah, like business expenses," I said.

"Right, exactly. But not *exactly* exactly. All right, I'm going to tell you something, but you have to keep it to yourself, okay?"

"No problem. I don't talk to anyone out here."

"Okay. You swear?'

"Yeah, I swear."

"Okay. I told you I did shipping for antiques and collectibles, and I do. Or I did. But I also move some other stuff that's not always legal."

"Like what?"

"Some drugs, some weapons, some stolen goods, some stuff they don't even tell me what it is."

"Okay. It's no big deal. I kind of figured as much."

"Yeah, I thought you did. And I appreciate you not prying. I'm not going to pry either. But let's stick to the subject for now, which is how I am fucked and how fucked I am."

"Go ahead."

"So Buddy calls me today and says he's been seeing a lot of helicopters and having to slip a lot of tails lately. Who fucking knows, right? Maybe he is. But he sounds real tense, not normal tense. Kind of screechy. And he says he can't come down for maybe another month. And that's a long fucking time. But I don't know what kind of shit he's running into up there. So then he lets it slip that he's been smoking meth all week and is higher than God's own shit. So I say, 'Hey Buddy, maybe the fact that you're all spun up is why you think the 5-0 is following you everywhere, you know?' I mean, it's not the wildest thing you've ever heard—that stuff makes people paranoid. But Buddy's not hearing it. He just goes nuts, saying he sure as shit can hold his shit, screaming it into the phone. Then he starts making all these crazy accusations, saying I just want him to get busted, that I'm just trying to get him to incriminate himself on a recorded line. Then he starts saying he's someone else, some weird name, Bob Muzzy, so they can't use the call in court, he says. I mean he's talking ten miles a minute, just crazy. So I say, 'Buddy, just take it easy, I'm your friend, you know. But you have to listen, I'm broke. And you have to send me some money if you want me to stay down here much longer, especially since I'm just sitting on so much shit.'

"So he starts going on about how *that's* my game, saying I'm going to blackmail him. And then he says he has ways to make sure I keep my mouth shut. I say, 'Buddy, it's not that at all, it's just that I've been here four damn weeks and I have no money.' I don't tell him about craps or the casino. I just say I won't be able to pay the hotel bill, and if I run out on it, the cops are going to get interested and *I'll* get fucked with all of *his* shit that I'm sitting on. And then I say again that I'm his friend and I'm doing him a *favor* by taking all this stuff down here and that sending some money is the *least* he can fucking do. But he's not hearing it.

"So I say, 'If you leave me out here high and dry like this, sitting on *all* this shit, then I will fucking get rid of all the stuff any way I can and skip town and I will not forget how you screwed me.' So he goes even crazier. And he's *screaming* into the phone now, like at the top of his lungs, that I broke *his* heart, that I was a brother to him until now. Then he starts sobbing. That's what it sounded like, anyway. Just crazy shit. He's whispering he's gonna kill me and take out my organs and do voodoo rituals so I'll go to hell and that he's going to find my lady and my kids and do the same to them. So I say, 'Listen, Buddy, you're higher than fuck right now and that's fine, it's cool, it really is, but don't say things like that. Really, don't.' I say, 'You don't know what you're saying. Get some sleep and we can talk this over calmly, like adults, like friends, tomorrow.' And he just tells me I'm not his friend and to go fuck myself and hangs up the phone."

"Jesus. Does he get like that a lot?" I asked, looking for a reason to be calm.

"Sometimes when he's all spun out he gets that way. But never that bad. I never heard him as crazy as that."

"So what's he going to do?"

"I don't know. Hopefully he'll come down, get some sleep and forget the call. He'll remember we're friends, and that we have a good business together."

"Are you scared of him?"

"Yeah. Hell yeah. I don't need him for an enemy. I'm an easy enough mark here as it is. And I've seen him do terrible things. I mean, I've *seen* it. I was in the room when he did them."

"Like what kinds of things?"

"Really bad things."

"What? Mixing paper and plastic in the recycling bin?"

"You think you're funny. But I'm talking killing, torture, stuff like that. Just horrible stuff. the kind of stuff just thinking about it makes me wish I'd never left Arizona. I mean, I never really bought into religion. But during some of these things, it felt like something bad was happening to my soul just by being in the room and not stopping him. But when you see a guy tortured to death or just killed while he's crying and begging for his life, you mostly just think 'better him than me.'"

"Jesus. So do you think he'll come after you?"

"I guess I don't know, really. Depends on how long he stays high and pissed like that."

"He knows where you are, even the motel you're at?"

"Yeah, he recommended this place," Guy said.

"What are you going to do?"

"I'm not sure. Maybe I'll give it a day or two to see if he comes to his senses. He has my cell number. I'll see if he calls."

"But you think he might come down here, come after you?"

"Sure. He would do it to keep me quiet and to get his stuff back. But really, he doesn't even have to come down here if he wants to fuck me up."

"You mean he could call his friends?"

"Yeah. There's that. Or he could call the cops. Wouldn't be too hard to drop a dime on me right now, holding all this shit.

That would fuck me up probably bad as his scraggly ass friends."

"Why? What are you holding right now? If you don't mind me asking."

"Cocaine mostly. But also some hand grenades."

"Hand grenades? Who the hell buys hand grenades?"

"You'd be surprised. You tap into the right people, especially out here in the desert, and they sell fast. You got the militia types out by Indio that buy them, survivalists up in Big Bear, idiot gangbangers in Riverside, meth-lab guys buy them for home security. Like I said, that shit can get you paranoid. My problem is that Buddy knows the customer base down here and I don't."

"So how'd you get stuck down here with all of it?"

"Buddy had to clear out a lot of stuff pretty fast. It was a complicated situation. We thought we had a snitch, or maybe a couple of snitches. We couldn't keep this stuff on our hands. We had to get it out of Fresno. But my little Inland Empire vacation was supposed to be over by now. I'm not a damn storage facility and I am not going to jail for this shit. I was just doing Buddy a favor like a fucking idiot," Guy said, looking at his shoes.

"So, what if he doesn't come to his senses?"

"That's a great question, a great fucking question. I'm trying to figure that one out myself. I have maybe another week, and then I'll be totally tapped for money. So I have to make some moves. I guess I'll sell the coke. That always moves fast."

"You sure that's a good idea?"

"Yeah. I know how the scene works. I know who to look for and who to look out for. They're all pretty much the same everywhere. I'll just find a bar here or in San Berdu, chat some people up, you can usually tell right off the bat who'd be interested, and sell to them."

"But isn't it risky?"

"Man, it's *all* risky now. If Buddy doesn't call saying he's sorry for threatening me and my family by tomorrow or the next day, then I have to assume that he's coming for me. I'll move the coke as fast as I can and get the hell out of here. I'll go to Vermont, see my little girls, maybe drive down to the Gulf

Coast. I have some old friends around Brownsville way. I could go on a real vacation. Maybe I'll go see my uncle in Phoenix about finally getting into construction. This shit should go for around ninety K, depending on how I cut it and how I sell it."

Like that, I was losing my only friend in the world. Guy tore the tab off the top of his empty beer can and dropped it in. It made a faint clink. He was sitting on the crappy motel chair, behind the table. He put his hands on his knees and leaned toward me.

"Listen, man, while all this shit is still shaking out, can you do me a favor?"

"What?"

"It's a big favor."

"What is it?"

"It would really be helping me out and the risk wouldn't be too big for you. And I *will* find a way to pay you back for it if you say yes."

"What is it?"

"Just keep some of the stuff in your room. I hate to even have to ask. But if Buddy does drop a dime on me, the cops won't get a search warrant for your room too. And it'll only be a short while. Just three or four days. I swear. I'll owe you my life, and then some."

I thought about a lot of things in the two seconds before I responded.

I thought about meth-crazed Yucaipa bikers blowing my head off. I imagined explaining myself and my cache of cocaine and hand grenades to the police. I thought of the weak reed of ordinary life that had begun to take root.

I also thought of all the empty days drunk and sober since I left Dizzy's ranch. I thought of my father and Mary Beth, of all the friendships I had failed, of all the people I could not protect. And lastly, I thought of Jack, of the hunting knife I left buried up beneath his ribs, crammed in what I can only assume was his crummy heart. I should be dead for that, if nothing else. I should at least be in jail, not enjoying Pringles, beer, cool desert air, freedom, tacos, farmers' markets, casino gambling, and human friendship like I was.

I thought of the feeling of my face curling into a smile or a laugh in the cold dawn, drinking with Guy and watching free men barrel down the I-10 in their eighteen-wheelers. I thought I was going to have to give back all this borrowed time to jail or the grave or some unseen, gruesome collector one way or another, sooner or later. I figured I might as well give it up for a friend.

"All right man, I'll do it."

"Really? You sure?"

"Yeah, what the fuck, right?"

"Thanks. You're a lifesaver. I swear it'll only be a little while."

"Don't worry about it."

22.

I worried about it.

In the harsh light of the late afternoon, more hungover than I expected, I remembered saying yes, but was still amazed to see the big trunk of hand grenades and the duffel bag of cocaine in my room.

I dimly recalled my noble reasons, but couldn't help but notice that Guy's plan seemed like a bad one, at least for me. My brain went through the motions of paranoia, but my heart wasn't in it. Maybe this was my half-assed suicide. But I decided to save my regret for the penitentiary.

Guy's plan, as I remembered it, was to sell off the coke and then just get rid of the hand grenades somehow, bury them in the desert, drop them in a river, leave them out in a parking lot, something. It was a shame though, because he had so many and they'd be worth a lot if he found a buyer, he said. It would only take a few days to sell enough cocaine to get back on his feet, he'd said. A week, at most. Then he'd go back to Vermont, or Phoenix, or somewhere.

We hung out two more nights before he kicked his plan into action. Two more nights in the same boat, hitting the snooze alarm on our real lives and watching the interstate for signs of danger. The clock was ticking loudly for Guy. Buddy still hadn't called. We drank distracted. It wasn't the cops and criminals and aliens and ghosts that made it hard to enjoy those nights. And it wasn't the illegal drugs and weapons stashed in my room. And it wasn't the stifled urge to tell Guy why I was really here at the Good Nite Inn. It was the future that pulled at both of us like a strong wind, pulled our thoughts far from each other and from Redlands.

Those nights, Guy drank less than usual and talked more about his daughters, saying vague things about the children he hardly knew. Natalie liked to draw horses. Chloe was younger and had the prettiest smile in the whole world. Maybe if he got things set up really good with his uncle in Phoenix, he could send for them. Maybe his ex could come, maybe she wouldn't be such a bitch if he was doing clean, regular work and putting food on the table. Everyone has to grow up sometime, he said.

The second night, Guy called it quits early. He said he was tired, that he had to get some sleep. Big day tomorrow. Buddy hadn't answered Guy's last-ditch phone calls.

Alone in my room that night, I crossed the police tape to think again of Mary Beth, the only bright face in that mass of shades. Dizzy's ranch wasn't her first go-round in a cult—or "nontraditional religion," if that's more your taste. She'd told me about her life toward the end of it, but it was a baddy. Left college after an OD, did the middle-class tour of east coast rehab facilities, where she met Steve; they joined the Moonies, had a Moonie marriage, and stayed clean and got straight jobs for a few years. After Steve came Irv, the meth-cooker. Then there was Raymond, who got her into Landmark Forum seminars, then Robby, the ecstasy king of Baton Rouge. Then there was Trevor, who got her into a snake-handling personal development church in Kenner. Mary Beth had a daughter with him, named Mary. The girl was still there, as far as she knew, probably better off, she said. Then there was Andrew, who flew shipments of heroin into Arizona in an ultralight. Then a few months in jail and a few more in rehab.

She kept it short and vague about each guy with the stuff, whether it was enlightenment or dope. The only thing she made clear was that each took something from her she couldn't get back, part of what made it possible for her to live. It was only when she came to Dizzy that she went to anything alone. She found a copy of Dizzy's *Final Revelation of Our Terminal Age* at a methadone clinic in Houston. She had never agreed with anything so much in her whole life, so she started writing to Dizzy. He invited her to the ranch. It was either that or wait to get hooked on a new thing and a new man, so she went.

Was there something I could have said to get her to come with me? Surely things could've worked out better than this.

Thinking of it makes me want something as big as the end of the World, just to wipe the slate clean. It almost makes me relate to Dizzy. The tension of being alive is a bitch, and like him, I want the ceaseless niggling jabs of the World and my mind to stop. I can imagine police coming down the dusty road to the ranch. Dizzy must have seen that he couldn't talk the tension away anymore. And his well-rehearsed Masada act, half fire drill and half high school graduation, was the only way to make the tension finally recede.

Armageddon sells because it works. It solves insoluble reality. And it takes the edge off a night that lingers too long in the shadow of a dozen dubious decisions. That's more than I can say for most things, especially since I lost the goddamn TV remote somewhere in the room. I don't know how.

23.

"Fuck it. He's not going to call," Guy decided in the afternoon. He spat off the balcony onto the parking lot below. The spit slapped the pavement and we walked to my room. He wasn't coming by to hang out, just to cut up some cocaine for the night ahead.

He said he was going to San Bernardino to scout out some bars. And I told him the Flamingo in town would probably work for his purposes.

"Thanks, man. I owe you big."

The next three nights I honed my disastrous relationship with solitude. I tried to drink, and pretended to sleep. The aliens began to snoop from the edges of everything. The third day, I woke and drove over to the beautiful old library downtown. But I got the bookstore blues before I could find anything to read.

From there, it was just a long impersonation of a human being. I ate a burrito at Cucas, sat in the big, airy café by the library with a cup of coffee for an hour. The people there were all acting excited or upset. I couldn't make out what they were saying.

Guy came over to my room on the fourth day. I was watching TV and eating a Domino's pizza, as was my custom. Guy had a woman with him. Not a bad-looking one, either. It was quickly apparent that they were both pretty coked-up, talking fast and loud, their hands dancing before them on distracted half-missions, laughing a lot for no reason, and walking around my room. They smelled like cigarettes, whiskey, stale sweat, and too-sweet perfume.

"Hey man, what's up?" was Guy's greeting. It was overenthusiastic and a little creepy. He said it more than once.

"Nothing much. Just taking a break from research."

"Right, research. I forgot about that. Hey Cindy, this is my friend I was telling you about. He's a professor. Oh, I forgot. This is Cindy. Ain't she cute?"

"Yeah ... she is. Nice to meet you ... Cindy."

"It's really Cinderella, but you can call me Cindy or Cin," she said, shaking my hand. Her manicured fingers were soft and cold.

"I like your name. You guys want any pizza or soda? It's all I have in the room," I offered, at a loss.

A blonde both natural and dyed, Cinderella wore very short jean shorts and a tank top. Her breasts were big and preternaturally spherical. Her thighs were smooth. Her face was pretty—nothing out of place, but nothing grabbed your attention much, either. Her dark black eyebrows were all that kept her face from being all California sunshine. She lit a cigarette and had a long pull at it. Blowing the smoke out the side of her mouth, you could see the lines between the lips and the chin of a person who frowned a lot.

"No, thanks. We brought up a bottle," Guy said, producing a mostly full bottle of Leeds' Scotch Whiskey. "And another one we forgot in the car. You up for some fun tonight?"

"I guess. Sure."

"All right, I'm just going to use your shower for a few minutes. I want to get washed up, okay?"

That was weird: Using my shower instead of his. Paranoia flared, but I was already a few steps behind on the evening and could only sit back and ride the weirdness. The trunk on the far side of my bed told me it was too late to put my hand back on the steering wheel now.

"Sure. Knock yourself out."

"Thanks, have fun, you two," Guy leered, winking as he took the whiskey bottle into the bathroom. He closed the door and the water started running.

"So," Cinderella said once Guy had closed the door. "Guy says we would get along."

Then she leaned, stumbled, and fell onto the bed. It was very matter-of-fact, the whole action. But after those months on Dizzy's ranch, I was used to mechanical and unnatural sexual advances and assents from women. Cinderella was Guy's token of friendship, and his repayment of a favor. And, with the sober and lonely itch so heavy on me, it was the kind of repayment I could really use.

"Oh," I said. "Yeah."

Not clever or seductive. But it didn't matter. She sat up on the bed, took her top off and squinted at me, as if she learned how to be sexy from a correspondence course. But that didn't matter.

She crawled onto me and we kissed. They say you can tell a lot about a person from a kiss. From Cinderella's kiss I could tell she done a ton of coke. Her mouth tasted like money, like the dirty dollar bill she'd been snorting through. So much coke that my tongue started to go numb from all the blow in her saliva.

Still, it would have taken more than that for me to have second thoughts. We got through the kissing quickly and got down to business. With neither lust nor tenderness nor rancor, we made love. That's not to say it was without enthusiasm. Cinderella was an athlete of sorts, eager to change positions and orifices throughout the act. She talked dirty and made more noise than was altogether believable. It was like porn, except for it being real.

Despite all the drugged abandon, Cinderella made sure I put on a rubber. She had one in her purse. I guess her recklessness only goes so far.

And she was beautiful in a way. The skin of her breasts was stretched so taut over the implants that her tits reflected the light from the nightstand lamp. She was the perfect and meaningless answer to desire, the one that makes you think you meant to ask a different question all along. Fucking Cinderella reminded me of California in that way. She even asked me to come on her face. Begged me to, actually.

Afterwards, lost in postcoital reverie, the last, catastrophic year of my life unfurled in the forgiving endorphin light. Cinderella wiped off her face on a sheet. Then she got up, lit herself a cigarette, and went into the bathroom. After a few minutes, Guy came out of the bathroom. Cinderella followed, still naked.

"What's up, man?" he practically yelled. He was wearing a towel and was now as high as hell.

"Just taking it easy. I was just talking to Cin."

"Talking! Yeah, good stuff, that talking," he snorted. "I told you that you were my man! I told you. Are you ready to have some fun or what!"

It's hard to enjoy, or even tolerate, the company of people that high unless you get high yourself.

"Yeah. Let's do it. Let the good times roll," I said, rejoining the world of the living once again.

Guy cut up some more lines on the dresser. We started

talking and snorting big lines of good, clean stuff. I didn't have to snort too much to get pretty high, but I snorted too much anyway. Soon my heart was fluttering like a drowning bird.

It was a special sort of night. Guy was excited and I was feeling pretty good and Cinderella wasn't getting dressed and I had the room at least for another five days. So we embarked on the long string of overenthused interruptions that make up a cocaine conversation. That night we burned through a sizable chunk of Guy's stash, which is to say we burned through his options and his chances. And that was part of what made the night feel special, important even. All coked up and cocksure, it felt like the crappy motel room was on the edge of the World, rolling the dice for all of humanity one last time.

It may have been just coincidence and desperation that kept us snorting and talking and drinking past noon the next day, but it felt like something more. It was love, of a sort, and sadness. It was like the night before college graduation, when everyone's packed and ready to say good-bye to each other for maybe forever and no one wants to go to bed. Because when they wake, everything will be irrecoverably different. It was all too much for me. So I put on my most earnest face and told Guy and Cinderella my story—the true one.

"Guy, I know you took some risks when you told me about your situation. And I want to tell you the truth too, because you're my friend. So here goes. I was bullshitting when I said I was a college professor."

I nervously swallowed a numbing clot of cocaine phlegm.

"Shit. You're not a cop are you? Shit," Cinderella said.

"No. No, no, nothing like that. Not a cop. Not a cop at all."

"But you're not a professor," Guy said.

"Not that either. It's a long story. I haven't told anyone. Cin, you seem like a nice girl. So I'll tell you too. But you really can't tell anyone what I'm about to say."

"Okay," her face said on its way down for another line. She was a high, hungry girl.

The coke had repaired my paranoia. I took a deep breath, then a big line. I was sweating. I got up, and walked over to the door, checked the lock and put the chain on.

"I killed a guy. And I am sort of responsible for a bunch of other people killing themselves."

"What? Are you like a terrorist?" Cindy asked, her bloodshot eyes opening wide.

Her panic was matched only by how damn out of it she was. She was already distracted by the time the question left her mouth. Her panic evaporated and she hit another line.

"No. Nothing like that. I'm a reporter, actually ..."

So, in rapid bursts, I told them my story, the recent part anyway. I told them about the assignment to cover Dizzy's ranch. I told them what happened, as near as I could figure. The police tape came off the scene of the crime and the cameras came running in. I told it straight, leaving out the dreams, hallucinations, and regretful asides as best I could. Maybe I should have been more circumspect. I could have waited until I'd gotten Guy alone, at least. But the cocaine and my own desolation after three days alone gave me the all-but-invincible feeling that I needed to tell the truth.

Telling the truth was nice. It was like opening a box of disheveled and dismembered dolls and putting them back intact, laying them down properly, with their clothes on the right way.

24.

"... don't know why. But my credit cards and my ATM card still work. I'm registered here under my own name. It's been a few months now. And the cops haven't come knocking. Maybe they're not looking for me. Maybe they think I'm dead. Maybe with all the death, I got lost in the shuffle. I have to get a little more rest, then I'll figure out what to do. I'm thinking maybe I'll just write the story, come up with some kind of alibi, and go back to work. Maybe in a few months."

"I knew that professor story wasn't true."

"Yeah? What tipped you off? Was it that I never did any research or that I didn't have any books in my room?"

"No man, you just didn't seem like college material to me,"

Guy said.

We laughed and kept laughing. And it *was* funny. Him supposedly moving art and rare collectibles and me studying the loser towns of California. Both of us lying, knowing the other was lying, and still becoming friends. He took another Ziplock bag out of the duffel bag, poured out another little pile and we laughed some more.

"So, okay, if the professor story didn't work, what did you think I was up to?"

"I thought you were just like, a good guy and you were kicking junk or having a nervous breakdown and just didn't want to talk about it. I should have guessed you were hiding out."

"A nervous breakdown, huh? I guess it's been a bad few months."

"Don't worry about it. I mean, I couldn't really get a read on you, except that something was going on."

"At least you don't have to go to work," Cinderella contributed from her pit of sniffling contentment, naked with her midriff covered by a sheet. She was laying half on and half off the bed. "Work sucks."

She had reached the place she wanted to be, and touched back down into our world only long enough to say something like "work sucks" or to sit up and have another line. Then she was back off in another more fuzzy and friendly world.

"Your story definitely sounds like a rough enough patch to me. But it could be worse, you know? You still can probably still go back to your job if you want. And that's good, clean work, right?" Guy asked.

"I guess so. I think so."

"I mean, you know what I mean. It's cleaner work than a lot of things. Just tell them you had a nervous breakdown. Happens all the time. And it happened on the job, right? Maybe you can squeeze some workers' comp out of them, say you were traumatized and shit."

"I just have to get myself together. It takes effort to come up with a story and then stand by it. I'm getting my strength up for that. That's what I'm waiting on."

"Man, I never would have figured you for a killer. I mean, whoa! You say you were a reporter, man. I don't know a lot of reporters, so I guess I could buy that. You just don't seem like a killer."

"Well, I killed someone. So there you have it," I said.

"I'm sorry, man. I'm just talking. I'm just running my mouth. But seriously, man, you're no a killer. Really, that was just, like, something that happened."

"So if I'm not a killer, what am I?"

"Don't think about it like that. I've met real killers. I know *killers.* I mean, I've known some of them too good for my own peace of mind. They don't get rattled by that kind of shit. They just don't think of it, of killing, like it's even a bad thing. It's just, neutral, to them. Like, take my boss, Buddy. He's just got different parts than us. Really."

"I'm not exactly broken up about killing Jack. So what makes me any different?" I pressed.

"You say that. But you're upset. Otherwise you wouldn't have slept through the last month. You're upset—you're like me that way. I remember being there when Buddy did somebody. It was terrible, and not just because it was noisy and gross. It was like by not grabbing the wrench or the pliers or the chain out of Buddy's hands, by just standing there, saying nothing and watching ... I still feel like I'm not totally human anymore. But that's just another day at the office for a guy like Buddy. And, I mean, just look at you. You haven't been able to even get back to your job since you killed that guy. You see what I'm saying?"

"Yeah, I guess."

"You might have killed a guy. But you aren't a killer, you know?"

"Maybe you're right. But for a guy who's not a killer, I've got a lot of blood on my hands."

"Man, it sounds like they were ready to do themselves before they even met you. They were tweaked to hell on God and whatever else that crazy bastard Dizzy was feeding them. You can't go around thinking it's your fault. You just saw that the shit coming down the pike. And you ran for it. You hardly even had a choice."

"I could have left more peaceably," I said. "I could have told them I was going. I could have tried harder to give them the warm fuzzies before I left. Instead, I freaked out first, and that escalated everything."

"Listen: All you can control is what you can control. Seriously, other people—you can't control what they do," said the man whose cocaine and hand grenades I was keeping by my nightstand.

"I know. You're right. What's done is done," I said, sweating now under the heat of Guy's attention. I changed the subject. "So what's your plan?"

"The scene is pretty dead here. Not a lot of action. I made a little dough, enough to move on. I figure I'll go to LA or San Diego and see some buddies I have out there. This is good shit and I could get some really good, fast money for it there. Then I'm seriously going far, far away. You should get out too."

He knew where he was going, but was being vague about it on purpose. You can't tell the cops or the criminals things you don't know when they come calling. And it seemed that Guy could sense the heat coming down sooner rather than later. He was at least protecting himself. And if that was too bad for me, then too bad.

I fought back waves of cold paranoia and tried to enjoy these last few hours with my friend. Because there would only be an awkward good-bye, a return of weapons and drugs, a handshake or a hug when we woke the next day.

And eventually exhaustion overcame the blow and whiskey and the big feelings. By the late afternoon, we were all done. The sunlight was dirty. Cinderella was well out of it, her mouth moving silently while she stared at the ceiling. Guy adjourned to his room next door.

I tried to get while the getting was good and made another go at Cinderella. She was off in her own world by this point, but awake and not unwilling. But all the blow had turned my manhood to a numb flap of clammy skin.

We were in bed for a few hours before I finally made my

way through the self-hating residue the drug inevitably leaves. My breathing and blinking chafed the air. The strip of light that scraped through the institutional curtains accused me. And I nagged God to sedate me away from the horrible thoughts I began to suspect all too strongly were true.

25.

Tangling and untangling unconsciously, Cinderella and I slept through the day and night, until nearly dawn the next day.

The sound of banging, of metal bending and scraping, of wood straining and splintering. I knew the sounds, had lived and relived those sounds. And in my drugged sleep, it could have been Jack in Las Cruces.

Four claps—clean, sharp and short, louder than anything except gunshots—stirred me back to Redlands. I heard footsteps running down the concrete balcony walkway and a car peeling out. Then moaning started, then yelling on the verge of sobs, pointless and wordless. Someone trying to slow frantic breathing by laying their vocal chords on it.

The yelling voice wasn't Guy's, it was higher and raspier. And it wasn't calling for backup, just shrieking. The backup had just run for its life. I closed my eyes then held Cindy close. The back part of my mind had it worked out before the front part had its pants on. Buddy's friends had come for Guy.

"Just shut up or we'll get shot too, you hear me?" I whispered.

It was like a movie, something that went straight to video. We were in mortal danger and I was calming her frail, womanly emotions, saving our lives with my cool head. The only difference was that she murmured nonsense and resumed snoring.

The yelling in the next room stopped for a moment. I climbed out of bed and pulled on some jeans. It was just after dawn and the orange disc of the sun had only begun to warm the air. The door to Guy's room was kicked in, the frame a splintered mess.

Early blue light shone through the wrecked door. A big biker type slouched under the window, wheezing, his long hair sopping up blood from the hole in his chest. I was careful to step over the expanding puddle of his blood on the carpet. He was a big guy, over six feet and fat. He moaned in shallow breaths. Noticing me, he started grasping for a big silver revolver that lay at my feet. I stomped his hand and picked up the gun. He let out a yelp, then went back to trying to breathe.

Guy was lying in bed as though nothing had happened. A beam of sunlight showed blood soaking through the motel blanket over his left arm. The lamp next to his bed was in pieces. I put the revolver down among the shards on his nightstand. Guy's breath whistled in and out and there was a little blood on his lips. His eyes were wide and focused hard on the doorway, the room's only source of light.

"Jesus, Guy, are you okay?"

His eyes went unfocused, like he was looking at everything all at once. Then he narrowed it all down to me.

"Oh, hey, man. What's up?" he rasped, either traumatized or acting cool.

"It looks like he shot you."

"Yep. Got me. Hard to breathe. Shit. Gonna die."

"You're not gonna die," I said, because that's what you're supposed to say.

"We'll see. Cold in here."

"It's always cold in the morning. Was it Buddy?"

"Yeah. One of his. Met the guy before." The words were a labor. He took some quick, whistling breaths to recover from the effort. "Don't call cops. Don't tell them anything, when they come. Bad for us both."

"What should I do?"

"Do what you want."

"I mean, about this. The shooting and the drugs and Cindy and the hand grenades and the police and whoever tried to kill you."

"That stuff is yours now. She's yours too. Just take it all and do what you think is best. I can't handle much now. Just fade away."

"How do I do that?"

"You're asking the wrong guy. I just got myself shot."

He tried to laugh. But he came up with a cough that bent his face into a silent, crying grimace. He swallowed the pain and whatever else had come up back down after a moment and marshaled his strength.

"Go to Oxnard, like you said. Keep hiding. Buddy and his guys aren't cops. They mean business, but they get distracted fast. Just ride it out for now. Cops coming soon. Act normal. Just be the guy next door. Tell them you're a professor. They'll think what I did. When they're gone, then run."

"Okay. Should I call an ambulance?"

"Probably someone already did. Guns were loud. Thin walls here. Just not enough time. Another day. Would have been gone. Now there's no time for you, either. Just get back to your room before the cops show. Act asleep."

"Thanks, Guy. I hope we meet again."

"Hey, you never know. Just get out."

It was then that I noticed the small pistol in his hand. It rested between his palm and the soft blue motel blanket like a remote control.

26.

The police came by before long. It seemed like there were a lot of them. A pair knocked on my door, just uniform cops taking statements. I went out to the balcony and answered their questions. The parking lot and the I-10 loomed behind them. I had a bag of cocaine, a trunk of hand grenades, and a sleeping stranger behind me. It still was early in the morning and you could practically hear the heat swelling.

Guy had already been carted off by then. I'd heard the paramedics fumbling in the next room. Maybe he was breathing his last in some hospital, gasping his last words or just suffering, silent and terrified, while death ate him up.

The cops were the first to ask me any real questions in a very long time. One nice thing about the World, is that you can pretty much count on it not to give too much of a flying fuck about you. That can be one of its most redeeming features.

After months of preparing for worse interrogations, their questions were nonetheless disconcerting. I upped my cover story, telling the cops I was a poet instead of a professor to seem even more off-kilter and harmless. The cocaine and hand grenades by my bed only amplified things. I was nervous and heard my own answers better than I did their questions.

"No. We said hello once or twice ... That was about it, really ... Never really noticed much out of the ordinary ... I guess he had a lot of tattoos, but that was it ... never saw anyone coming or going ... a poet ... writing a big piece, an epic about the Inland Empire ... no, doesn't pay much ... used to do advertising ... a lot of internal marketing, nothing you'd seen ... some family money, and grants, mostly ... probably leaving later this ... maybe go out by the Salton Sea ... no, never saw anyone come or go ... just heard the sound, like firecrackers ... can't believe it was so close, next door ... just figured it would be safest to stay in the room ... she slept through it ... that's so true ... scary is right ... you just never know ... was it drugs, do you think? ... next time I'm going to shell out extra money for a nicer motel, that's for sure ... If you have any other questions, don't hesitate to stop by ... I'll call if anything comes to mind on this ... thanks ..."

They didn't seem to suspect anything, just thanked me for my time and left.

When I was young, I always thought I was lucky. When I heard the Nativity story at Christmas, I thought that's how it must have happened with me. And that chosen-one feeling never totally went away, stuck with me even in the long stretches when events seemed designed to repudiate the notion.

And after a murder, after holding out the foot that tripped dozens into their graves, with a duffel bag full of cocaine and a trunk full of hand grenades in my room, I tell the police that I'm writing the poetic epic of the Southern California desert suburbs. And they suspect nothing. It's enough to make it seem that the

World is opening up along seams I'd never guessed at. Every day since Las Cruces has been impossible in the courts of my mind. And as the cops left, I began to suspect that those days haven't been for nothing.

27.

With Guy and the guy in his room carted off in ambulances, the stuff of Guy's room bagged and sorted by the police, and the door boarded up until a carpenter could be called in, I resumed my life on the lam.

Sometimes you get years to hash over the most trivial shit. You mutter and bore all your friends with what some woman said, or the size of the raise they gave you at work, or the unlikely success of a colleague, or the criticism of an acquaintance. Other times, you have to decide your fate in an hour. This was that second one.

"Cin. Cindy. Cinderella, get up."

"Huh? What time is it?"

"It's like eight."

"In the morning?"

"Yeah?"

"It's still early. We don't have to check out for like, hours. I'm going back to bed, honey."

"Cindy, babe. Guy got shot. They just took him away."

"Who?"

"Guy. The ambulance took him. They took Guy. Someone shot him, like an hour ago. The cops were just here."

That woke her up.

"Oh, shit. Are they still here? It's not my shit. You have to tell them."

"They're gone, for now. They don't think we had anything to do with it. But when they all leave, I have to get the hell out of here."

"Where you goin'?"

"I don't know, but I have to go soon. I was thinking of maybe going to Oxnard." *Shit. I shouldn't have told her*, I thought. Three cheers for the world's worst fugitive. "Or maybe back east, to Colorado or something. Maybe Brownsville."

"I'm about done with this town, too. Can I come?"

"Sure. I guess. You want to?"

"Yeah, I guess. You still partying?"

"Partying?"

"Like last night? I mean, you still have the coke, don't you?"

"Uh. Yeah. I do, actually. So yeah, sure. I'm still partying. You really want to come along?"

"Yeah. Can I?"

"Sure, I guess."

She wanted the coke bad enough to go wherever with me on a moment's notice. And I wanted the company enough to go along with it. Not a lot of dignity here, but it would do. I didn't ask Cinderella if she needed to stop by her place to get her things, or if she was worried about missing work. And she didn't bring it up. The coast seemed clear. So we loaded up the car and got on the 10.

Maybe in Oxnard I'd figure out what all this luck has been for. Maybe this unexpected freedom would unfurl in a way that meant something. Maybe I was still high, but I felt blessed with a luck too profound to culminate in just a lousy Pulitzer entry and the uneasy embrace of the World. I did some lines with Cinderella to get up for the long drive ahead. It was quicker than coffee.

It was a hot, smoggy day and I kept checking my rearview. But if someone was following, I'd have no way of knowing. Cinderella must have forgotten what she told Guy and me the night before, because she told me most of it again in the car. And it was pretty much what you'd expect. Rolling westward, I heard how: Cinderella grew up in Riverside with her mom and was studying to be a nurse. School was okay, but boring and the people were lame and stuck up. She took up dancing—the naked kind—to pay the bills while she was in school because it was good money and it's her body, etcetera. But she still couldn't pay her bills, and some of the guys at school found out she was

97

dancing and thought they could treat her like a whore. One of them tried to rape her at a party in front of his friends. But she got away and then she had another guy she was seeing smash up the would-be-rapist's car. She left school. That let her work more and save up some money. She already had nice tits, but she had them enhanced to make more money. But that was another bill and it didn't make her as much extra money as she expected. She's not sure about going back to school. Being a nurse isn't so great anyway. It's not like being a doctor, and that's *so* not going to happen. So she mostly dances now and hangs out with her boyfriend, who lives in Redlands, and who can go to hell. He never does shit except take her money and sit around getting high all day. She has to find a real man, one with a job and money, who doesn't want her to work. Work just sucks, and a husband's one of the only sure ways to avoid it for good. That or the lottery. But she never meets those kinds of guys, probably because she parties too much. Anyway, that will come later. Now's her time to do what she wants and have fun. It's not like she has a kid or anything. She should be partying and having fun and making money, which is what she's doing, so there's really no problem.

For all of Cinderella's protests that she enjoyed partying and fun, her spiel made it sound as though her life was already over and the only thing left was to sort out the blame.

Cinderella's life story forced an uneasy fact on me: That other people are just like you. They're also scared and sensitive and awake. They also want to not hate themselves. They also assume that the world started when they were born, revolves around them, and will end or won't matter when they die. Every single one of them. I know that you already know that. Everybody does. It's obvious. But hard to swallow, for me and, from the looks of it, for most people. If you're strong enough to look at people that way, it'll give you a bastard of a headache. Look at every face, at everyone who's in your way, and imagine that they see and feel and know and worry just as much as you. They even matter to themselves as much as you do to yourself. Maybe more.

Just try to imagine it.

The Buddhists call it compassion. I call it picking at a weak spot. Still, I was trying it with Cinderella, even if just because it was a long car ride and I didn't have anything else in the World to do.

"I mean, I'm just having fun. And that's what you're supposed to do when you're twenty-three. I don't have to support anyone but me, so I can do what I want, mostly. But it's like, you have to keep it self-contained if you want to keep having fun. Like with Guy, when you go out there and start talking to strangers, telling them you have this and you have that—that's when people say 'oh, he has this,' or 'she has that.' That's when you get the wrong kind of attention. And then they come after what you have. I mean, I have fun, I party, but I keep it to myself a lot. Sometimes I go up on stage and I'm high or I'm drunk. But I never tell anyone that, because they'll think they can take advantage of me. And I like to party. But I'm not like some of the girls there. I'm not a whore. I'm self-contained. But Guy, like, wasn't self-contained. He probably, like, let whoever shot him know about the stuff he had. And that's why they came after him. I know Guy's your friend. But you see what I'm saying?"

I didn't see the benefit in explaining to her who had shot Guy and why. I just nodded and watched the road.

You could tell Cinderella would turn mean at a moment's notice. It reminded me of my mother. It was the kind of weather they don't have meteorologists for. And when you're a kid, it's the kind of weather they don't make umbrellas for, either.

I can't really blame Cinderella. She had to know I didn't think much of her and that I wasn't going to do her a jot of good in the long run. And she couldn't snort anything to distract herself from those facts—at least not in the car. I think she only told me her life story so she wouldn't feel so scared or so cheap.

> *Why would you be angry at the Cosmos?*
> *Well, who said you would see it as a*
> *Cosmos?*
> —E.J. Gold, *American Book of the Dead*

28.

Oxnard, Calif.—After we made the turn north onto the 101, I felt safer. We were in LA and I felt assured that worse than us was happening all around. I pulled off the highway and bought some beer at a gas station and some plastic travel mugs to drink it from for the rest of the ride. It took the edge off.

Lack of sleep and lack of drugs had taken their toll on our moods. The conversation took on the quality of two people making the best of their situation. But it couldn't stay that way, unfortunately.

"So, did you know the guys who shot Guy?" she asked me.

"No. Did you?"

"No. What do you mean?"

"Nothing. Just kidding." A long and laughless silence ensued.

"What did you tell the cops?"

"Nothing. Just that he lived next to me and I didn't know anything about what happened."

"So you didn't tell them about Guy and the stuff?"

"No. It wouldn't have been a good idea to tell them much about it, you know?"

"Yeah. Totally. You want a cigarette?"

Still, the drive relaxed me. With Cinderella riding shotgun, I could barely think of things. I put my hand on her bare thigh. She didn't mind. That kept me aroused enough that my mind didn't wander far. The ambiguous and dangerous situation clarified itself better in the windshield than in the plumbing of my brain.

Cinderella didn't find the drive all that relaxing. She was

jumpy and annoyed the whole way, chewing gum, drinking beer from her plastic mug, chain-smoking cigarettes, and eating potato chips, loudly.

"So, last night, did you really say you killed a guy?"

"You don't remember?"

"Yeah. I remember. Mostly."

I knew I couldn't trust Cinderella. So I started talking like a lawyer.

"I said that last night. But I said I didn't mean to kill him. I mean, I said I did *mean* to do it, but I didn't, like, plan it. I said it was self-defense."

I was as bad a lawyer as I was a fugitive. And I could tell from her face that my talking like a lawyer wasn't helping her trust me. But I'm not smart enough to know how to fix things like that.

"So this guy you killed, he was going to kill you?"

"Yeah. What happened was a lot like with Guy. I was just lying in bed, and this guy, Jack, started kicking in my door. He had a gun with him. Luckily, it took him two kicks. So I got to the door and stabbed him as soon as the door flew open."

"So, the guy who wanted to kill you, was he just after you because he was after your stuff?"

"You mean the coke?"

She really didn't remember much from last night, I guess. She tucked the "killer" part away and let the details drift downstream.

"Yeah."

"No. I didn't have any with me then. I never had any with me. I was just holding the stuff for Guy and he said I could have it after he got shot."

"Oh."

Cinderella's face betrayed her: She thought I shot Guy. That was a story she could understand. I didn't know how to talk her out of that. And because she hadn't said it, denying it would look bad.

"The guy, not Guy, but the man, Jack, who broke into my motel room, he didn't have anything to do with drugs."

"So why was he trying to kill you?"

I really couldn't bear to tell the story twice in a week. And I guess I just didn't think enough of Cinderella to go to the trouble.

"I was doing a story on a group he was a part of. They thought I was going to write something bad about them. So they sent this guy to kill me."

And there she was again, with that damn I-don't-believe-you-but-I-won't-tell-you-I-think-you're-lying "oh."

So we went from getting-to-know-you, back to making-the-best-of-it, the killer and the cokewhore, riding into the sunset.

I wondered what the hell I was going to do with Cinderella. She didn't trust me, but she was also a little afraid of me. I had that. I tried to project my thoughts back to Long Island, to the firemen in the bars and the commuters hurrying and striving for their bigger houses, newer cars and better towns. The town had its center, with its diners, bars and movie theater. The highway had its mall. The train to the city zoomed above it all, loud and fast. I may not have liked it, but it made sense. I think of a day in fall, wearing a sweater, walking home from high school. It was probably the best time of the year, but when you're as unhappy as I was growing up, things being familiar and making sense only makes them worse.

I decided to break the souring silence and put things on friendlier terms.

"So, you ever think of going back to school anytime soon?"

"Nah. I really don't need that headache. Nursing's a good job for when you're older and don't want to have fun anymore. But it's a lot of work. A lot of blood and people crapping themselves. And at first, you can't even choose your hours. You just have to take what they give you. And that sucks, because when you're starting out is when you make the least money."

"So, what about your job back in Redlands? Did you call them?"

"So now you're my mom?"

"Hey, I'm just asking."

"Fuck that. My job sucks. And anyway, they don't care.

Girls flake all the time. It's no big deal."

"Which club is it?"

"It's the Hustler Club—like the magazine. It's near the motel."

"How is it?"

"It's expensive, so that keeps it nice. There are gentlemen's clubs in LA that are way better. But it's hard as hell to get in there to work on good nights. The guys who book those places want money and other stuff to let you work there, unless you're like a famous porn girl or something. And I don't do porn. And it's a long drive to LA anyway."

"How many strippers are there at the Hustler Club?"

"They're called dancers. The girls there get all mad if you say stripper instead of dancer, because it makes them sound like whores. But that's bullshit. I guess we dance, but it's not like it's *Dancing with The Stars* or anything. No one pays to see dancing, they pay to see tits and pussy. And anyway the girls there are full of shit, especially the ones who get mad when you call them strippers. A lot of them are the ones who also fuck the guys at the club for money. So they really are whores. You really never been to the club?"

"No. I never went."

"I mean, whatever. It's not like I should talk. I guess I'm a whore. I'll fuck just about anyone, if I want to. And I don't even get paid. I get the short end of the stick a lot. And the short end of the dick, too. Ha. I should charge. You probably think I'm a whore."

"I hadn't really given it much thought."

"You do think I'm a whore. I can tell. Just a whore for coke. You think you're, like, so much better than me, and I'm just a whore."

I've had women talk to me like this before. They want to let you know they are not what they seem, that they're smarter, more perceptive, freer, and more confident than they seem. They want you to think that they have some secret reservoir of self-esteem and freedom you will never be able to reach. But they don't. They're almost always exactly what they seem. It's mostly just a cheap way to see you squirm. The only good answer to women when they get to talking like this is to slap them in the mouth. But I was never tough enough to take my own advice.

"Come on, you're not a prostitute. We didn't discuss a price for this trip. This is just a party, like you said. We're having fun."

Hearing the words come out of my mouth depressed me. Her gambit was working, and I was on the defensive, the worst place to be with a woman like this. "No, but Guy said I could have as much coke as I could handle if I did you. So there, I am a whore. And you were thinking it all along. I could tell. You won't look at me the way you would look at other girls."

This fucking conversation could go on for hours, I realized. Cinderella was loaded for bear on misery and eager to pick at me.

"Cinderella, I don't really give a shit what you are. My goddamn best friend just got shot. I'm driving through LA with a bag of cocaine big enough to put us *both* in jail for a decade apiece. You want to call yourself a whore, go ahead. I don't care if you want to call yourself a fucking *giraffe*, as long as you keep your shit-jammed head in the fucking car. And I don't know what gave you the idea that *I* was all that interested in dealing with your fucking self-esteem problem at this point in the day. So just shut the *fuck* up and let me drive."

There. I knew I had it in me. I'd answered her real question, telling her she was a piece of shit, that I didn't care about her, and that I was in charge. Now life could go on in terms she understood. I didn't even have to hit her. Cinderella was quiet for a few minutes, then she was ready to play nice.

"So, are you really a reporter?"

"Yeah. I was. I guess I still am."

"Redlands and Oxnard are strange places to pick for a vacation."

Maybe it's as strange as taking off to Oxnard on a moment's notice with the friend of a strange drug dealer who was just shot half to hell a few hours ago, I didn't say.

"Yeah. I'm just taking it easy, staying under the radar."

"Because you killed that guy?"

"Yeah, mostly."

"But when we get there, you still want to party, right?"

"Yes, definitely. I already told you. We're going to party."

"Okay. Don't you worry. We're gonna have a lot of fun. Just leave it up to me. But if we're going to party, why are we going to Oxnard? I know a lot of fun places in San Diego, or like, Santa Barbara."

"Listen, I like crappy towns. I want to relax without a lot of pretty people walking around thinking they ought to be having the time of their lives. I can't deal with that shit right now. Crappy towns take the pressure off. There's nothing to do there, so I don't feel like I ought to be doing anything. You see?"

"That's depressing. I know *I* want to have the time of *my* life. You *said* you wanted to *party*. So what's up?"

Now she was angry. This is what happens when you tell anyone what you're thinking. That's why I usually avoid it.

"Cin, don't worry about it. We *are* going to party, big time. I'm sure Oxnard is a lot of fun. It's by the ocean, and no one will be looking for us there. I guess I'm just a little tired. Just forget about it. We're going to party hard up in Oxnard."

"That rhymed!" she giggled and clutched my hand harder to her warm thigh.

29.

Oxnard. The name sounds like Middle English for ugly. It wasn't so bad, just a half-crummy town on the ocean, less a beach than a place to load and unload trucks and barges. Like so many places, it was what they probably call a good place to raise a family. Like Redlands, Oxnard was somewhere between two places you might want to be, a little valley of obscurity. From here, you could take the 101 south to LA to earn a living, or you could take it north to Santa Barbara for a vacation. I passed the biggest plain of car dealerships I ever saw when I was coming off the highway. It went almost to the horizon.

The Oxnard Vagabond Hotel was nice enough, even if it

wasn't really for Vagabonds. It was about twice as much per week as the room in Redlands.

Getting settled in the hotel, I brought the duffel bag and the trunk full of hand grenades up to the second floor. And the grenade trunk was damn heavy and Cinderella didn't bother helping. So it banged on the concrete steps as I dragged it, imagining how I would explain my own lame death in eternity— hauling a trunk full of grenades up the stairs of a motel—not even my own grenades—grenades I was holding for a friend. Still, I felt better with them in the room.

The morning's conviction that this was all part of a plan had passed. And I was enmeshed in the plan forged in Cindy's noisome heart, to snort through the pounds of cocaine left, fuck, and watch the motel TV until we run out of powder or the wheels come off. That may sound romantic to some of you, but it was really just the path of least resistance. And it wouldn't accomplish anything that won't have to be un-accomplished later.

Cinderella did a quick few lines, then she took off her clothes.

"What do you want to do?" she asked, naked.

Sex was the last thing on my mind. And I had seen Cinderella naked for so much of the previous night that its effect was lost on me for the moment.

"I might take a nap for now. How about you?"

"I want to go swimming," she said.

"Did you bring a swimsuit?" I asked.

"No, but I have one of my work outfits in my purse."

"Does it, you know, cover everything?"

"Yeah. It's fine. It's just like a small bikini."

"Uh, okay."

"Or I could go nude. Would you like that better?"

"Later. I'm just tired right now."

Cinderella put on her outfit. It was a white g-string with sparkly stars on it that slung over her shoulders, covering her nipples on the way up. So much for a low profile. It was the latest chapter in the annals of the world's worst fugitive. She grabbed the last two beers, her pack of cigarettes, and a towel, gave me a quick peck on the lips and went down to the pool.

I tried to nap, but I couldn't stop thinking, scheming. Maybe ditch Cinderella. Maybe turn myself in to my editor and use Guy's nervous breakdown excuse. I still couldn't figure out if that was the safest route or the most dangerous. But none of those ideas appealed to me as much as the vast ambiguity of my situation. The big destiny thoughts of the morning could survive only in this murk.

So I decided to go shopping. After all, I'd promised Cinderella a party. Booze and coke and TV and fucking, a real party that would blot out our mutual distrust of one another, along with everything else.

I stopped at the pool, where Cinderella was already done swimming. She was wet, stretched out dozing on a chaise lounge, a cigarette ashed into her first beer. Her goodies showed through the damp, white stripperwear. It was quite a sight, if you hadn't already seen too much of it.

There weren't a lot of people by the pool, just some teenage boys and their obese mother. The boys were tense and nervous in the face of so much wet, nude woman revealed. They were trying to see as much as they could of Cinderella without being caught by her or their mom. They were torn between wanting to get Cinderella's attention and not wanting her to move.

"I'm going to the store. You need anything?"

She squinted up at me.

"Newports, maybe some Bud Lights, and those chips that come in a can. You know which ones I mean?"

"Yeah, Pringles."

30.

Yesterday's expansive mood returned when I passed through the supermarket's automatic doors. So I got a cart. I started loading it with everything I'd need for Cinderella's grandiose and indolent plans—cases of beer, the big bottles of whiskey, vodka, and tequila.

It seemed like a good idea. And you have to trust yourself, even if you shouldn't. It's a poker game against your self-destructive impulses. And you're never certain playing a strong hand and when you're bluffing for the wrong reasons.

The little brown fridge in the room was for beer and mixers. So I went for non-perishable food—candy bars in packages of twenty four, crackers, Slim Jims, boxes of cookies, bags of popcorn, jars of orange nacho cheese. Then I remembered Cinderella said she wanted chips, the kind that come in a can.

It took me a minute to find the chip aisle. And that was so big it took me a while to find the Pringles. When I finally did, I discovered that there were more than a dozen varieties of Pringles on the shelves. Long tubes, short tubes, some red as blood, others green as lawn, blue as the sky, orange as nacho cheese in a jar, and on and on. They were like a rainbow over Guy's grave—and more than that—a sign.

The tubes flabbergasted me. *Those chips gave so much comfort to Guy and others in situations more and less dire than his*, I thought. I marveled at how many different flavors of Pringles there were. It was like looking into the light refracting inside a strange diamond. It was like looking into a great garden.

But Pringles are not flowers, not accidents of nature. They require real human effort to conceive and manufacture. Men and women woke early, on cold mornings, dressed, and drove to work. They discussed each new flavor in long meetings. Scientists mixed the organic and the inorganic to create safe, nonperishable flavors and chefs mixed and remixed those elements to get those flavors just so. And all along the chain, each person had to care. Each had to give up weeks and months of their lives for these chips. And all those hours, laid end to end, added up to a human lifetime, and probably more than one. A Pringle man, the Pringle men, sacrificed, for us.

And yes, they did it for money. But the money was almost incidental. They did it to make people happy. They cared. For this salty trifle, they *cared*. For each new potato chip, a whole life had willingly been given. I know this isn't a radical discovery. But it was radical, and almost miraculous, to me, at that moment. I mean, I couldn't be bothered enough to do the barest minimum for myself. I hid from the World. But not the Pringles makers. And in the chip aisle, stunned and on the verge of something, I asked the air: How did they care? How the fuck could they muster the wherewithal to wonder and worry about whether or not people were less happy for not having Mexi-Pizza Pringles?

The answer hit me like a hammer from heaven, like the whole sky balled itself up into a fist and came slamming down on my head.

The answer was Love.

And it buffeted me from all sides, there in the Albertsons. I felt that Love like I'd been plugged into the wall. The colors surged on the packages. The logos and the faces in the brands gazed at me like expectant lovers. The Pringles, the canned tuna in oil *or* water, the twenty kinds of mustard, the diet fettuccini, the heat-and-serve turkey meatloaf dinners, and low-carb chocolate mint cookies were themselves the emanation of a massive and overbearing Love that shone though the shelves and said: *Hello, we've been waiting for you notice our real selves for a long time. Hello there. We love you. Come try us. We exist for you. Hello. We are sorry and we forgive you. Hello. We love you.*

And in that moment, trembling over the cup-holdered handle of my plastic shopping cart with tears welling in my eyes, I could see it clearly. This was the Love that would chew up the whole World and spew it out as so much trash and excrement just on the chance that it would make us happy. There was nothing It wouldn't do, no forest nor idea, no edifice nor god that this Love would not defile and destroy for our ever-iffy happiness.

I wandered the supermarket from there, my mouth trembling, my eyes watery and wild, forgetting my cart, surrounded by this Love. I was consumed. I overflowed with the Love emanating from the long aisles of soda and paper plates. I ran my fingers along the shelves fully stocked with so many kinds of pickles, lost in the very Love I had spent most of my adult life repudiating. I began to cry a little. Whatever real sympathy I had for Dizzy and his cult, it was with how they seemed to deny this Love too. In my own way, I'd loved his promises that the end was near, loved his hatred of the World. Even after my father's own maybe-suicide, I loved suicide because it proved, spitefully perhaps, that the rude and ham-handed Love of the supermarkets and shopping malls and televisions and the whole human World could fail so completely, and be so stridently discarded.

But in the light that poured in from the high-piled aisles and from the cartoon faces of the cardboard display stands, I surrendered. And the World showed itself to be not reality, but rather, a slow explosion of Love. In that light, my life was just a wound that had refused to be healed. And though I'd spent my life despising that Love, It was willing to help me hate It, if that's what made me happy. If I cursed It in song, then that Love saw that I had such songs, if they made me happy. If I cursed Love in long meditations, It gave me books that elucidated a similar hate, if they made me happy. It was willing to scan the centuries so I would have company in my misery, if that made me happy. And it made this company accessible, even free in libraries.

I repudiated the Love with liquor, mocking its advances and come-hither gestures with idiocy, vomit, and a slow suicide. But Love kept the bars and liquor stores open late to overserve me. Love gave me generously and without reservation every means by which to hate and degrade both It and myself, if that made me happy. Pringles man died not to redeem my sins, but to make them less inconvenient.

Turning the corner into the frozen-foods aisle, I bumped into another man, better-dressed, older and balding, but also weeping quietly. We regarded each other suspiciously and kept walking.

Far from my cart, in the frozen-foods aisle, I was forgiven, not because I deserved it, but because that was what the supermarket's Love was, and what It did. It forgave my whole life in an instant, without my even asking. It was so unlike everything else I had ever experienced. I could hardly breathe.

By a massive shelf of multicolored party napkins, I realized

110

how flimsy all of my sins really were, and began weeping full-on. It was a feeling like I'd never known. I was forgiven, free, new, and loved. I turned the corner onto forty yards of multicolored plastic juice bottles. So many kinds of things to drink, just for me. The tears washed a crust from my eyes. The fingers fell from my throat. And I saw that they were my own.

I wept for all the Love I'd ever known and repudiated, or just botched. The love of my parents, of women, of girlfriends, of Mary Beth, of Cinderella, of my coworkers, of my friends, the last of which may well be dead now. I wept for how I'd hated myself for so long and how I'd hated the World and how I'd hated God himself if He was there at all. I shook and shuddered where I stood.

My eyes blind with tears, my knees gave out. I didn't stop open my eyes until a crowd had gathered. I looked up and saw the many concerned faces of the people standing over me. I wanted to tell them the wonderful thing that had happened. But my face was clenched with sobs and my voice was tucked below my heart.

The word *ambulance* from the crowd broke the spell. Paramedics, police, doctors would come to help me with a love made of drugs and confinement. And I wasn't ready for that yet. I had to take this feeling out to somewhere it could breathe. Leaving my cart and all my hopes of a successful shopping trip behind me, I got to my feet and ran sloppily out of the supermarket. I sprinted across the blacktop to my Pontiac, tears and sweat on my shirt. I sped out of the parking lot, tears resuming as I drove.

I drove around through Oxnard's downtown, not going anywhere in particular, just to calm down a little. I wanted to soak in the feeling of Love and look at the World through my new eyes. I wanted to pin this Love on all the things I saw, like a mnemonic device, so that I wouldn't forget it ever again.

While I drove, I decided I'd try to find a beach to take Cinderella to later. Maybe I'd buy her a proper bathing suit while I was out. Maybe I'd find another supermarket and try to actually buy some things. I would learn my way around Oxnard and savor what was left of my spiritual revelation at the same time. That was it, I'd multitask.

31.

I drove toward what I thought was west and hit sailboat marinas, container ports, and chain-link fences. I hate to be of so little faith, but suddenly the scenery didn't seem so much like the outward manifestation of an all-powerful Love. It was all either poor and neglected or charmlessly new. Every man I saw on the road seemed to be spitting on something. I followed the chain-link fences, waiting for a clear opening to the Pacific. Instead, I came to a Navy base.

I kept driving until I realized I was lost, somewhere around the KFC and the El Pollo Donut. I couldn't find the 101 and I panicked a bit. The Mexicans standing around on the corners of the wide streets suddenly seemed like they were just waiting for their chance to pull me from my car, rub dirt in my face, take my college degree away, and leave me by an on-ramp to sell oranges to passing cars. The radio didn't help, the love songs all seemed cloying, desperate, the dance music seemed like malicious brain surgery and the Mexican stations were too sinister to bear. I gave up on finding a beach. I gave up on coaxing my little surrender to the overflowing Love of the World any further. The tide had receded, revealing again the shipwreck that I admiral around town. I was tired for real.

I found a taco stand and stopped for a burrito and a beer. That put the kibosh on the ecstasy and the panic. That was a relief. Truth is, big feelings don't fit with the rest of my mind. Middling-to-bad moods are where I know how to live, if not all that well.

I remember Dizzy talking about a feeling of searing, overwhelming Love. In one of his teachings that I was allowed to attend, he told us of a sort of love that drowned out the senses and crippled the body with remorse and joy. At the time, I thought he said it to keep the ranch's ex-Jesus-freak contingent happy. As a rule, he didn't talk about love very much. But that

112

day, Dizzy told us that this feeling of unbearable love is as near as we will ever be to knowing how God feels when he destroys the World. It is the feeling of God overjoyed to set us free, pained to hurt us so thoroughly and sad to have let us go so wrong for so long.

But somehow I doubt that's how Dizzy felt when he had everyone on the ranch kill themselves.

Leaving the tacqueria, I was calm enough to get my bearings. I found the 101 and took it the two exits back to the Vagabond. On the way, I stopped at a gas station minimart for beer, condoms, cigarettes, and some bags of pretzels and chips. This little bit of shopping left me a little moony as I drove off.

Back at the motel, Cindy was sleeping in the chaise lounge by the pool. She must have jumped in the water again. You could still see her pubic strip and her nipples through the damp and sparkly white outfit. The teenage boys were still there, still pretending not to gawk and pretending to swim. I walked to Cinderella and dropped a pack of cigarettes on her bare belly. She grabbed them and murmured but didn't wake up. That was probably for the best.

Then I got an idea of how to occupy myself. I drove over to the hardware store down the road. And, embraced by its strong, paternal Love, I bought a Master Lock and a small bolt cutter.

Back at the motel, Cinderella still slept, gawked-at and peaceful, by the pool. I went up to the room, locked and chained the door and closed the curtains.

32.

Until then, I wasn't too curious about the trunk. Guy said it had hand grenades inside and I took his word for it. That was weird enough for me. But so much had happened, and so much seemed possible that afternoon that I cracked open a beer and cut the lock on the trunk.

There were no surprises inside at first, just dark-green hand grenades. It looked like there ought to be about eighty or maybe even a hundred of them, resting in neat rows on layers of black foam egg-crating. They looked innocent of their purpose, round, neither dull nor shiny, like eggs recruited into a war without their knowing.

I picked one up. It had nice heft. I thought of the Love of the supermarket and how It gave us whatever we wanted, even ways to murder each other, if that's what made us happy. The grenade was cool as hell. My mind flailed through a thousand scenarios in which I might need it. But no dice. Then I tried to think of a way I could set one off, just for fun, and not get caught. But I couldn't come up anything realistic, at least not in Oxnard. I was a kid who met the toy that was his match. And I wanted to know how many I had. I took out the top layer of grenades, twenty of them. I put them on the bed and peeled back the egg crating.

Now, I know that credulity is for the crazy or those on their way. And I know that the same goes the same for you as it does for me.

But by now, I know the hiss and whisper that accompanies the appearance of the unreal, the ghosts and aliens and so forth. And there was none of that. So I can swear what comes next was no hallucination. And so you can take this at face value as part of my story, or simply as the archaeological ruins of a wrecked mind. But here goes: It wasn't just grenades in the trunk.

Below the first layer was a gold box, about the size and shape of a shoebox, nestled neatly into a rectangular hole cut through the layers of egg-crate foam and hand grenades. There was another layer of foam and grenades beneath it.

I took the box out of the trunk. It was heavy, almost solid. It gleamed yellow and white metal. The lid was a low, rectangular pyramid and the sides were etched with sideways-looking hieroglyphics. But the pictures weren't Egyptian.

The scene on one of the broad sides depicted a dark gold limousine, fleeing a bright platinum explosion and crumbling buildings. It was all very intricate. The fat man in the back of the car was expressionless. But there was one platinum drop of sweat, or a tear, rolling down his puffy cheek. His chauffeur had the head of a frog, with a huge mouth and big, blind frog eyes below his chauffeur's cap.

The other broad side of the box showed a procession of the species, starting with the mosquito and moving through the snake, the fish, the bird, mouse, dog, monkey, and then man. The last figure, after the man, was a flame. Each figure with hands or forelegs reached out to touch the next figure, peacefully, calmly, except for the man. His dark gold eyes squinted in fear. He withheld his hand from the flame.

One of the narrow sides was blank, a perfectly smooth, pale gold mirror. I looked at my tired, stubbly face in it and looked away.

The other narrow side was the one I liked the least. It was the familiar slim form of the alien, with its big black eyes and slit for a mouth, staring out at me. I could see the room reflected in its large, smooth eyes. The alien extended its emaciated arm to shake hands with a skeletal specter that barely rose from the surface of the box. Cradled in their shaking hands was a fat infant depicted in dark gold, with blazing white eyes.

That pissed me off the same way my own hallucinations did, as the lazy escapist fantasies of a failed mind. It made me hate the box. Some mind as ruined as my own, but even worse for lacking the ability to distrust itself, cast this stupid piece of malnourished religiosity in precious metals and loaded it into a trunk full of hand grenades. I thought of poor Guy, and got even angrier. If they'd killed him over drugs, I guess that's just an occupational hazard. But if they came from Fresno for this silly goddamn box, that was just too goddamn much. Fuck those deluded idiots and fuck all of California for making them and for letting them live.

My rage glossed over the real question: Exactly what the hell was going on? And what had I gotten myself into?

It was right about then that I seriously worried for the first time in a while. The bikers might be willing to write off a trunk full of hand grenades and a few kilos of cocaine as acceptable losses. It's that kind of business, I would think. But a gold box inscribed with their LSD-and-Star-Trek mystical code would probably have an interested party attached, who might be more persistent.

Between my credit and ATM cards, my paper trail hadn't gone cold for a moment since I left Dizzy's ranch. Any private detective worth his salt could find me in a day or two, for any client with a few dollars. There was also Guy. And he was helpless if he was still alive. It probably wouldn't take too much leaning for him to tell that interested party where I'd said I would go and what kind of place I'd be staying in. That would be right fucking here.

It was time to come down to earth and make some plans. First off, I'd have to relocate my extended party with Cinderella, maybe to Nevada, to another hiding place. Carson City came to mind. For all its flaws, taking a week or two to drink, fuck, and get high with Cin was still the best plan I had going. A momentary personal inventory was enough to tell me I still wasn't ready to go back to Mo, New York, and the human condition.

And if she wasn't into Nevada, I could just give her bus fare and the rest of the blow and cut her loose. I would get rid of the grenades and hold on to the gold box to placate whoever wanted it, if they ever found me. I could leave the grenades in a parking lot somewhere and call the cops to go get them. After that, I would play out the string on this squalid romp until I was ready to return, penitent, or just fed up, to the World once more.

That was the plan I came up with in the few numb seconds before opening the box.

33.

The World is not a mirror. It is not a shotgun leveled at your heart. It is not here for your benefit or for your education. It is not a letter addressed to you, regardless of what the Hindus or the Jungians or the hippies say. The World is a procession of things and situations that mostly have nothing to do with you. You just happen to be there for it. Sometimes it matters that you're there, sometimes not. There is no destiny you are fulfilling, no fate you meet, no true self you become.

No one wants to learn that. It took me a while to figure it out, and a while to accept it. But opening the gold box, I was jolted into thinking the other thing. The inside of the box was lined with crimson velvet, like the inside of a jewelry box.

Resting on the velvet, strung together in an open-mouthed oval were Dizzy's teeth. Next to the teeth lay something else that I'd been trying not to think about for the last few months, the silver-and-blue handle of the hunting knife I'd left buried beneath Jack's ribs in New Mexico.

I recognized Dizzy's gold-capped front tooth from his otherwise surgically perfected smile. Removed, you could easily tell the false teeth from the real ones and the molded or filed-down ones from the natural ones. Not a lot of natural ones. The knife handle I knew from my lengthy recapitulations of those moments in Las Cruces when I made Jack a corpse and myself a killer. This was the murder weapon, all right. The handle still had dried blood on it.

But there was no need for me to recall. Beneath the oval of Dizzy's teeth was a gold plate, engraved: THE MOST HOLY TEETH OF DIZZY OF NEW MEXICO. And beneath the knife handle, a similar plate read: INSTRUMENT OF THE ASCENSION OF DIZZY'S DISCIPLE JACK.

Sometimes the strangest things of all just aren't that surprising. Reaching into the box, it felt like I was reaching out and finally touching my real life. Maybe I was going just crazy. But at least I wasn't afraid.

I picked up Dizzy's pit-boss teeth. They were strung together on an elastic string, like candy jewelry. After all the craft that went into the box—the gold, platinum, and velvet—the cheap string surprised me. I put the teeth on like a bracelet and snapped it against my wrist, as if to wake myself. The teeth rattled. It felt like they gave me some kind of power. The knife handle had a nice heft to it. Whoever had prepared it for the box had cut off the blade cleanly, right above the handle. When I gripped it, some of the dried blood came off gummy on my sweaty palm.

Feeling powerful, I stood up on the bed, with a suicided guru's teeth on my wrist and my neutered murder weapon in my hand. I tried to fathom how Dizzy and Jack had come back to me through a circuit of coincidences as these macabre good-luck charms. I checked my sensitive palate for reality and I could taste that this was real.

Some of the grenades rolled off the bed onto the thinly carpeted floor. But I wasn't afraid. I stood there awhile, in the bumped-through quiet of the motel room and stared off, as if I could see through the wall, past the town and out to sea, to the destiny this squalid mystery was leading toward.

Despite the lack of sleep, the loss of a friend, and the dissipated visionary experience from the supermarket, I felt strong and awake. I stood on the bed and stared. I knew at that moment that whatever happened to me from here on out was not just a wild and irresponsibly told anecdote, not an accident. And I was neither its innocent victim nor its imperfect witness.

From there on out, the World would indeed be a mirror, the harshest and most honest kind. It would be a shotgun, leveled at my heart.

34.

That's when Cinderella came back from the pool.

She was wearing her stripper suit and carrying a hotel towel and her cigarettes. She opened the door with her key, but the chain on the door stopped her.

I let her in. She stopped a foot inside the door to take in the scene, following the knife handle in my hand to the bracelet of teeth on my wrist to the hand grenades on the bed and floor, to the gold box on the night stand. I think I had my shirt off by that point. Her face indicated this was not something she had signed up for, but she didn't say anything.

"Oh, hey. What's up?" I asked.

It was all I could come up with.

"Wh-what's going on?" she stammered.

I smiled at the strangeness of it all, at the sudden intrusion of meaning into the day. I shut and rechained the door. I grabbed Cinderella and kissed her hard. It took a moment of kissing before she kissed back, but she eventually did. She pulled away and giggled, nervous and frightened, but turned on. Or at least faking it better than she had.

I started taking off her damp, spangled outfit, giddy and confident. My palm was still gummy from the blood on the knife handle when I cupped her taut, spherical breast. I could tell she was afraid, and I pressed my advantage. We made love like we meant it on the bed, next to the trunk. No sexual gymnastics or show-offy dirty talk this time. She was quiet and seemed honest in the sounds she did make. I stayed above her, up on my arms the whole way through. It felt like I was making love to the whole World, fearlessly, on top. Hand grenades bounced off the bed and thudded onto the carpet as we went at it.

Let them detonate now, I thought. There has to be a Valhalla for people who die like this. We could've been the last man and woman having the last screw in the last crappy motel room in the last shabby town on the last planet that mattered in among an infinite sprawl of galaxies. The thought made me harder. She made more noise each time a grenade hit the carpet.

What this was like for Cinderella, as later events will show, I will never know. Probably just another routine fuck with another dangerous and crazy man on the way to whatever it was that she actually wanted. When we were done, Cinderella pecked me on the cheek and broke out more cocaine from the duffel bag. She cut up some lines on the nightstand next to the gold box and started at them with a rolled-up dollar bill.

"Want some?"

"I'm just going to take it easy for a minute. But go ahead, help yourself."

She said nothing and twirled her blond hair behind her neck. She was still naked. She hit two quick lines and scrunched her face into two hard blinks directed at the wall. Her eyes opened wider. She bent over for another two quick lines. I suddenly felt very lonely. I watched her bare ass like a voyeur while she snorted a few more lines off the dresser.

The sun was setting and I really was beat. Anyway, it seemed like she was having a fine party on her own. She turned

119

the TV on and paid me no mind and snorted some more, smoked cigarettes, and changed channels next, so thoughtlessly nude, like a billionaire child throwing money into the street.

Sleep came beautifully, reassured me that the supermarket's Love had made Dizzy, my dad, and Mary Beth truly okay. The Love that struggled clumsily to reach them through potato chips, deodorant, floral-printed paper towels, face creams, and plastic forks had finally found them through me.

I remember smiling as I fell asleep to the sound of Cinderella changing the channels.

35.
Air-raid sirens wailed in the distance. I've been in a lot of towns that liked to run the sirens out of Cold-War nostalgia or something, but I never really understood it. Nonetheless, I woke rested and calm, like a guy in an ad for a hotel. Checking the clock, I saw it was six o'clock at night and I'd been asleep all day. The TV was on a cop drama. But the volume was way down. I turned on the nightstand lamp.

The room was a big mess. Too much for the maid and probably too much for the local cops. It was an FBI-sized mess. Beer cans, chips, cigarette packs, a big, dirty coke baggie, hand grenades everywhere and the gold reliquary box. I had a dead man's teeth on my wrist.

Cinderella wasn't there. And the cocaine was gone. The money in my wallet was gone. My car keys were gone. I went out on the balcony, and the Pontiac was gone. The ashtray was full. What I wanted wasn't a drink, but a hangover. I wanted to feel wretched enough to deserve this betrayal-wrecked awakening.

It all closed in fast. I was a sitting duck in a hotel room with a trunk of grenades strewn about and a solid-gold hieroglyph-inscribed box. Cinderella was nice enough to leave all that behind. I can't say I really blame her. It must have spooked the hell out of her once she had a second to think about it. So she took what she felt she was owed, and then a little more, and took off.

At least she left my drivers' license, ATM card, and most of my credit cards. Beyond that, I had no car, no cash. The one really nasty thing she did was to take my shoes, just to slow me down. The maid would show up in the morning to call down a whirlwind of authority on me. But my strange adventure would have to continue. And it would have to start with shoes.

I took a deep breath, pulled on some pants, snapped the bracelet of Dizzy's teeth against my wrist and put the hilt of the knife in my pants pocket. That got my nerves straight. I got dressed and called a cab from the room.

The cabbie was a fat man in sweatpants, with a huge gray T-shirt and an old LA Rams baseball hat who was visibly unhappy to pick up a guy with no shoes. When I got in the car and told him where I wanted to go, he just idled and said nothing. I said I'd double the fare. He started driving. The cabbie breathed so heavily that it was like he was snoring while still awake. He got even less friendly when I said I had to go to an ATM to pay him. He expressed his displeasure by breathing even heavier. He was unhappy and seemed to have a talent for spreading it around.

At the Wal-Mart, I gave him $80 to get me some shoes and a pair of socks. The shoes cost $40 and he forgot the socks. He kept the change and I didn't say anything. I had more places to go and I didn't need to attract attention by getting into a fight with this fat bastard over $40. I was vulnerable enough already.

To cap it off, I rented a car, another Pontiac. It was newer but smaller. At the car rental place, the sleepy proprietor put my driver's license into a box with a red light in it. I imagined my Social Security Number running off like a centipede to the cops, FBI, CIA, ATF, Homeland Security—all those guys. A red square would flash on the computer of some public servant. And that would be that. My safari into ambiguity would give way to a simpler, darker journey.

But no dice. Paranoia is largely a hopeful impulse. We want someone to be watching. And no one was watching the Oxnard Dollar Rent-A-Car, it seems. The cabbie breathed heavily as he counted the money. I tried to act like this was just another

Wednesday night for me. We parted ways and I drove off in my Pontiac.

So I was back where I started. Cinderella was at least someone to talk to. I drove past the sprawling plains of car dealerships to Denny's. It was a new, twenty-first-century Denny's, full of snappy, well-lit optimism, not like the Denny's that shared a parking area with my hotel.

The Denny's All-Meat Skillet was substantial, but I was still grinding my teeth with hunger and anxiety when I was done eating. So I ordered the chicken-fried steak, potatoes and all. Then, to the waitress' mild disbelief, I ordered the Moons Over My Hammy. Then I slowed down. Grease seemed to seep from my pores, and I was starting to get that hot, nauseous feeling that almost felt like safety. I lingered in the booth over a Denny's sampler basket of fried appetizers for another hour or so, trying to drink enough Coke to balance out the soporific effect of all the food.

"Quite an appetite tonight," the waitress said, bringing me more Coke. Free refills at Denny's. She was middle-aged, with brown hair and a big butt.

"Yeah," I stammered. "I'm celebrating. I just met my Weight Watchers goal."

I don't even know why I lie sometimes.

"Really. Wow. So that really worked for you?"

She was suddenly very interested in the conversation. *Shit*, I thought.

"Yeah."

"How much did you lose?"

My mind reeled for an answer. *I lost a million pounds ... a billion tons ... the weight of the universe ... I lost my shirt ... my shoes ... my service ... the weight of all the hopes and fears they say you should have ...*

"One hundred eighty pounds."

"Oh my God! How long did it take?"

It took twenty-nine years ... a lifetime of systematic abandonment ... eleven years of progressively worse decisions ... an instant of murderous horror ...

122

"Uh. Just over three years."

"Wow. I guess it really works. I did Weight Watchers for a while. I just couldn't make it to all the meetings. You know how it is. They want you to go in to be weighed every week. And it's just hard to find time, especially when you have a job like mine where the hours always change. I lost some weight. But when I stopped going, I ended up gaining it back. It's hard."

"Yeah. You have to be persistent. That's what they try to stress."

She leaned back and took a breath. She cocked her head back and looked at me with a mix of pride and awe, as if I had cured cancer or discovered the meaning of life. She shook her head without saying anything. It was absolutely bizarre.

"Well, *you* did it. And that's *inspiring*. It really is. So you just be careful not to gain it all back now. You know how hard it is to take the weight off."

She smiled and tried to take my shifty eyes in hers. I looked down at my basket of fried shapes.

"Yeah. I know it. This is just a celebration. I haven't eaten all day."

I couldn't tell if she was talking to me out of boredom or attraction. It was slow in my section of Denny's. And she had that Southern California blandness that made her hard to read.

"What's that on your wrist?" she asked.

Jesus help me, I thought.

"These ... these are teeth ... on a string ... it's a bracelet a friend made ... it was a ... a present, for my birthday, a few years ago."

"Really? Like baby teeth? They look big for baby teeth."

"They're actually ... uh ... monkey teeth. I was in the Army ... in the jungle ... in South America ... training ... and a monkey attacked my friend ... it had rabies ... we think. I shot it before it could bite him. So he pulled the teeth out and put them on a string and gave them to me for my birthday."

"Wow. That's really ... unique."

"Yeah. It really is. It's got a lot of sentimental value. He even put some gold on one of the teeth."

123

"If you were in the Army, shouldn't you be on a base somewhere? It seems like they need everyone they can get, with all that's going on."

I wanted to ask her what she meant. I'd been flipping past the news on TV ever since Phoenix. No use watching other vultures gnaw on the bones I'd once claimed. I even avoided the Weather Channel. And now, deep in a lie, my profound ignorance of the life of the nation was not something I wanted the waitress to help me with.

"I was discharged with a disability a few years back. I have a bad back. There's actually a rod in it."

"Oh my."

"Yeah. Two of them, actually. I should really get home and do my exercises for it now."

"Okay. Can I get you anything else?"

"Maybe just a chocolate milkshake and the check."

Waitress gone, the Coca Cola and the grease and the gravy muffled my nerves. And it was still early enough to have a whole evening to contend with. I had to put the grenades back in the trunk and lock it up before the maid showed up in the morning. Also, I had to check the news to see what was going on, and get out of Oxnard.

I would wait until morning to hit the road. The 101 to Denny's from the rental car place was just one exit, but it had taken me more than a half hour. And the way people were honking, wringing their hands out of open windows and driving on the shoulder made it seem worse than just Labor Day holiday traffic. Really bad holiday traffic, maybe with a few accidents, and a jackknifed tractor trailer thrown in. It seemed like it would take me a while to get back to the hotel.

The waitress came by and gave me a chocolate milkshake, the check, and a smile like a face forced into a fist.

In the half hour it took me to choke down the last chicken fingers and mozzarella sticks, I decided to call Mo, if my luck would just hold out another few days. The supermarket's Love made me feel strong enough to endure the million-round fight called workaday life. Goofed-up on that feeling as I was, I could have started my own cult. I'd call it the Church of Surviving the Caring Other (COSTCO). I could probably even have gotten corporate sponsorship.

I decided I could probably endure Mo's onslaught, the office, all of it. And it probably wasn't too late to write up the story for our Pulitzer and all the good stuff. I was tired of being so lonely and crazed. I could hear the hissing, whispering engine of craziness starting up again.

Things were looking up. I paid for my meal with three crisp twenties and left. I walked out into the orange light of the shadowy parking lot. As I approached my car, though, a guy with an Atlanta Braves baseball hat pulled down over his eyes stepped out from behind a van.

"Excuse me, mister, do you happen to have any jumper cables?"

His voice was shaky. He leaned against the van as soon as he had my attention.

"Uh, I'm driving a rental. I don't know if they gave me any," I said.

"Could you check?"

Something was off, and I gave him a closer look. The guy was in his late twenties, but dressed like a teenager, in a worn-out T-shirt with a surfer on it. One of his arms was covered in tattoos. The other one was gone, with a bandaged stump barely poking out of the T-shirt sleeve. The missing arm, the hat pulled low, and my own acute self-absorption are why I didn't recognize him right off. But I came around.

"Guy?"

"Excuse me?"

"Is that you?"

"Yeah. Hey man."

It definitely was him. I was happy to see my friend alive after all. But he was acting strangely.

"What's up? I was worried about you. I thought you were dead."

"No, man. Something else happened."

"But you're out of the hospital."

Guy shrugged, tried to smile. His attention seemed to drift past me and I heard footsteps, too close already. I ducked down, but the cattle prod was going for my ribs anyway. My muscles all clenched and unclenched violently. I hit the pavement. I think he said sorry. Then I was zapped again and blacked out.

> *The Population Reference Bureau predicts that the world's total population will double to 7,000,000,000 before the year 2000.*
> *"I suppose they will all want dignity," I said.*
> *"I suppose," said O'Hare.*
> —Kurt Vonnegut, *Slaughterhouse Five*

36.

The Compound, Alaska—It could have been a day or a few hours or just a minute chock full of dreams. Sometimes it was like sleeping. Sometimes it was like being high—vivid and vague and pleasantly scary all at the same time. And sometimes it was just a fucking nightmare, like being buried alive. In a rising panic, I'd be in hell, or the aliens would vivisect me, or the nuts from the ranch would interrogate me.

Some of what I remember probably did happen, the dull parts, I guess. I was strapped to a stretcher and put in a big, cold metal room. I think it was an airplane, from the noise and the scraps of conversation around me. I remember something went wrong with that. A woman got yelled at, and they had to cut off the tip of my nose because of frostbite. I remember a lot of noise and blood getting in my eyes.

There was a middle-aged woman with stringy blonde hair and a dour expression who wore a crimson robe and chain-smoked cigarettes. She was always around, it seemed. Her job was to change my diapers. She didn't pay me too much mind while she worked. And she didn't seem to like me too much.

I didn't like her either. She was always getting her cigarette too close to my balls while she was working. Sometimes I smelled burning hair. But who knows. Hers was the only human interaction I could be somewhat certain wasn't a dream or a hallucination. Too drugged to speak much, I still had moderate control over my bowels, so I'd try to crap on her hands when she changed me. Aside from the transactions within my continuous, elaborate hallucinations, trying to crap on her hands was the only way I had of expressing my opinion.

But I was usually too out of it to even try that. I would come to and suddenly have a beard, or be in a different hospital-type room, or the diaper woman would suddenly seem older and thinner.

Most of the time I spent at a beach house from my dreams. Now, everyone was there: Dizzy, my father, my mother, the aliens, Mary Beth, Cinderella, the cult members, coworkers and sources from Long Island, Texas, Massachusetts, and New York, old high school friends and acquaintances, kids I knew from grade school, Little League, and preschool. As the months went on, the house became more crowded and the sea grew more unpredictable. It would rise up unpredictably, over the roads. A rogue wave would bring me the newspaper. By the end of my time as a deeply drugged near-vegetable, the water from at high tide covered the kitchen floor. But it didn't much bother anyone. We went for drives around town. We fixed up the house and ran errands. We had ordinary, pleasant conversations over dinner. And occasionally, I'd find myself alone with one of the guests, and everything would get real quiet around us. They'd say they were glad we had some time alone. They'd say there was something they were meaning to tell me. And in that heavy quiet, they always seemed serious. A lot of what they said then didn't make much sense.

Mom said she was surprised to hear about my promotion, because she never thought I would amount to much. But she was proud, she guessed.

One of the aliens showed me a path it had made between a series of birds and house pets it had cut sloppily in half. It promised me descendents more numerous than the sands of the beaches if I'd walk down the bloody aisle with it. I said I'd think about it. The alien gave me its card, which read "Alien" at the top. The writing below moved around when I tried to read it.

My father told me a story about how once, in a fit of rage, he had thrown a perfectly good sandwich on the ground, and kicked it. He said wasting the sandwich made him sadder than he had ever been and he never got over it. He had Sandy, the golden retriever, with him. Sandy looked happy enough.

Jack said soon it'd be my turn to get in the game. No one wanted me in there, but everyone else was injured, he said. It would be my one shot, and he just hoped I wouldn't fuck it up like I'd fucked up everything else.

The biker I found on the floor of Guy's motel room told me about a kid he knew in high school who would dip lottery tickets in liquid LSD and sell them so you couldn't cut them up into hits until the lottery was called and couldn't turn the ticket in if you won. He bought acid from the kid anyway, he said.

The Human Resources lady from the newspaper who arranged for my rehab said that even though I was still covered by the company's health insurance, I should be careful.

Dizzy told me he really does miss being special. And, despite all the obvious advantages of being dead, he envied me. He gave me a big weird smile and a thumbs-up, with both his eyes looking straight at me for the first time.

Cinderella told me she thought we should just be friends.

The woman from the front desk of the Redlands Good Nite Inn handed me a snow cone with a straw in it and said, "Welcome to Alaska."

Mary Beth said she was sorry about what happened to my nose. She told me she'd met someone in her new place, and then asked me to give her back her stuff, soon, please.

It went on and on like that. Each time, what they told me seemed important to them and seemed important to me. It may all seem like dreamy word-salad crap, the settling of personal scores via drug-induced hallucinations. But I was crapping myself in an incoherent fog for months. And I ought to have something to show for all that time. Anyway, the part about Alaska turned out to be true. That's where I really was—diapers and all—having my beach house dreams.

Using the diaper and the room as my main criteria for sifting reality from everything else, here's everything I figured out in those months: I was in a windowless room with new corrugated metal, bare fiberglass insulation, and pale blue sheets for walls. The room was part of a sprawling steel building. I was on a steady, intravenous drip of something that kept me crap-myself incapacitated most of the time. And we were way out in the Alaskan wilderness.

Over time, I either developed some resistance to the drugs or they lowered my dosage. I started to wake up.

"We're laying low until the revelation is complete," Guy told me one of the first days I was awake for more than a full hour.

He said other things, but they scurried off to shady corners of my mind where I couldn't find them again. Guy had changed since that night in the Denny's parking lot. He was thinner, paler, with dark rings under his eyes. But I had a diaper on, so I guess he was doing better than me.

Guy told me about the revelation in the room with the corrugated metal walls. So I took it to be possibly real. I wanted to ask him ... well, I wanted to ask him a few things ... but the drugs slowed me down before I could do anything but loll my head like an idiot and let out a little moan.

37.

Then one day, my right foot was gone. It was a neat job, just above the ankle. Not much blood showed through the gauze on the stump. After being lost in my own mind for so many weeks, the loss was more amusing than anything.

After that, though, the drugs really began to ebb. I went from paralyzed to stupefied to stupid to scatterbrained to just drowsy and itchy and irritable pretty quickly. I got my speech back and I could use a bedpan. I never saw Diaper Bitch again.

Despite the jumpiness, helpless rage, insomnia, physical weakness, and constant itch, coming down was a relief. Despite a rocky friendship with reality, I embraced the consistent narrative of my dull days struggling with solid food, staring off into space and resuming independent bowel movements. The food was cereal in fake milk twice a day, with rice and beans for dinner. But I was glad to be eating like a big boy again.

Given a mirror to shave with, I saw a deformed mess. The muscles in my face had melted, leaving the eyes oversized and haunted, and a mouth afloat in a stubbly puddle of pale fat. My nose looked like a rat had started to gnaw it off and then found something better to do. Reality was dull and unpleasant. But it was reality.

Guy was the only one I knew there. But I met some new people, some Eskimos, some not, who fed me and put fresh gauze on my stump. Diaper Bitch must have been a specialist. I tried flirting with the new girls a little. I can't imagine I cut too dashing of a figure, irritable and ugly and winded after a walk to the bedpan. Anything to fill the time, though. And you never know. Some women dig helpless men.

The real thing I was looking forward to was things making some sense. So the next time I saw Guy, I had some questions ready, starting with *what happened?*

"Yeah. We cut your foot off," Guy told me.

"But why? Was it infected or something?"

"No. Someone wanted it."

"Who?" I asked.

"I don't know."

"You don't know who wanted my foot?"

"I don't really know them that well, no."

"Well, did they say *why* they wanted it?"

"No. Not to me, anyway."

"But, Guy, you know, I need that foot, you know, to walk. If they had asked me for it, I would have said no way. 'No way you can have my foot.' So I'm pretty upset about this, you know? And I feel entitled to know why they cut it off. I mean, I'm pissed. It was *my* foot."

Somehow this wasn't registering with the once quick-witted Guy.

"Well, dude, you didn't say anything at the time," he responded.

"That's because you and whoever the hell else is up here, doing whatever the hell you're doing, had me totally incapacitated here like some damn veal calf."

"I thought you were just sleepy."

"No one is that sleepy."

"Well, whatever. Man, I wish I was on half the shit you were on. You got to miss the worst of it, really."

"What the fuck do you mean, 'lucky'? I have no goddamn foot."

"Well I have no arm, asshole," Guy said, wiggling his stump. "And it didn't get chopped off carefully in surgery while I was out on the good, heavy drugs."

"What? Are you saying that you getting shot was my fault? You knew what was coming down the pike. And I even stuck my neck out for you while you stuck around too long."

"Man, I *wish* I had known what was coming down the pike. I forgot all about fucking Redlands. Getting shot was the luckiest thing ever happened to me."

"What the hell are you talking about? What came down the pike? And why are we in this place? And how long was I, uh, like that?"

"You mean how long were you in a diaper blowing spit bubbles?"

"Yeah, that."

"You've been like that since I got here. And that was like six months ago, I think. Time is funny up here. For a while, it seemed like it was night outside for weeks and weeks. Now the days are starting to almost feel like days again."

It's odd, but my first thought was: Jesus, I must be thirty.

"So what the hell happened? What happened after you got shot in Redlands?" I asked. I tried to be forceful. But I could barely hold my head up. And I slurred my words. I was getting drowsy.

"A lot happened. And I changed in the biggest way I could. I really did. I'll tell you the whole story another time. You're

132

getting sleepy."

"Goddamn sleep."

"Don't knock it. Sleep is the best thing going right now. And anyway, don't worry. Just relax, really. Whatever happens next is pretty much out of your hands anyway. I know it's out of mine."

My hands were so heavy. So was everything. If anything was in my hands, we were fucked.

"Guy?"

"Yeah."

"We're still friends, right?"

It was a whisper barely strong enough to get past the thick saliva in my mouth.

"Yeah man. You may be the only friend I have. And I'm sorry about that thing back in …"

Guy's words became raindrops hitting the roof of a car. And sleep gently removed the million questions that fought to be asked. But for the first time since I opened the crate of hand grenades, I felt hopeful of answers. Little by little, reality was resuming respectable dimensions.

And Guy was probably right. Sleep was the best thing going.

38.

It was a tidy stump, just above the ankle, a little raw and pink, but clean. It was an alien thing—the stump. So much for making a run for it, I thought.

And there was a bonus. Whoever cut the thing off apparently had a creative streak. Around the base of the stump, they tattooed: THE HEALTHY WILL NEVER FIND TRUE HEALTH, NOR THE SANE EVER BE HONESTLY AT EASE. Thanks, guys. Really, you shouldn't have.

The inscription bewildered me. It was one of Dizzy's. I remember seeing it painted on the wall of his audience room. It was a favorite consolation for his unfixable flock.

First the gold box, then the tattoo. I'd had my Dizzy story ready—get-rich guru turns apocalypse nut—with all the derision that entails. It was the only editorial view I could have. I spoke to my readers and I spoke for them. And the goal of my readers was not truth or transcendence. Their goal was to live. So I informed and entertained. The information helped them survive and entertainment helped them want to. That's what I was paid for. My own goal was also just to live, more or less.

And that made Dizzy a joke. Because, to be frank, after the last few thousand years of ripping each other off, no one was really buying religion, ancient or new. That's why we used the word *charismatic* for people like Dizzy. It was a way of saying that hard-core religion consists of a talented but unbalanced huckster selling the hell out of something that doesn't exist to a pack of dupes.

That's why Mo was so hot on this story. We could bring our readers religion in terms they could not ignore—sex and violence, Mo said. We could deliver Fraud Our Father to our readers in a police report. We could catch Him in the act of murdering His flock. Churchgoers and noisy atheists alike relished the thought of God brought to trial. Like the men on the posters at the DMV, He was, at the very least, guilty of being delinquent on child-support payments. Only He was a few millennia in arrears, Mo had cracked. And I went right along with him. It beat covering politics or the crap on TV.

In the World, Dizzy was a sideshow, but in the compound, he seemed to be the headline act, at least at first. Looking at my foot, I realize I'd missed something big that was going on right in front of me at that ranch. Maybe a more intrepid reporter would've gotten it. But before Dizzy and company called it a life, someone was watching. Someone with the wherewithal to collect Dizzy's remains and the murder weapon that felled his number two, someone who could drug me, ship me up to Alaska and cut my foot off with impunity.

You have any ideas who that might be? I don't.

Guy hurried by the door to my room the other day. From my drowse, I tried to flag him down. But he kept on moving.

I flirted with one of my nurses for some answers. But flirting mostly meant smiling and a bit of small talk without drooling at that point. She was a big, cute Eskimo girl with shiny black hair. But when I asked who ran this place, she just smiled a calm, knowing smile and shrugged her shoulders. When I pressed, as charmingly as I could, she said my boss would tell me everything.

So I had a boss. That was big news. It didn't explain much. But it was something.

The next day I got Guy's attention. I avoided the larger questions and asked him about my boss.

"News travels fast around this place," he said.

"Yeah, I guess it does. So I'm going to have a boss?"

"I guess so. Everybody has a boss. But yeah, that must be why they woke you."

"Who is he?" I asked.

"I only met him once. We work in different areas. He seemed like a nice guy, though. I forget his name. He says he knows you. You'll meet him soon."

"When?"

"I think pretty soon. You probably need to kick the rest of what's in your system. I wouldn't worry, though. Judging from the chow you're getting, they must need you for something. Support staff only gets that stuff once every few weeks."

I had a bowl of rice with Spam and a little ketchup in it. I hadn't touched it.

"I'm not too hungry, you want some?" I offered.

"Really?"

"Yeah. Go ahead."

"Oh, wow. Thanks man. But don't tell anyone."

"No problem. So what do they need me for?"

"I dunno. You said you were a reporter, right? Maybe they want you to write a story. We have a lot of editors and stuff here."

"Will they let me go home then?"

"What do you mean?"

"Will they let me go? Like, after the story?"

"Home?" Guy asked, raising his head from the food, and furrowing his brow.

"I mean, will I be able to go back to my life, my job, you know, home?"

"That's a good one! Home! For all your time in Stupidville, you haven't lost your sense of humor. I'll give you that, man."

Guy went back to really shoveling down my dinner.

"I don't get it. Guy, what's going on?"

A long-muffled fear and panic rose in my voice. Guy could hear it.

"Jesus jumpin' Christ, man," he said sadly through a mouthful of food. "You really *don't* fuckin' get it? You really don't know?"

"Hey asshole, I obviously don't. So how about filling me in?"

"There's nowhere to go home *to* anymore, man. It's all gone. My daughters are fuckin' gone, my bitch ex is gone. Buddy's gone. Everything we liked or hated or thought we would get around to one day is wiped the fuck out."

"What do you mean?"

"I mean that all the stuff they said would happen, it happened."

"What stuff?"

"Fuckin' all of it. The plagues, the bombs, earthquakes and volcanoes, the alien invasion, the angel's fiery sword leveling the cities and towns. The zombies eating each other. The nine-hundred-foot-tall Jesus H. Christ kicking over office towers like God-fuckin'-zilla, you know?"

"No. I don't. I don't know. What line of shit are they feeding you here?"

"I wouldn't believe it either. But I saw it and it's no shit, seriously. You were lucky. You missed most of it. It all hit at once. It started getting bad right around the night we got you at Denny's. You missed the bombs by maybe a day."

"What bombs? And who is this fucking 'we' that zapped and fucking kidnapped me?"

"Kidnapped? Hey man, I'm sorry about how it went down. I

136

am. They were in a hurry, and they were right to be. But don't you think you might want to thank us? I mean, we saved your ass."

"Saved me from *what*? From having a foot?"

"I can't believe I'm the one who has to spell it out for you. The whole World went crazy and burnt right up. I saw it with my own eyes, and on TV. This is really it. I mean, it's the end, game over, *that's all folks*."

"We're still here."

"It's not, like, totally over yet. There's us, maybe a few other pockets. But the cities are gone, most of the suburbs, anyplace by an ocean or a river or a volcano. I don't know if you were supposed to know this yet. And I wish someone who knew more about it could have come in and told you already. I'm sorry, man. Just get some sleep for now. It'll be a few more days and you'll be totally out from under the shit they had you on. Then they'll put you to work," he said.

"Guy, come on, you're my friend. Just tell me what's going on. If you can't tell me, just say you can't tell me. Just don't lie. Don't feed me a line."

"I know what you're going through. It took a while for it to all sink in for me, too. But I ain't lying about this one. Really, scout's honor, cross my heart and hope to die."

"Guy, how did you wind up here?"

"I was picked, like you."

"Okay. But why'd they pick us?"

"I don't know. It's not like I was particularly deserving. I don't even know how they got me past the cops and out of the hospital. They took me out to this old, like airplane hangar, way out in the desert. I was half dead by then, shivering and screaming and wishing I could pass out when they amputated my arm. No fucking anesthetic or anything. I almost lost my damn mind from the pain. While I was getting over that, they said that they'd chosen me. They said that I'd cried long enough and hard enough on this earth. They said I could help them. They showed me the things that were on the way. Terrible things. And they said there was a way, that I could dodge what was coming to all

137

mankind. I knew that the cops were probably looking for me, and Buddy, too. Then they said they wanted my help picking you up. I'm sorry about the cattle prod, man, but that wasn't my call."

"Who said all that to you?" I asked.

"I don't really know them that well."

"But did you ever meet them before that?"

"No."

"What did they look like?"

"I don't know. Nothing really sticks out about how they looked."

"And they, they were people, right? Like human beings?"

"Like I said, I don't know them that well. And man, I'm sorry about your foot. It could have been worse. We all lost a lot these last few months. I don't even want to think about what happened to the girls up in Vermont. They were living by a river out there, I forget which one. But from what I heard, those towns by rivers didn't do so good. And who knows what else might have gotten to them. The more I hear about, the more I hope it was the river."

"I'm sorry about that, if it's true."

"Thanks. How fucking crazy it all is. Remember how fucked we were in Redlands. No money. People trying to kill us. Fucking stupid Cinderella. Now it's the World that's totally fucked, and us sitting pretty! Well, maybe not pretty, but we're not half as fucked as the lower forty-eight, Europe, China, you name it. Not yet, anyway. I mean, we're sitting out the kind of shitstorm we can't even imagine. The Feds, the cops, Buddy, and his jerkoff psycho friends, bitch Mandy and her bitch mom—they're all dead or dying down there."

Guy was excited to find a happy thought to mine. A piece of rice shot out of his mouth with the last word. It landed on the edge of the emptied bowl. He stopped talking to pick it up carefully with his fingers and place it back into his mouth.

"Guy, seriously though, who do you think it was who took you out of the hospital? I mean, after you got shot in Redlands. How did they get you out? There must have been cops around.

You couldn't just ..."

"Listen, man, what happened back there doesn't matter anymore."

"Okay, fine. I guess it doesn't. But who was it?"

"Who's involved with this place and this thing we're doing up here—that's a whole other story. And I'm not really the one to tell it. It's way above my pay grade. You'll meet your boss soon and he'll straighten you out."

The conversation was my biggest exertion in months. And it wasn't getting me much of what I wanted to know—the who, how, when, or the why. Guy talked about his job up here, fixing engines, digging a basement, acting as a lookout on the roof of the building. The women were friendly, but a little strange, he said. Then he said he had to go, and left.

I watched from my bed for some evidence of the apocalypse. I listened for proof in the conversation of the people passing people by my room. But there was nothing—just an echoing voice now and again, the sounds of a food cart moving down the hallway, the occasional flicker of a body walking by the doorway in the fluorescent light of the hall.

39.

Over the next few days, it started sinking in, like Guy said it would. Maybe I should have been more skeptical. I could've applied Occam's Razor. But Billy Occam had been shrugging his shoulders ever since Oxnard. So I took Guy's word. He was my friend, after all. Even if I was taking his word on that, too.

Humanity being 86'd from the bar of the World probably deserved more reflection. But I was really anxious and excited about my new job. I wondered excitedly about my new boss. Would he be wearing a robe, military garb, a business suit, a tinfoil hat, or would he just be a naked alien? I wondered about the job, the duration, compensation and benefits.

By then, my dosage of downers, painkillers, and general obliviates was down to almost nothing. I itched all over. One day all I did was scratch until I was a crying mess. The sweet Eskimo girl I'd been flirting with sat with me a few hours and said nothing when she brought my food. That was nice. Other days were less extreme, but miserable exercises in ignoring myself, ignoring my itch and my panicked thoughts. Yeah, Guy, really lucky to be here.

But overriding all that was a sense of my life starting again. Even if it was mopping the floors, all I wanted was to be busy until it was my turn to walk down the devil's throat. I realized, while scratching maniacally, that I wasn't afraid of death. I realized I never was. I was afraid that everything would start to get good after I died. I was greedy and jealous more than I can say I ever loved being alive. If Guy was right and everyone else really has lost, why bother staying in the race? That was probably the only nice thing about the apocalypse.

Guy came by a few days later. He looked worried and paler than before. He hurried through the conversation.

"Sorry I haven't been able to talk more lately. I'm just really busy."

"What are you up to?"

"Just working. Doing some double shifts for a few people who got sick. Just trying to stay on board a little longer."

"What do you mean?"

"They're doing some cutbacks, like, layoffs this week."

"But why?"

"We're running through the supplies too fast, I guess. The last shipment never made it, and they underestimated how much everyone would eat. So they started cutting some projects and cutting staff."

I guess the end finally found its way up here to Ice Station Elect.

"Where are they sending the people?"

"You going to eat that?" Guy asked.

He was eyeing my breakfast. My jaw was finally strong enough for a too-chewy lump of corn syrup in a gold wrapper called a PowerBar. It was for active lifestyles, it said. It tasted like wet, sweet dirt. But the withdrawal had made it almost impossible for me to eat.

140

"Go ahead. So where do they send them?"

"Thanks man. I haven't had one of these in weeks. Seriously. *Starvin*. Um, the layoffs?"

"Yeah."

"They just send them off, like, into the wilderness. They give you a little food and some extra clothes and tell you to start walking, just to go away. If you aren't out of sight after an hour, they start shooting from the roof."

"Are you fucking kidding me? Where did you hear this?"

"I didn't hear it. I'm one of the shooters. Me and two other guys. It was just a few days ago."

"Jesus."

"I know. It sucks. I was surprised. I'm still a decent shot, even with just the one arm. The other day, one of the other guys ended up shooting this old guy, one of the editors. He just wouldn't leave. He said he was from *The Economist*, this loud, English prick. I didn't really know him when he was here. He kept yelling that he had to finish his *important* work *his* way and that he would *not* be bullied, all in his funny accent. We warned him a bunch of times. I even took a few warning shots, even though we're not supposed to. Then one of the guys shot him. Fucker got him in the thigh. So the English guy starts begging for help and apologizing and promising shit if we'll help him. He was like that for like a minute. It was bad. The other two guys were just laughing. I never thought that kind of shit was funny, so I just finished him off. No reason to leave him like that. Dumb fuck."

"Jesus Christ. Poor guy."

"Yeah, I guess. Poor everyone, you know?" Guy mused.

"I guess so."

"I felt bad, but what does it matter anymore, you know? It's going to be me walking off into the snow and the mud sooner or later. I'm just shooting for later. They say it's not so bad up here in the summer, and that's only a month or two away. At least now it's not dark and freezing all the time."

"When did they start cutting people loose?"

"I think two weeks ago, or so. It's hard to get a grip on time up here. I really don't know how they expect us to survive out here in fucking boondock Alaska."

"So no one is going to stay here, like, long term?" I asked.

"I don't know. I don't think so. Someone said they're going to bury all the books here and then torch the buildings. But I heard that like, third- or fourth-hand, so I'm not sure. Smart money says everyone here is probably fucked one way or another."

"Even the bosses?"

"I don't know. Who can even guess with those guys?"

"Okay, but, Guy, do you have any idea why we're even up here?"

"Like I said, I don't really know. And anyway, it's not my place to go into that so much. I'm just a little worker bee. But I think you're going to meet your boss any day now. He'll give you the straight dope on it, as much as you're entitled to, anyway. They aren't always so chatty about what's going on here. But he'll probably tell you more than they told me. They're certainly feeding you better. But I gotta get back. I'm scheduled for more digging. Thanks for the food, man. Hang in there."

Guy left with the rest of my PowerBar.

I was alone, and it all sank in a bit more. Clueless and helpless, I seethed at the aliens and the asshole cultists with nothing better to do at the end of the World than drug me out of my skull and cut off my damn foot, seethed at Guy for selling me out to these nutters, seethed at Jack for coming after me that night in Las Cruces, at Cinderella for stealing from me, at Dizzy for killing off all those weak, but not-so-bad people, seethed at the dead devotees who desperately wanted the apocalypse as revenge on the reality principle for the pain it had inflicted on them, seethed at Mary Beth for being so miserable that I couldn't reach her, and seethed at myself for not going after that Pulitzer.

Who knows? The story might have shattered Dizzy's mirage of holy prescience for whoever survived, the assholes who had me. It might have called down a rain delay on the apocalypse. Who knows? The story would have shown the pretensions and the suicidal hopes of those apocalyptic assholes in the harsh light

142

of our readers' perspective—a perspective well-bowed to the reality principle. My story might have helped people deal with the apocalypse when it came. Who knows? But instead, I ate Domino's pizza, jerked off, and got drunk, while God splashed gasoline around the whole World.

Not that regret matters here in the rapture. There are no charming anti-heroes in the Book of Revelation. I checked.

40.
"Long time no see."

My boss in this perverse place and time, it turns out, is my old boss, Mo.

He sat by my bed. His narrow, crooked face was more pitted and gaunt, his beard white where it'd been black and yellow where it'd been white. His blue, button-down shirt was stained and threadbare—but it was Mo. His presence confirmed everything I'd been told. If Mo was here, going along to get along, in my crude little hospital room, then it must be the end of the World. It all sunk in a little deeper.

"Yeah, I know ... long time ... uh ..." I stammered.

"It's good to see you too."

Mo seemed hurried, distracted, and a little pissed. I guess understandably so.

"Hey, Mo, I'm sorry about just taking off like that. I tried calling a few ..."

"Come on. I don't give a crap about that. You can't think I care about that, can you?"

"I don't know. I really don't."

"Then just let me do the thinking for both of us, okay?"

"I guess so."

"You're crazy if you think I don't have bigger things to wring my hands about here than your latest unprofessional freak-out. I don't want to hear about it or think about it or know about it. We've both been laid off by the paper. And, like everyone, we have been laid off from the whole damn world. I take it you've figured out that much by now."

143

"Yeah. I heard. I just wanted to say sorry about flaking out and all. Things got really out of hand."

"You are damn right. You want to know just how out of hand they've gotten? Every town between the Pacific and the Rockies big enough to sport a Wal-Mart is a smoking, radioactive hole. Washington DC was overrun by snakes, literally this time. Manhattan is a goddamn ship of the dead in the middle of the Atlantic. The South seceded then begged to be let back in the Union, after it got what was coming to it. And America got off easy, compared with what I heard from overseas."

"Yeah, I heard most of that. So there were some disasters and everyone freaked out. But that doesn't mean it's the end, does it?" I asked.

"That's almost a good question. And the answer is yes. It's all over but the shouting. And I have it on good information that worse is on the way to cut the shouting short."

"Okay. So let's say I believe you. Let's say I buy it. What's your point?"

"My point is that I have no time, patience, nor use for your bullshit. Now I'm not going to sugarcoat it: There's no Pulitzer to be had, there's just about nothing to be had. The story of the century is that the story is over. And there's going to be nobody to read about it for a very long time. That said, you and me have a lot of work to do and not much time to do it. *Capiche*?"

"I guess."

Then Mo saw my foot stump with the tattoo sticking out from under the sheet.

"Jesus. Are you all right?"

"Yeah, mostly, except for the foot. I think I'm mostly off the drugs I was on."

"I *mean* the foot, did that happen here?"

"Yeah. Same with the nose. I think the nose was frostbite or something. I was hoping maybe you could tell me what they were thinking with the foot."

"I had nothing to do with it. But I'd heard they did things like that. Jesus, I'm sorry about that. Management has its own ideas about how to treat the staff. I don't always agree, but this isn't the type of place with a suggestion box. You're okay otherwise, I mean, mentally? You can function, you can write?"

"Yeah. I'm pretty together."

"Good. Because this isn't the paper, in case you haven't noticed already. If you freak out, flake out, or fuck up again, you won't have a Human Resources department to save your ass. There's real work to do and real consequences if we don't."

"Gotcha, Boss. So, tell me, what are we doing?"

"I am glad you asked. Because this is probably the only good news you will hear for the rest of your life. Are you ready?"

"Yeah. Hey, drumroll please. What is it?"

"We're writing the story for the distant time when people will be able to read again. We're going to give them the tip of the burnt end of five millennia of civilization. We're going to tell them how this story, our story, and history came crashing down, what it meant and what it means."

"Well, I've been asleep for most of whatever happened to everything. So I don't know what I can add."

"That's fine. It's almost better that you didn't see what happened. You're writing a very important book in the story."

"Sure. Great. What part?

"It's a major piece of the story. 'The Gospel of Dizzy.'"

This was not the sort of book deal I had in mind when I flew out from New York.

"What if I don't want to?"

"Let's just say ... let's not get into that. You don't want to know and I really don't want to be the one to tell you."

"Awfully early for the threats, isn't it?"

"What I will tell you is this—you want to write this piece. I can't promise you money, awards, promotions, or any accolades that you'll ever hear. But this will be the only chance that you have to actually *matter* before you die just like everyone else."

"Okay. So if I do write this piece, what then?"

"Not much. You live a little better and a little longer than most everyone else here in the compound. But, from what I can gather, there is pretty much nowhere else to go. Even this place is a dead end. Just not yet."

"Great. Just great. Thanks a ton for waking me up."

"Spare me the sarcasm, all right. I saw my wife and daughters killed back in New York. So I am very far from finding your biting ironic bullshit cute."

"Hey, Mo, I'm sorry to hear that. I really am."

Mo nodded, and had a private sigh.

"But what does that have to do with this business, with me writing a gospel of a fraud who had his followers murdered?"

"I'm glad you asked. You see, by all the reasonable standards, I shouldn't give a damn about your project or anything else. My life is already, for all intents and purposes, over. But I keep going. And I *do* care. I care because this is bigger than the personal tragedies behind us. This is the biggest thing anyone in the whole World is a part of right now. Something I do today, something I'm part of today, could determine the fate of all human civilization down the line. I *know* my life will not have been a waste. For all the wonderful things in my life before, I never had any reason to imagine I'd be part of such a thing."

"All right, Mo, I'm listening. Tell me more."

"The World below is still burning and will burn for a long time to come. An apocalypse actually takes a while."

"Rome wasn't destroyed in a day," I offered.

"Nice. I wish we could use it. What we're doing up here is building a library, probably the last library for a very long time. The DNA of a civilization is in its books. They give shape to human civilization and, if you're so inclined, to the human soul. What we're trying to do is to keep that DNA intact, maintain the thread of consciousness through the current succession of catastrophes and the catastrophes to come. But we're also trying to genetically engineer, to stay with the DNA metaphor, the next civilization. We have more than a hundred fifty editors and even more support staff working to that end, both here and at a few other, scattered locations," Mo said.

This was my new-employee orientation.

"And how are they deciding what books to keep and what to

146

get rid of? What sort of purge is this?"

"I don't know. I'm actually pretty low on the totem pole. And it's not my area, anyway. I'm not one of the book guys."

"So what are you doing?"

"I'm a newspaper guy. Me and a few other editors have been watching the wire services, the satellites, and the radios for the last few months and drawing together a book on the last days drawn from that. The final dispatches came through about two weeks ago."

"You mean there's no more news?"

"None. We have access to the satellites, radios, and phone lines—and all of them have gone silent, except for the occasional voices over the shortwave."

"So now what?"

"I'm almost done with my part of the editing there. Then it's me and you—we're going to work together, just like old times, on the 'Gospel of Dizzy,'" Mo said, excited.

"Huh. I guess that makes sense. But there are a few problems. For one, I only knew him a few months."

"Don't sweat it. You knew him better than anyone still breathing, and you did your research beforehand. And anyway, it's a gospel. Most of Jesus' disciples didn't know him much more than a few months. And they probably didn't take as many notes as you did. Also, J.C.'s gospel writers did their work forty to a hundred years after the guy died, so you're a much better source."

"I guess, but the other problem is that I didn't like Dizzy. I never really bought his line of bullshit. I mean, I wasn't really supposed to. He knew that, and he never trusted me that much. It's like having a gospel of J.C. as written by a guy from the Roman census bureau."

"Don't overthink it. You'll be fine once you get started."

"And there's something else. I mean, come on, Mo. This guy wasn't a damn messiah or a prophet or anything. Just some suicidal, megalomaniacal ex-banker. You're smart enough to know that. He was full of the worst kind of vague and New-Agey shit. I mean, the guy was a joke. What did you call him before I left—our 'Suicide Star Search winner'?"

"Something like that—maybe it was 'the Suicide in Our Savior Star Search.' So what? So we joked around about it," Mo said.

"So you believe he's a prophet now? You can't be serious."

"He was right about this mess."

"Come on, Mo. Don't blow smoke up my ass. You know some loon or another has been predicting the end of the world for the last two thousand years. Someone had to get lucky. Dizzy was just the asshole who hit the jackpot on the prophecy lottery."

"Prophecy lottery—good one again. You're on a roll. And I see your point. But the bosses want a gospel. And you're the man to do it."

"Who are these damn bosses?" I asked.

"They're not so bad. But let me deal with them. It'll be easier that way. Just write about Dizzy in a way that fits a gospel—with wisdom and truth and miracles and parables and so forth. I can get you a copy of the New Testament if you need a general template. They just finished editing it down the hall."

"So you want me to lie?"

"Come on, you know better than that. There are no lies. But spin it. You're a pro. Leave out the bullshit and accentuate the holy parts. Embellish a little where you need to. That's not dishonest. It's professional. You know how it's done."

"What if I think most of what Dizzy said and did was bullshit?"

"Would you please stop being so childish. Come on. It no longer matters who Dizzy Sheehan was or what he was about. And it matters even less what *you* think he was about. Focus on what should survive about the man and about what he had to say. Don't think of the petty New-Age dictator. Think of the people who will read this and have to figure out how to live. Don't think of Dizzy. Think of the story. Think of the readers. You have a great story, a front-pager like no one's had in two thousand years. And I just gave you your angle. The thing should write itself," Mo explained, with a gleam in his eyes.

"So I should just make stuff up?"

"You have creative control. I'm sure you overheard things or 'forgot' things that were meaningful and important. We're well out of libel range. Listen, we could do this without you, but I want you on board. And more importantly, the bosses want you on board. It's basically just a big feature story. Just keep it in simple language. Small words and short sentences. The readers will probably be half-literate at first. They'll have endured a few generations of immense hardship, from what I hear. I'm thinking no more than 20,000 words."

"And Dizzy, who's he supposed to be in this?"

"I don't know, exactly. But why don't you try holding your nose and playing up the whole destroyer-of-a-sick-world/new-hope-for-a-reborn-world angle? Just give them what he said, or what you think he said, what he did and why it mattered. Just bring the content, and the readers will bring the devotion. I know you can do it. You're a pro. And there are a few perks if you do decide to write it."

"Yeah, yeah, yeah. You already told me—a few more days alive and the cheap immortality of being read."

"Other than that, you'll have a bigger room, to work and live in. And better food. So what do you say?" Mo asked.

"Can I get a room with a window?"

"Yeah, I think a room with a window just opened up."

"All right, I guess I'm in."

"That's great. We start tomorrow."

"Okay. But, Mo, what happens when the gospel is finished?"

"What do you mean?"

"I hear supplies are running short. I hear they're cutting staff."

"Where did you hear that?"

"News travels fast in this place."

"I guess it does. The cuts are mostly the result of projects ending. But the place is still running well on the whole."

"You sound like a spokesman for a company that's doing layoffs."

"I guess I'm a company man."

"So what about when our project is done? I mean, this

gospel sounds like a pretty big deal. What happens to us then? Will we get any special consideration?" I asked.

"Like I said, I don't always agree with Management's methods. And I don't know what happens when we finish. I heard they throw the people out into the wilderness. I don't have any reason to think we'll be any different. It's May now, so it's actually not that cold. People getting the boot actually have half a   chance   out   there."

"And what about us?"

"Well, I don't think there are any more supplies on the way. That's probably why our deadline was moved up two weeks."

"How long do we have?"

"Still plenty of time, like nine weeks. It should still be summer if we finish on time. So there's a chance we could survive, just not a really great one. The sooner we finish, the more warm weather we get out there."

"So, really, tell me, who is running this place?"

"I don't know them that well."

"But you believe them? You believe them that the World really is at an end? You believe them, that we're doing the right thing with this library, this gospel?" I asked.

"I do. I don't have anything else left to believe. And they ... they got me out of New York when no one could get out of New York. They found me and they knew what I'd gone through. They knew I wanted to die. They told me there was a reason, that there was one more thing I had to do, and it was the one thing I had prepared my whole life for. They said it would redeem me. They've been right so far. They've done things and known things no one could. And that's the only kind of credential worth respecting nowadays," Mo said, more sincere than I can ever remember seeing him.

And that's how I got up to speed on my situation: Our World's aflame and I have nine weeks to write my spurious gospel for its next tenants. Then they expect me to melt into the tundra with their acorn of a library.

I decided to seduce my Eskimo nursemaid.

41.

The next day, I followed Mo out of my room. I was slow on crutches and he had to keep stopping so I could catch up. Opening a door, we left the infirmary and crossed a balcony over a big, open office space of low cubicles, lit by strong white lights that were strung from a ceiling about thirty feet high. It looked and sounded like a newsroom, with people talking intently over cubicle walls, or goofing off by a drinking fountain, or ignoring the noise and typing hard for a deadline. The only sound missing was the ringing of phones, the running to answer a phone, and the schmoozing or badgering of a source.

After a tortuous trip down the stairs, I was worn exhausted. But from there, it was just a few doors down a hallway down which the office space echoed.

"Here you go. Home sweet home," Mo said, opening the door.

The room was what Mo promised—a bed, a metal desk with an old laptop and some notebooks on it and a window that looked out on an expanse of sparse tundra. There were still patches of snow and ice around which the earth outside bloomed in a dull sort of way, brown with flecks of color—little leaves and flowers, sprigs of grass and patches of moss rolled off to the distant mountains. Everything surviving tenuously.

After so long on my epic, windowless nap, the sunlight seemed a miracle. There were colors and shadows in my room that the fluorescent lights hadn't permitted. I was back among the living. If this was my last home, I could do a lot worse, I figured. Mo's voice vanished for a moment before coming back into focus.

"... should write it up on the computer. There's a file of news articles on Dizzy on it if your memory fails you. And we have Xeroxes of most of your old notes from the ranch. They're in the folder on the desk. You can use the notebooks for drafts and outlines. I'll check your copy every few days. There's a toilet down the hall. Just bang on your door and someone will help you over there. Otherwise, they'll bring you meals to the room, so you don't have to crutch around too much. Okay?"

"Looks good. But there's something I need. And I mean this. I need it or else I can't work."

"What is it?"

"Tell whomever or whatever's in charge that I want that Eskimo girl, the young one, who feeds me most days to keep bringing my meals. Otherwise, I'm not going to be able to write a word. I'm serious."

"Okay, I'll see about it. But a word to the wise: Watch it with the ultimatum talk. You're not in a union shop anymore. But I don't think it'll be a problem. Just so long as you focus and get your work done."

"No problem. I'd just like to have her around."

"Okay. I understand. Just remember, the sooner we finish this, the better chance we have of getting out of here while the weather's still decent."

"Okay, but I've heard that freezing to death is actually a pretty good way to go. You go numb, euphoric, hallucinate nice things, and then you just sort of fall asleep. But if you've cooked up a better way to go, don't be shy. I'm all ears at this point."

"I'll bet you are. Now get to work. I'll check back in a few days."

Mo left. The last time I saw him was back in New York, at the paper. The part of the office I'd worked in wasn't that different from the bullpen we'd just walked by.

That day was cold, and I'd packed the last of my stuff into a storage unit in Queens. I stopped into the office to pick up my laptop. Mo was busy, running from one meeting to another, disheveled, distracted, and intense as always. He stopped at my bare cubicle long enough to wish me a quick good luck. For him, that was a tearful good-bye.

Then I caught a cab to LaGuardia. The cabbie didn't have any folkloric cabbie-wisdom for me. He was talking Urdu into his headset and I was listening to music on my headphones. The World withers, that's how it ends, I thought snottily as the US Airways terminal came into view like the cathedral for a diocese of shopping malls. They say Nero fiddled while Rome burned, and imagine what'll burn now that we have satellite TV and surround sound. It was a nice, sneering pop-culture apocalypse. It sounded good. I may have sensed I was full of shit at the time, but I had no idea just how full.

Realizing I'd never see New York again, I can almost make out the vast dimensions of how stupid I was. Almost. That'll take a while to sink in, too.

The room was quiet. I looked out the window for a minute and thought of my Eskimo nursemaid. Then I started up the computer. It was an old laptop, the kind the paper would have given you as a loaner. Smudged gray plastic.

42.

They gave me coffee with breakfast in the new room. And it seemed that they'd spiked the food with some kind of amphetamine. So I was rarin' to go. And rarin' in more than one way. My Eskimo nursemaid's name is Nuna. I found that out on her first visit to my new room. Secure in the knowledge that I'd be dead by this time next year, I started flirting with her as best I could. My talking so much made her nervous at first. I just kept my mouth moving, saying whatever came to mind to keep her in the room. She brought my meals every other day. A cult-looking girl with a bad smell to her and an older Eskimo woman with all-black teeth split the other days.

Like the older Eskimo woman, Nuna's teeth were also starting to go bad, a darkness coming in around the edges. But it wasn't that bad, really. Her round face and steady way of looking at me with her dark eyes calmed me. Her skin and hair glowed in the sunlight of the room. Even if I made her uneasy, she smiled when I smiled at her. Maybe her eyes didn't seem to smile along with the rest of her face, but it was a start.

I know I was missing a foot and a chunk of nose. But I did have the whole if-you-were-the-last-man-on-Earth thing going for me.

Though I tried to work, I daydreamed about her a lot of the

time. In my daydreams, I was a lost Arctic explorer on the verge of discovering the Northwest Passage. My foot got sheared off by an iceberg along the way. Something like that. Damaged and doomed in the harsh Alaskan wilderness, Nuna finds me. We fall in love. She brings me into her Eskimo tribe. I overcome their suspicions and we wed and rear Eskimo children. I live out the rest of my days in indigenous bliss, slowly forgetting all the aspects of the Big Western Hurry I was born into. We would be in love—a big, speechless kind of love. We wouldn't have *issues*, or anything else we would have to talk about. We would look at each other across the igloo and just know. We wouldn't even have to smile at each other.

But the real Nuna never lived in a tribe. Talking more yesterday, I remembered to ask her questions to keep her interested. She was at the university in Fairbanks, studying to be a hospital administrator, when the heavenly boot came down.

"I left school in Fairbanks before anything bad happened. I went to see Mom. Rob left and Mom was sad. I went to be with her."

"Who's Rob?" I asked.

"Mom's boyfriend. He's a bad guy, especially when he drinks. And he drinks when he's not working. He called my mom some names and then left one day. She was upset, so I went home to keep her company. I was with mom in Koyukuk when the news about the disease came on the TV. It said the miners got it first. It came from under the ground. The disease sounded terrible. It ate people's muscles, their skin, everything. The pictures on the TV of people in Fairbanks made mom sick and we had to turn it off."

"So what did you do?"

"Mom said not to go back to school and I agreed. We stayed in the house for a week. The supermarket sold out of food and no more came in. People started living on the fish and the animals they could catch. There was enough and everyone shared what they had at first. After a month, there were no more shows on the TV. We already knew about all the troubles down in the lower forty-eight. But we had been okay so far. All of this worried

Mom. Some of the radios still worked. But the news on them just got worse, for all of Alaska. Then the news wouldn't come through on the radios anymore. It was just people talking. Some of them said things that were even worse than the news."

"So how did you wind up here?"

"After a few weeks, a man came. He offered us some work. He said there was plenty of food here. And the people in the town were acting strange, suspicious, very angry and crazy. Mom was still worried about Rob and I thought a new job would take her mind off it. We decided it would be good to leave and work for a while. It was only a short plane ride. And the man said he would pay for our flights."

"Who was the man?" I asked.

Her gaze hardened a little and her back stiffened. Her face, usually so unexpressive, betrayed her. She squinted, not sure if I was trying to trick her.

"It doesn't matter," I said, trying to calm her again.

"I should get going."

"No—I mean, stay for a little."

She did. We had a minute or two of silence. It wasn't uncomfortable, but it wasn't comfortable, either. She was a lot more at ease in silence than I was.

"You're very pretty. You know that, don't you?" I said to break the quiet.

It seemed to surprise her, who seemed so far beyond surprise. She even blushed.

I did, too. I was all jumpy from nerves and the speed in my food and a strange sense of pressure that this might be not just mine, but all of humanity's last chance at anything like the kind of love that preoccupies us so much. She looked at me, not sure what to do.

"Thank you. You're nice," she said.

And her eyes smiled too. I reached out, took her hand and held it. For a moment, the World rearranged itself with us in the center. We seemed to sit there for a long time. She looked at the clock, because we cannot yet reside in timeless bliss or in death. Then she leaned down to me and wiped a speck of food from a

155

corner of my mouth.

"I have to go now. But I'll come back tomorrow, okay? I promise."

"Good. I want to see you again, soon."

Nuna turned around and looked back at me on her way out the door and smiled, awkward and happy.

43.

I sidled up to the desk again, stared at the computer screen and felt professional again. I took out a notebook and a ballpoint pen and started drawing the shape of an outline.

Only a few minutes into my grand task, boredom closed in. I was distracted and needed a distraction. I knew it wouldn't work, but I tried to go online. It didn't. I hunted through the files on the computer for a video game, porn, something to read, anything to entertain myself. There were big word documents marked "Final UPI," "Final AP," "Final Reuters," "Final BBC," "Final Dow Jones," and so on. I opened one. I read through the AP document, which ran chronologically from the time I was in Oxnard. Then I read the AP document and the end of the BBC file.

Reading the early reports, I was envious. You could hear how excited the reporters were about the big stories they got to cover. But in the beginning, they thought they were making their careers with those stories. And it showed. They were there, right at Ground Zero, strutting their stuff. They tapped good sources, got snappy quotes and interesting angles on what was going on. Their stories were provocative to the point of fear-mongering, which was funny because, skipping ahead, I could see their later stories struggle to seek out a contrarian note of calm or hope.

I wished I'd had the chance to cover some of these stories, like the house pets of St. Louis in open mutiny, murdering their masters.

I wished I'd even had the chance to ponder it. But I already knew what it added up to. Mysteries are supposed set us free from reality, in some small way. That's why people seek out the weeping statues, the strange lights in the sky, the levitating yogi. But when a mystery has you in its sights, well, that's another story. When it's not confined to a Ripley's-Believe-It-or-Not anecdote, a mystery is just something you don't have a chance in a million of dealing with successfully. And it took a good while for just about every reporter covering the onslaught to learn that much.

For all their stories and commentaries, the reporters learned only one important thing about the mystery that was taking place. And they learned it too late.

What they learned was that the mystery does not like us.

Three quarters of the way through the news documents, the reporters had lost their enthusiasm for the story, even as it got bigger and stranger. Ground Zero was suddenly inescapable, and just about no one had the appetite to cover it anymore. When the White House couldn't be reached for any kind of comment anymore, and the death of a few hundred from a pack of bipedal pigs in suburban Illinois didn't warrant more than two quick paragraphs, you could tell they were just mailing it in. Hearsay passed unquestioned, quotes repeated the obvious, unnamed sources would be quoted saying they didn't know what was going on.

Wit and humor vanished from headlines. "Undertakers Overwhelmed," was the best anyone did by then. "Six thousand Dead as Suburban Plague Jumps City Barricades," was the dominant tone. I kept reading and chewed on my ballpoint pen until I drooled blue ink. I looked out the window, but the view rebuked me, saying *there's nothing to see here, get back to work.*

Reading through the World's death rattle in clean, inverted pyramids, a few things surprised me. I really didn't think things could disintegrate so fast. And I don't mean just the buildings kicked over by the nine-hundred-foot Jesus, gnawed down by steel-eating insects, or toppled by a hydrogen bomb from the People's Republic of China. In just eight months, the roads, power lines, farms, cities, airports, most of the people, and any sense of civilization vanished one way or another. And the news disintegrated right along with it.

Some of the last news reports from Reuters are just pleas for food, first aid, and general help transmitted to its subscribers. Later pleas mentioned sexual favors from the staff. Hardly a proud final moment for journalism. For those of you keeping score at home, the BBC held out the second and bowed out with a short, polite good-bye. Bloomberg lasted the longest, quoting the going rate for a pound of semi-fresh human flesh at the very end.

Another surprise was that virtually no news reports dared refer to the long string of seemingly unrelated catastrophes as the apocalypse. Maybe someone in the government asked that they refrain from it. Maybe it was the advertisers. You would get phrases like "this is the eighth natural disaster to strike the Denver suburbs in the last three weeks," but almost nobody, except maybe the evangelical neighbor of a woman eaten by a giant snake, ever called it Armageddon. And that part was added just for laugh-at-the-yokels local color.

The columnists were the first to be overwhelmed. Too much was happening for them to pick one theme and chew on it. The news outpaced them. I can't imagine that anyone really cared about what they had to say, anyway. But they kept cranking out the opinions, with their smug little photos. Editorials during Armageddon were by turns hilarious and maddening. One columnist cried racism for when the fire departments let a building full of zombies burn to the ground. Another complained when an army unit fired on a fleet of fire-spewing flying saucers. One righteously denounced the religious persecution of the Air Force for trying to slow down the nine-hundred-foot Jesus with air-to-surface missiles. Another columnist claimed that the president made a mistake by not imposing martial law earlier. Then the same columnist railed against martial law as being un-American. One sternly chastised the FEMA director for an off-color remark she made about Chinese people. One bewailed the whole of Western civilization for having created atomic weapons. Another columnist in the same newspaper reproached the United States' failure to launch its nuclear missiles sooner. One mocked the new emperor to rise out of the East. Another lamented no longer being able to get a good tuna steak. More than one columnist ridiculed the preachers for crying Armageddon, when they could have organized their congregations to fill sandbags. It went on like that right up until the Revelation had all of them right between its molars.

I was hoping for some clarity at the end, some sense of exactly what had happened and why. But I had no such luck, not in any of the documents. The horrors kept coming, faster, weirder, and worse. And any string or speculation that might connect or explain them seemed to disappear with the next calamity. Bombs all over the West, plague and pestilence and livestock revolts in the plains, angels torching Los Angeles, snakes in Washington, zombies in Texas, earthquakes in Florida, monsters in a New York a thousand miles adrift, volcanoes in Maine, Saint Francis directing an onslaught of birds on San Francisco, whales attacking Boston.

Zombies! But why not, really? Whatever were all those Other People to you anyway?

Nine-Hundred-Foot Jesus! What's an apocalypse without J.C. making an appearance? But didn't the sneak previews make it seem like he had more than just a cameo?

Nuclear Bombs! Good bread-and-butter annihilation. Have your whole World destroyed without leaving your home-cooked sense of reality—not a bad deal.

Angels with Fiery Swords! What? Did you think you were special? You get done in by heaven's civil servants.

Plagues and Famine! Nice and traditional.

Floods! Even more traditional.

Alien Invasions! Well, we were pretty much done with the planet anyway. I hope we get our deposit back.

A Meteorite Collision! And you thought those crappy blockbusters were just a waste of time and money.

Six Foot Frogs! Jeez. Don't ask me. You know, I just work here. And just barely.

I guess nobody ever had a chance of knowing what was going on. Everyone with any credibility was waiting until all the facts were in. And all the facts never made it in. A huge frog ate

159

the facts. And a volcano sprouted beneath the task force looking into a recent revolt by cars, trucks and kitchen appliances.

And if *they* couldn't get a handle on what was happening, I doubt anyone ever will. Whatever happened in those last days of reality was either smarter than us or just more senseless than we can accept.

I tried to think of all the people I would miss. I thought of the bars, the casinos, the apartments, the beaches, the hotel rooms. I thought about the times I had been untwisted enough to enjoy those people and those places. And I told myself they really were gone forever. I pulled as hard as I could on my own personal sympathy cord. But the motor wouldn't catch.

My imagination just shut down as I read to think of the human lives crystallized in those body counts. They had fought and wondered why they bothered fighting at all. And then they died. Everyone I ever knew—they were all gone.

But I got to have a good job, and maybe even a cool girlfriend (I crossed my fingers). There was still no fucking justice.

44.
At my desk, the tundra bloomed dimly. Blooming wasn't its strong suit. A stand of trees clustered at the foot of far-off mountains. I waited for sunset to work, but it never seemed to come. The sun crept across the mountains, casting long shadows toward me, then swung around the horizon and out of view. The shadows stretched and receded, then spread out before me. That shadow was the first idea I got of the building's real size and it was big, the size of a shopping mall.

To calm my amphetamine-and-apocalypse breathing, I took a fresh ballpoint pen from a desk drawer and told myself to get to work. But my mind wandered back out the window into the warm summer tundra with Nuna. I was with her and the tribe, making sealskin coats for winter, eating fish and penguins, living in igloos, watching the aurora borealis like a big TV at night. I'd be an outsider, but all the more welcome for it. The tribe would make me a new foot out of whalebone. They'd inscribe the tribal insignia on it like you'd sign a cast. Nuna and I would make a brood of children who ate blubber and played in the snow. We'd discard the World and all that we'd been in it like a broken harpoon.

But to have the barest chance of reaching that fantasy life, I'd have to write. I scratched "DIZZY" across the top margin of a notebook page. And there I stalled. Dizzy was the most broken harpoon, the most hare-brained of all the fads to fall into the fire. I took a deep breath to reconnect with my inner professional.

So, I tried starting the book when Dizzy was still with his family in New Jersey, after he resigned from the bank. He'd chased the World's idea of success as far as he could. And though he got what he was after, he still wasn't happy. So he condemned the world. I read that as he did, and called it *spiritual hunger*. Then he took his toys and went out to the desert. I called that a *hermitage* and planned to find a simpler word later. Then, when the people outside of his control became too much trouble, he solved that problem like he solved all the problems in his cosmology, with annihilation. I guess I'd call that an "ascension," to make it sound like he did the right thing.

As a reporter, media-relations flaks were often my natural enemy. But there I was, maybe the worst flak in history, telling timeless lies into a tenderly naïve new epoch. But a job is a job.

I started to sketch an outline. By the time I started typing, I thought I had the tone and the story pretty much figured out. It wasn't inspired any more than remembering how to ride a bicycle is inspired.

In the peaceful days of the last president of the United States of America, John Dizzy Sheehan left his home and family in New Jersey. With a group of sixty-two disciples, he settled in New Mexico, one hundred miles from the city of El Paso, Texas, to set up paradise on Earth and to instruct mankind before its final horror began.

Mo was right. This thing would write itself.

45.

From there, I started putting out a thousand or so good words a day. Mo was happy. And more importantly, Nuna came by every day. She brought me little presents, extra food and stuff like that. Our backs were to the wall, but were falling in love. Innocent as children, we held hands and talked quietly. We kissed carefully, like we were just discovering how to do it.

"I called all my friends in Fairbanks when the news started getting bad," Nuna told me one afternoon, her beautiful, moon-round face stoic as she spoke. "I told them 'Come to Koyukuk. It's safe here.' But they wouldn't come. They said they would just stay on campus. Men from Washington DC were coming to fix things. They said they'd see me when I came back to school. I called a few weeks later and they said they wanted to come to Koyukuk, but the men from Washington wouldn't let anyone leave then. The next time I called them, all I got was voice mail. I invited them to come to Koyukuk on their voice mails. But no one called back."

Telling the story, Nuna was calm. When the sunlight through the window hit her hair, it gave off a silvery glow. On those afternoons, she was the most beautiful thing I had ever seen.

"Then soon their voice mail didn't even pick up. Mom was upset. She kept talking about Rob. He wouldn't be okay if things like phones didn't work. She started crying that he was dead somewhere and that we should try to find him. We had to bury him the right way. She started drinking again. And Mom shouldn't drink. And I have to tell you something else."

"Okay, go ahead," I said.

"I hope you don't get upset."

"No way I'd get upset."

"I had a boyfriend, too. He was my fiancé. I met him at Fairbanks. His name was Freddy. He bought me a ring with a diamond in it. He stayed in Fairbanks when I went to see Mom.

He had to write a paper. A few weeks after the phone and the TV and the radio stopped working, I gave up on him. I just knew. Mom was crying over Rob. I thought that was silly. 'The world's not going to live for us, Mom,' I said to her. 'And we can't die for it.' But she kept crying. She was drinking. I took the ring off and put it in a drawer. I thought it would help Mom. But it only made her cry harder. You're not mad, are you?"

"No."

"I know men can be jealous," Nuna said.

"It's all right. We're here now. The rest doesn't matter. How's your mom now?"

"She's mostly all right. I thought here she would have things to do and wouldn't be reminded of Rob. She also can't drink here, so she's a little better. But she doesn't eat as much as she should, sort of like you."

She pinched my stomach and laughed.

There was a silence. Nuna smiled. I took her hand. And then I told her my whole story. Almost the whole story. As a courtesy, I went light on the details about Mary Beth and left out Cinderella completely. The telling felt different with Nuna. All the shame and guilt vanished from it. Through her, I had found some sympathy for myself.

When I was done, she squeezed my hand and looked in my eyes. She didn't say anything about it. So neither did I.

We changed the subject, and talked about the situation and the prospects on the compound.

"I guess Mom and me'll go to Koyukuk, when it's time. I hope they'll still fly us back. If not, I don't know if Mom can make it all the way back. She's not very strong. I hope Koyukuk is still okay."

"Huh. I wonder what I'll do."

"Don't joke. You'll come to Koyukuk too, of course. Stop being silly," she laughed and kissed me.

"I might not be able to make it, with my foot being, well, gone."

"Of course you'll make it. Even with your injury, you could make it. You are young and strong. And I'll help you. I will help you forever."

I believed her.

"Maybe all this will work out for the best. I already met you. And most of my old friends should still be in Koyukuk, I think."

We didn't talk too much more about the real future after that. I don't think either of us honestly expected to survive much beyond our time in the compound. We were just too much in love to admit it.

Sometimes, we'd just look out the window, hold hands, and say nothing. It was then, I think, that I felt the closest to her. Our dread made us look into each other's eyes harder, speak more honestly, and enjoy each other more. Even with time being short, it was a little more than a week of talking and kissing and staring out the window before we'd made love. It was a new experience for me because it meant something, and that almost superseded all the ordinary enjoyment of the act. Her body was strong. Her hips wide, breasts big with the nipples pointing down. She wasn't a fashion model, but she was a real woman, and a good lover.

The sex was simple and strong. It was like we'd reinvented the sexual act, freed it from a long servitude as an obligation, an entertainment, and a meal.

Nuna was my muse. When I was writing my grandiose and dishonest tract on Dizzy Sheehan, it was Nuna's face I saw above the computer screen. I knew that each lying word brought me closer to her. So I wrote quickly and I wrote well enough that nobody would ever ask me to write the damn thing again.

There I was: I had good love and I was doing good work. There wasn't much else to say. Misery makes you loquacious. Happiness shuts you up.

It was the happiest I'd ever been. Funny, really.

46.

In hindsight, I should've seen it coming. My speed-dilated senses were acute enough to hear the activity growing fainter outside my door. I should have noticed the spattering of voices becoming sparser, more distressed. And I could have inferred something from how the amphetamine dosage in my food was being increased until I could begin to taste faint, bitter traces in my food. But I was so high, so in love, and so wrapped up in my gospel. And things were going too well for me to think they could go any other way.

That's the way it always seems just before the floor drops out.

"The story is good. But it's a little thin. Management doesn't like the disciple stuff. And I think they're right. I mean, this isn't supposed to be a Platonic dialogue."

"What were you thinking, more of a bubonic dialogue?"

"Good one. But listen, I'm serious. It needs work. I mean, I liked the Mary Beth character, but management doesn't like the smart-aleck stuff. She comes off as wiser than Dizzy in places. I'm cutting most of her stuff out. Also, this Jack guy is vicious. What's the point of keeping him in it? I mean, it hardly fits for a holy man like Dizzy to keep that kind of human Rottweiler so close. I'm cutting him out entirely," Mo said.

"I thought I made him pretty human."

"Not human enough."

"But you said you liked it."

"I do, I did. It's good stuff. But it reads, I don't know, too much like a novel. The characters are too flawed, especially Dizzy. They want it to be more gospel-like, more straightforward. They want Dizzy to be more *likable*."

"I thought I was making him likable."

"They want him to be more likable. Maybe give him a pet, or an orphan he takes care of."

"Are you serious?"

"Unfortunately, yes. And there's too much with the disciples, and not enough preaching, not enough prophecy."

"But the gospels I read had a lot of disciple stuff."

"Well, read them through again. Those disciples screw up, get corrected by the Savior, and then forgiven. They ask questions, and then sit and listen as the Savior struts his stuff. They're more like literary devices than three-dimensional

165

characters. No one wants to hear about the actual freaks on the actual ranch. They served no purpose in life and they serve no purpose here."

He had a mug of tea with him. And judging from his eyes, he looked like he was tweaked on the same stuff as me. And I was ready for another dose, which had me in a bad mood. Nuna hadn't come with my food. No one had, actually. Now this shit.

"Okay. So you want a puppy and you want more prophecy. Great. How much? I mean, where do all those cuts leave us?"

"They leave us coming up short, by a lot. Just get cracking on adding more philosophy, aphorisms, instructions, parables, and so on. Really showcase how wise Dizzy was. You can bring the disciples back in later, but go easy. They can have personalities, but only insofar as they each bring different sorts of questions to Dizzy."

"All right, I'll see what I can do. And what's going on? Why the hell wasn't there any breakfast? I'm ... starving."

"I don't know what that's about. There were more cutbacks this morning. A bunch of editors along with some support staff were laid off. Maybe the reorganized duties aren't up yet. We're getting up on deadline. It's just us, a few others, and some support staff left now."

"Where's Nuna?"

"Oh, right, her. She left as well."

"What?"

"Yeah. Someone told me to tell you that she left today."

"You've got to be fucking kidding. Tell me you're kidding."

"Sorry. She was laid off, dispersed."

"You mean they fucking *dispersed* Nuna? I told you I couldn't work without her here. What the fuck?"

"I thought this might upset you, so I checked on it. They didn't disperse her at first. I did what you asked of me and made sure they knew when you started work how she was special to you. At the time, they told me Nuna would stay on as part of the last batch of support staff."

"So what the fuck happened?"

"What I heard was that they had to lay off Nuna's mother.

And so Nuna asked to leave with her. And so they let her go. That's what I heard. And I'm sorry about that. But we're getting near the end here."

"What the fuck?"

"I know, it's too bad. I don't want anyone to suffer more than they absolutely have to, even you."

"That is total bullshit," I roared. "Why didn't she come to tell me, to ask me, to say good-bye?"

"It's just standard procedure. Once it's decided that someone is laid off, they're put outside. No one's allowed to make the rounds and say good-byes. It's a safety thing. There are no deviations from the dispersal protocol allowed, under any circumstances. That's the rule from on high," Mo said.

"Fucking *dispersal protocols?* Can you even *hear* yourself? There are like twenty people left on the fucking *planet* and you're telling me about goddamn virtue of obeying *standard procedure.* I can't believe this shit."

"I know. But what are you going to do, rebel? Go on strike? Quit? There is nowhere else to go, nothing better to go to, and really, if you think about it, instead of just flying off the handle, nothing better to *do*, in light of our situation. You have two choices, finish the gospel, or don't. Welcome to reality, asshole. We saved you a seat."

"Go ahead. You can fucking have your reality. And congratulations, Mo, you found a way to be the planet's last brown-nosing stooge. You should put it on your resume when you get to hell," I spat.

"I'm *sorry* about what happened. But these guys, they will get what they want out of you, one way or another. They have a bad side. Not everyone gets dispersed, I know that much. You have to suck it up for, I don't know, like *two weeks* and finish this thing. Just keep it together that long."

"I can't believe this shit," I said.

"Believe what? That your girlfriend of like, *a month*, chose her mother over you? That the World ended? That you have an opportunity like no one's had in two thousand years? Well they're all true. And if you don't like it, then I have good news:

167

We'll be dispersed soon enough."

"Thanks, Coach. Real rousing stuff."

"I'm just trying to help you here. What did you think? You were going to marry the girl in the compound *chapel?* You thought you were going to have a *future* together? It's a little late in the game for this, but you have to grow up."

I slumped down in my chair and turned toward the window, half expecting to see Nuna walking out toward the distant mountains. I was numb and paralyzed with anger.

"*Anyway*, what I was *saying* is they want more of Dizzy's cosmology, his metaphysics, his moral philosophy, that kind of stuff. You already have some of that in there, and it's good. We just need more of it spread across what you've already written. I've marked places in the story where this or that kind of insight might work well."

He picked up a dog-eared stack of papers jabbed and slashed with red ink and waved it at me.

"You just have to plug the insights in. With the parts you don't know, don't remember, or don't understand, just don't be afraid to write what you *think* he said or what you *think* he meant. And don't be afraid to be vague. Be really vague. Let the asshole bishops of the distant future hash out what Dizzy really meant. I know we're changing direction here. But you're still doing great work. Everyone thinks so. This is the home stretch. Just keep it up."

Nothing stirred out on the tundra. I could hardly move. I was all clenched up with nowhere to go. I slumped in my chair and muttered. Mo was talking fast, with dramatic inflection. Looking at him, I could tell that my protests didn't have a chance. So I said what came to mind.

"Shit, shit, shit, shit, shit."

"I know you had a thing for the Eskimo girl. And I know this is hard right now. But I lost my family. I lost my home. I lost my retirement, my position, everything. I know what it's like. But listen to me, this is bigger than you or your gripes or your goddamn feelings," Mo explained.

"Whatever."

"Hey asshole, this is Armageddon, not Woodstock. It hurts now and will probably hurt right up until you die. But when you do die, the pain won't matter at all. Only one thing will matter: *The work*. The work you do now will matter. If you finish strong and finish soon, I promise it will hurt less. And when you're drifting off to your final frosty reward, you'll be able to say that your life wasn't a complete goddamn waste. Because right now that's what it is—a self-pitying, lazy, pathetic waste. Being able to say your life *meant* something may not sound like much to you now. But just try dying without it. I know you. You're a pro, and a pro is someone who does good work on a bad day. Well, here's your bad day. And who fucking knows? Nuna's a local girl. If we wrap this up soon, you'll at least have a *chance* to catch up with her somewhere down the line. But if you choose to be a *child* about this and do nothing, then I doubt you'll have chances at all."

I stared at the floor.

"I knew this was a bad idea. I knew you'd flake. Why do you think they kept you in dope and diapers all those months? Why do you think they cut your foot off?" Mo said.

"Golly gee, Mo, that just makes me want to work all the harder for these mysterious lunatics."

I stared at my hands, numb and sick. I'd been humanity's last chance for real love, not to mention its guiding light toward spiritual and cultural rebirth. But that day, I was just the last schmuck on the planet stuck in a job he hated but couldn't quit.

Mo sat across from me, waiting for the silence to bring me to my knees. But it didn't. My last hope had left the building. Now all that was left for me was to aggrandize the same assholes who had bored me with lame lies, amputated my foot, deprived me of my love, and who would soon send me to my death. Somehow, the situation didn't feel all that unfamiliar.

"I've said all I have to say. I'll check in to see how you're doing in a few days. It can be a lot harder than this, but it doesn't have to be."

Mo turned and left, still full of righteous steam. He left the door open behind him. He was humming, loudly, as he walked

169

down the hall. It took me a minute to name the tune, but it came to me. It was Whitney Houston's "Didn't We Almost Have It All."

47.

Three days into my eating/writing strike, they sent a vacant, willowy girl over to my room, after a dinner I wouldn't eat. I didn't want to look, but she had a pretty face, though her eyebrows were plucked completely clean. Her name was Bianca, she told me, sitting next to me on the cot. She made herself available to me in the noncommittal way of girls who are used to being passed around. She asked if I wanted her to make me feel better. I didn't say yes or no. I didn't say anything.

She started undressing. She had big but taut breasts with nipples that stared straight into my eyes. Bending over to put her clothes on my desk, she had a nice ass, round and compact. I looked away, into the darkness out the window. She came back to my bed and put my hand on one of her breasts. It was firm and warm and real. I gave it a little squeeze. I told her that I was busy and that she had to leave. She lingered a few minutes before dressing. I told her I was serious and raised my voice. She dressed and left, as indifferent as she was when she entered. After she was gone, I jerked off to the thought of her.

Management trying to make me happy was worse than them threatening me. They were just trying to love me into doing the only awful thing I was being kept alive to do. And I was going to do it, just to avoid that love. I guess they knew what they were doing.

Maybe that was the real tragedy of the now-defunct human race—the inability to be loved. But we'll never really know what went wrong with us, especially after I'm done writing my big lie. And that was the plan.

I started eating again. They must have expected I wouldn't eat much, because they upped the speed in my food to almost toxic levels. I ate a whole day's food at once and then lost half a day, talking to ghosts and aliens, old dead friends in long conversations that made no sense at all.

Coming down, I ate some oatmeal with just the right amount of speed in it. And I felt good, like a stone in my chest had been dislodged. So, high as a kite atop the flaming planet, I began to sort through Mo's marked-up copy of the gospel. I plugged in the gaps with my memory of Bartlett's *Book of Familiar Quotations* and what holy books I could recall or reconstruct. Where that failed, I inserted my own pearls of wisdom, whose profundity I can't guarantee. When you're as high as I was, everything sounds good.

Then, about halfway through, I found my opening—a dull spot in the gospel that would support its centerpiece—*Dizzy's Sermon in the Supermarket.*

Dizzy wandered the aisles, addressing a crowd that followed him, the cashiers, clerks, bag boys, and the products themselves. Wandering down the corridors of food, Dizzy described the way people ought to live, how they ought to feel, what they ought to think of the World and what they had a right to expect from their lives—all the stuff people want to know definitively and never ever can.

For a bag of chips is useless unless opened and eaten. And so it is with ourselves. We must be opened and devoured to ever truly matter.

Maybe a little high-falutin, but it's supposed to sound like that, I think. And anyway, I liked it. You try writing a gospel.

The megadose of speed also helped me remember, or at least confidently imagine, the things Dizzy had told me. The real Dizzy had never looked as good, nor sounded as wise and snappy as he did in his *Sermon in the Supermarket.* He was damn profound. He put everything in its place. His words calmed and excited me all at once.

After a dozen or so pages, the supermarket took over the sermon. The miles of aisles of soda and deodorant and toothpaste and cat food and paper plates surged from their place in the background and spoke with their own voices. My own episode in the supermarket in Oxnard asserted itself. And it emerged as the transcendent physical expression of an overbearing Love that sought as best it could to address every imaginable want of the limited creatures we would always be.

I named the soup mixes, their makers, and who each brand was meant to please in a feat of galloping photographic memory. I described their labels and explained what the colors of the boxes were meant to convey. I followed the same method of explaining the whole twenty-four-aisle supermarket as a vast and orgiastic explosion of Love for a fallen, frail, and fragmented people.

Wise men with dubious reputations you will always have with you. God's love will always be around, and always in question. But fifty varieties of yellow mustard on one shelf you will have with you for but a short while.

You get the idea. It was a long sermon.

The prose poured forth for a few days. Three or four I think. I choked down the meals just for the drugs in them, typing with one hand and eating with the other. When my eyes burned too badly, I closed them and kept typing, accidentally banging out a few pages of pure glossolalia. I did not care.

It wasn't journalism and it wasn't gospel writing. It was something else. The words demanded to be written. I was just their employee. The sun stalked around the horizon as it always had, disappeared from sight, coming back, and then doing it again. I was immune to it all. I knew I was going to die. And I had to get this out of me before I did. I was a million leagues below the sea, sending telepathic telegrams to the rare fish of the future who might one day sink as far as I had. I was writing the real arcana of my inaccessible soul. All my rage and despair found their rightful place on the computer keyboard. I dared not stop.

In the frenzy of the last day, I forwent my meals altogether. Without the drugs, exhaustion finally found me. I struggled to keep awake as I completed the joyfully frivolous litany of the anxiety-relieving snacks, celebrity magazines, and impulse buys at the cash register.

When I was done, *The Sermon in the Supermarket* contained

fifteen pages of Sermon and more than a hundred of Supermarket. I crawled to my bed when the section was over.

My fingers echo-twitched from the keyboard as I drifted off. And I knew I'd probably missed the mark on Dizzy's gospel. But I'd made something else—a proper Last Testament for the World. It pleased me to have found, albeit too late, the thousand reasons why it was a bad thing that the World had passed. Didn't know I had that in me.

Hell, I may have even written the founding document for my imaginary Church of Surviving the Caring Other (COSTCO). Maybe no one would ever see a supermarket again, or get my little joke. But I could still chuckle.

48.

Lying in bed, I knew he was there. I could hear him breathing and sighing occasionally, like he was trying to wake me by accident. I could hear his keystrokes. But I pretended to sleep. At first he typed a lot. Then just hit the scroll keys. I stayed very still and listened to him curse quietly to himself as he read the document on the computer. His exasperation helped me remember what I'd written over the last few days.

I sat up to face the music.

"You were sleeping, so I figured I'd give it a read."

"Oh. Hey. What's up?"

"I always knew you were a little sketchy. But this is really something else."

"What? Dizzy's Sermon? I've been working on the, you know, the metaphysics and philosophy and whatnot."

"I don't know exactly how to tell you this. And I'd be surprised if you didn't know it already, but what you have here is absolute shit. Completely useless horseshit. I told you to take the piece in one direction and you drove it off a fucking *cliff*. Speaking of shit, what is that stink in here?" Mo asked.

"Piss, I think. I may have had an accident while I was writing."

Mo jumped up from the desk chair. He looked down and his

mouth curled into a snarl. He started pacing.

"Jesus Christ! Well, my friend, that piddle is probably the best work you've done all week."

"Sorry about that. I was on a, uh, roll," I shrugged.

"I know you were. When they told me you were working, I thought, thank God, the boy has suddenly come to his senses. But look at this thing. You really have lost it."

"I did what you said. I wrote the gospel of Dizzy."

"Oh, *come on!* Don't bullshit me of all people. I don't care if you want to fuck the help. I don't care if you want to piss yourself in your chair. I really don't. It's when you deliberately and *spitefully* fuck up the whole project that I have to put my foot down. I don't know if you're stupid or out of your mind or what. But now you're going to have to start your rewrite over again from scratch."

"But I wrote what Dizzy said," I lied, hoping against reason that Mo would leave me alone.

"I mean, *fine*, you flaked on the story. You flaked on a very expensive year-long investigative project that most reporters would have crawled over their mothers for. And, okay, you *killed* one of the major players you were supposed to be covering."

"I didn't know you knew that."

"I didn't, not until I got here. I just knew you flaked out, you fucked up. You fucked me and you fucked you. Because that's what fucking *losers* do—they fuck themselves and then they take everyone who ever tried to *help* them along for the goddamned ride. And all of that doesn't matter now, it's *okay*. Bygones really are bygones now," Mo said, visibly trying to calm himself down, and mostly failing.

"Wow. So you knew about that?"

"Just shut up. Just shut the fuck up. This," Mo said, banging his knuckle on the plastic of the computer screen hard, "this isn't okay. This. This has to penetrate the jadedness and naiveté of the coming centuries, which will make the jadedness and naiveté of *our* century look like a fucking make-your-own-fudge-sundae birthday party. This has to be perfect. But you're good at what you do. I know, once you take your head out of your ass and take a deep breath of air, you can pull this off. Diaper time is *over.* Playtime is *over.* You have to suck it up before there really is no going back. Surely you can string together two weeks of good work."

When someone is as mad as Mo was at that moment, there are a few ways to play it: You can argue. You can apologize. You can tell them to go fuck themselves. I reached into my depleted bag of tricks and decided to keep playing dumb.

"I thought that's what you wanted. Metaphysics, little sayings, meaning-of-life stuff. You know?"

"Oh, I'm *sorry.* I guess it's *my* fault. So let me make it crystal clear to whatever part of your degenerate alcoholic fuck-up brain that still functions. A hundred-some-odd pages about a fucking supermarket *isn't*—that means *is not*—what we *want.* It's not what anybody wants. It's not anything. It won't make it through five minutes, never mind five thousand years. I could barely read ten pages of the shit."

"I thought Dizzy said some pretty timeless things there in the supermarket. Did you read the part about the potato chips? The closing part, with the analogies? I think you need to give it all a second read before you really judge it," I said.

"I know you aren't this stupid. By the time people, whoever is left, get the wherewithal to start reading again, they'll be lucky to have horse-drawn wagons. And you give them silly parables about true wisdom as fucking *dental floss.* How are they supposed to relate to any of this *stuff*? I mean, what the hell is wrong with you?"

I know Mo doesn't come off well in all this. But bosses never do. And I felt a shot of sympathy for old Mo then and there.

"Well. I guess I'm sorry. But it wasn't my idea to write this thing in the first place. I guess I screwed it up. But I've written everything I know about Dizzy."

"It's just *how* you wrote it. It won't be a hard rewrite. I'll look over your copy hour to hour. We'll do it together. It's just ..."

"Mo, just stop. I'm finished here. I'm not the right guy for this job. I'm just not. I'm done. I'm a fuckup and I'm ready to die. I can't write another word or do another fucking thing. Really. I'm just done. Can't I just go wherever I'm supposed to go now?" I asked.

That's when Mo teared up. His hand, the one on his beard, started shaking. I've probably worn the adjective—surprising—down to nothing. But this was that.

"Okay. Okay."

"Mo, I'm sorry. I just can't."

"Did I ever tell you what happened?"

"What do you mean, Mo?"

"With Diane and the girls?"

"You said they died."

"That's all?"

"Yeah."

"Well, I'll tell you now, how it happened. The trains weren't running that day, so I worked from home. The police had things in order, at least on the Upper West Side, so I went out to get some groceries. There wasn't much, even at Zabar's, but I found a few things to bring home. The rest of the day, I stayed in with Diane and the girls. I read the papers that I could find and did the crossword puzzle in the *Times*. It was November and it was raining. But we still got a lot of light in that apartment, so we didn't mind the hours when the electricity was out. That night, Diane cooked dinner. Pasta with a little chicken. After dinner, we played Scrabble with the girls. We all went to bed early. I was restless from sitting around the house most of the day, and I couldn't sleep. I just looked up at the ceiling and tried to decide on some things for the Sunday magazine. The entire population of Brooklyn had vanished entirely two nights before. We were either going to lead with that or the saucer fleets over Kansas City."

He took a deep breath to steady himself, ran his hand through his sloppy gray hair, looked at the floor and raised his voice.

"So when I heard glass breaking, I was out of bed like a shot.

Something had broken through the living-room window. I first saw it in the kitchen. It was built like a man, but broader, with no neck. Its head was of one piece with its shoulders. And it had enormous black eyes, big as softballs. It was a six-foot-tall frog. I saw it well enough to know that for certain. I did what any father would do and I tried to scare it off. I yelled at it, but it kept coming. So I ran at it and punched it right on the nose, as hard as I could. Besides hurting my hand, I don't think I did much damage. It grabbed me and spun me around to the ground then slammed my head against the hardwood floor until I was unconscious."

Mo winced as he said the last part.

"I remember lying there, knowing I had to wake up, but not being able to. It was like I was fighting against a ton of darkness and it wouldn't budge an inch," Mo said. He looked at the floor and chuckled faintly. "Sort of like you. You were drooling in idiot storage for what, seven, eight months?"

"Something like that. I'm hardly the one to ask."

"You and me, we slept through all the crucial parts. And like you, I'm here to talk about it. The only difference is I woke up and my family was gone. You woke up and the better part of the World was gone."

"That's us—apocalypse buddies?"

"Just give it a rest, okay, asshole."

"Okay, fine, what happened after you were unconscious?" I said, reluctant to enter the little sympathy trap Mo was building.

"The frog-thing killed all of them. From the looks of things—and I did *not* look away—it had tried to eat them, but didn't like the taste."

Now he was crying a little. The emotion was honest. But the honesty was still part of his pitch. He sensed my skepticism and collected himself quickly.

"We slept, you and me. We slept while *everything* was taken from us. Only difference is I could have done something about it. Maybe that's why I care about trying to make something right with the time I have left. Maybe you just never cared at all."

"No. It's not that I don't care ... I care. It's just that ..."

177

The Last Bad Job ... Dodds

"I *know* you care. I know that under all your cowardly cynicism and your alcoholic self-absorption, you have a good heart. You want to do the right thing."

"Mo, I appreciate your optimism, and the pep talk, and everything. But it's wasted on me. I'm really done here. I'm all out of whatever. I have nothing left to say about Dizzy. It's not me being lazy or flaky. I'm just emptied out, completely. I mean it. Really, I'm just done."

"Okay, I know you're tired. But listen. I haven't made my point yet."

"I thought that was your point—making things right and such."

"No. That's only part of my point."

"Okay. Go ahead."

"Now there are things we know. We *know* that evolution takes thousands of years to produce any real variation in a species. So how does Central Park produce a fucking *frog man* in a week, while no one's looking? So, let's say it's not evolution, let's say I was hallucinating. But we *know* there were a hundred sightings of the same homicidal frog men uptown that month. So let's say it was a government project, some genetic experiment by the Pentagon. But Manhattan's hardly the place for the sort of research facility that would produce those *things*. So what the hell killed my family?"

"A frog man?"

"Yes. But where did it come from? How did it come into existence? Why did it break into our apartment?"

"Beats me. What's your point?"

"I ask because the frog man is just the tip of the iceberg. What about the rat men downtown? What about the population Brooklyn just vanishing, Manhattan floating out to sea, as if it wasn't a trillion-ton rock, and the sudden plagues, zombies, and floods? What we don't know is the most important part. And I'm so befuddled that I'm willing to believe that it's because we're sinners in the hands of an angry and imaginative God. And we were a Society for Ethical Culture family, second generation. So the sinner thing wasn't going to be my first guess."

"Well, no one knows. So what's your point?" I asked.

"My point is this: I thought I'd accumulated, through education, reading, and experience, a pretty solid idea of what goes on and how things happen in reality. Now I realize that I never even had a *fighting goddamn chance* of knowing what was going on. And what I didn't know wound up destroying my entire life. This library, this gospel, is about giving people that chance."

"Mo, thanks for the speech. It's a good one, but I'm really done here. Not changing my mind. Do what you have to with me," I said, staring at the mountains.

"Listen. This won't do. They need the gospel and they need it soon. Raiding parties have crossed the Bering Strait and they burned one of our libraries a week ago. They're crossing Alaska before they head south. We need this library done and buried in the next week and a half."

"Then what?"

"What do you mean?"

"What do we do?" I asked.

"We fend for ourselves for as long as we can. This book, this library, is all that survives. I know you weren't there and you didn't see it. But to be alive is not normal anymore."

"So I'm dead in or out, right?"

"Pretty much."

"Just get out of here. And, you know what? I like the *Sermon in the Supermarket*. I think it's better than anything Dizzy ever actually had to say to anyone. It's better than whatever pack of lies you assholes wind up saddling future unfortunates with. Your Gospel of Dizzy is bullshit. And I hope, for the sake of the future, that it never sees the light of day," I said.

"That's really too bad. Now you're on your own. I'm sorry it had to end like this."

"I'm not. Take care, Mo. I'll see you in heck."

"Back atcha, Scoop."

And with that, Mo was gone.

49.

In a place like the compound, you become very sensitive to routine. And any break in the routine is unsettling. It's called being institutionalized and there's nothing all that interesting about it. It's actually the opposite of something interesting.

Being institutionalized, I woke knowing that something was in the air. Then breakfast didn't come. No one answered when I knocked to use the bathroom, either, so I used the bedpan. I tried to go back to sleep some more, but it was more like hiding under my blanket. Then a pair of men I'd never seen before with pale, plain faces came in and took the laptop, the notebooks, folders, and the pens. I was finally fired. And though I was ready to die, losing my job still upset me somehow.

A light rain fell outside my window. It was silent in the hall. No one stirred in End of Times Square down the hall, as far as I could hear. Around the time I would have expected dinner, another group of pale, plain-faced men came for me. They picked me up from my bed without a word and dragged me out of my room. I didn't resist. They took me down the hallway, away from the silent offices, past the bathroom I used, down another hallway to a room I had never been in.

The room was dark and cold. From the light that came through the door with us, I could tell it was a big room. And I could make out a table in the back, and in front of it two posts with big spheres on top of them.

The men stripped me down to my boxers and undershirt with indifferent efficiency. I didn't resist. They sat me down in a big wooden chair and strapped my arms and legs to it. One of them injected something into my shoulder. Whatever it was, it made me wake way up, more than even the speed had. And unlike the speed, the new drug did its work without making me happy at all. It simply amplified everything. And everything, at that moment, was unpleasant.

The seconds passed like hours. I heard footsteps leaving the room, each one a boom and squeal that stripped my nerves. When the men closed the door behind them, it was completely dark. Alone, my breathing, pulse, and blinking all noisily hushed and thudded. I sat there for what seemed like months—the doomed and lame veal calf of the final revelation of a dead age.

After eons of darkness, the lights on the posts in the center of the room sprang on, too bright for my eyes to have a chance in hell of adjusting. I blinked wildly and I clenched my eyes shut. But even then, the light was too bright. It reminded me of everything all at once, summer and childhood and that lit tunnel they say connects the hospital bed with heaven.

Sounds, like papers shuffling or feathers rustling, were all I could make out besides the blinding light.

Questions began to issue from the light.

"Who was Dizzy Sheehan?"

It sounded like a woman's voice, the kind you'd hear on the mass-transit system of a strange city, polite but firm.

The whole thing reminded me of something I couldn't put my finger on. And whatever they had boiling in my veins made the words hit me like a prison dropped from space. The question reverberated as dumb syllables. In it I heard a dozen riddles, a dozen bad puns, a dozen useless digressions and rhythmic codes. This was a very strong drug. It was all I could do to focus enough just to speak.

"He was a banker from New Jersey who decided he was God's final messenger. You already know that. I already wrote it."

I could feel every muscle from my temples to my scrotum pull to annunciate the words. I could feel my gums holding my teeth in place. I could feel my skull holding my brain in. My ribcage thrust upward and crashed down with each breath, like an ocean wave covered in a layer of steak and old wood. Blinking, I could see the dead cells floating across my eyeballs like the seagoing ships of the sixteenth century.

Upon finishing my sentence, the lights and the drugs seemed to intensify simultaneously. The air warmed up all around me. I could feel my pores open and the first drops of sweat form on my forehead.

After about two years of suicidal devotees, half-hallucinated aliens and ghosts, of having a foot amputated and a historic destiny foisted upon me, this was the crowning moment. And if the two blinding globes of hot light were a hallucination, then they had to be the last hallucination—The High Throne of the Great Psychotic Core. But it's hard to question a hallucination that scares you. Real or not, it was a very raw nerve that I was in the presence of.

"Who was Dizzy Sheehan?" the same voice asked again.

It was like someone had pressed a button to repeat the question. The lights grew brighter. I clenched my fists and the drugs made my atrophied muscles feel like iron under a blanket of bacon. The hair bristled on my head. I was angry. All my fear turned inside-out. It felt like power.

"Who the hell are you? And what the fuck do you want?" I yelled. Spittle shot from my mouth, landing on my chin and on the floor.

The lights, somehow, grew brighter. They stayed that way through another pause that seemed to stretch on for hours— lights so bright that they also impinged on the other senses, seeming loud, pungent, and concussive.

"You know who we are. We are the mask on a face you cannot see. We are the ones who know what you have hidden for so long."

It wasn't the recorded voice. It was thinner, like the voice of a child with a cold. It was scarier than the recorded voice. My fear was turning to anger.

"What the fuck does that even mean? I am so fucking sick of these bullshit wishy-washy fucking riddle answers. Who the fuck are you?"

The lights grew brighter and hotter still. My mind reeled. People came and went in the light, floating like broken toys on a lazy river. I saw my poor dead father pleading with me, blood squirting from his eyes, the TV remote still in his hand. I saw Nuna give me an evil look and turn away. I saw Guy trying to talk though feces poured from his mouth, saw Mo crying clumps of sand, saw myself as a child, saw the aliens staring expectantly and checking their watches, saw the ghosts lurching miserably after each other in a ring, saw Dizzy sweep his arm through the air.

"Tell us about Dizzy," said the recorded voice.

"You fucking loser freaks! Fuck you! What the fuck is wrong with you? Couldn't you think of anything better to do with yourselves? It's the end of the world and you want to know about that loser? He was a lying goddamn asshole who led a bunch of halfway decent people to their deaths. There. So what the fuck does that make you?"

The lights kicked up another notch. Light and heat like I never imagined.

After a few minutes, I started talking just to keep from being cooked alive and to forestall the crushing sound of the voice. I said a lot. I told them about the supermarket, about Guy and his kids in Vermont, about Mary Beth and the lake, about my father and the robbery at the cigarette store, about Cinderella stealing my shoes, about the years when I never saw noon sober, about Nuna and the Eskimos who were carving me a whalebone foot. I just rambled.

It didn't do me much good. The lights just intensified, burning me like the summer sun, then like an oven. When I finally got around to Dizzy, it must have been 250 degrees in my chair. At the mention of Dizzy's name, it cooled. I said he was bald, said I didn't like him much, said the women at his compound were easy but indifferent, said he sent a guy to kill me, said he killed all the people on his compound.

But I couldn't remember much more about him or what he said life was all about in that moment. So I started making stuff up just to buy time and stay alive. I said that he played half-court basketball to teach his disciples about the end of the World and that he would take five or six steps to the hoop and no one would call a foul on him. I told them that he was a friend to long-distance truckers, and had said his successor would come from among them. I said that he often warned of his bastard daughter in Bangkok who would bring one thousand years of darkness to the world if she wasn't stopped. I told them about the underground castle he'd built with his mind, but had lost in his divorce. I told them about his Air Force of pigeon men. I went on and on, telling whoever was behind the lights about secret money hordes and about armies of clay figurines and mummified harems buried underground who would come to life at the end of the World.

"This is a waste of time," said the reedy voice from behind the lights.

The lights dimmed and the room cooled instantly. It was suddenly chilly and dark again. In the darkness, I heard the rustling sounds and the squeak of rubber. I never saw their faces. Two of them held my arms. A third jabbed me in the shoulder with a needle that seemed to be two feet long.

Then they left me in the darkness, tied to the chair. The injection hadn't done anything to counteract the first drug yet. My senses were still dilated and I could hear more rustling and the sound of opening and closing doors. I could feel the friction in the door hinges. Soon everyone was gone. I swallowed from fear. It felt like a tsunami in my throat.

I have about a minute to live, I thought. I grasped for a prayer, a saying, an aphorism or memory, anything. I wanted to ride into death in the right frame of mind. I ransacked Bartlett's, my memories, everything. But nothing was quite right. It was like trying to find a high school yearbook quote. Everything was too trite or too obscure. Every good memory was tainted by what came before or followed. In the end, I couldn't find anything worth saving from the burning house of my life. That second shot began to move faster than my thoughts. I remember slumping in my chair, still hunting out a mantra that wouldn't misrepresent or mislead me.

This is it, I thought. It was the best I could do.

"You know what's coming back?"
Warren said. "Everything; then it's going
away for good."
　　　—George W.S. Trow, *Within the Context of No Context*

50.

The Alaskan Interior—Bugs buzzed. Other than that, it was so quiet I could hear the blood rushing in my ears. It was not too cold and not too warm. Before I opened my eyes yet, I could tell that I wasn't dead. The hard throb in my shin-stump told me as much. Long masked by drugs, it thumped something awful now. I blinked a big, sharp chunk of sleep into my eye and sat up to discover a headache, like the queen of all hangovers had been hiding behind the other discomforts. It said hello.

Not heaven. I knew that much.

The sun was clear and bright, hovering just above the horizon. The tundra still bloomed with leafy trees and flowers. I was laid out about fifty yards from the burned-out husk of the compound. It looked like the fire had been out for a few days. Inside the blackened perimeter, I could make out the frames of a bunch of metal municipal-type desks, like the one I had. But there was no one around as far as I could see in any direction.

I was dressed—overdressed actually. Next to me, they left a pair of crutches and a big old hiking backpack. Inside was some water, more clothes, a tarp, a sleeping bag, and a lot of those awful PowerBars. My severance package.

My stump hurt like hell, so I pulled the boot off that leg thinking the cool air would help. They'd attached the boot to my long underwear with a pair of clips. The whole getup was overkill for the fairly warm summer day, but I'd probably need it all later. The boot was too heavy. Checking inside, I pulled out some balled-up socks, and underneath that, a white foot—ivory, I think. It had a vague shape, like a mannequin's foot.

There was a compass carved on the sole of the foot, with an arrow marking a spot on the compass. "Sunset tonight. Best of luck, from You Know Who" was written in calligraphy beside the arrow. The writing was brown, like scrimshaw.

A farewell present from everyone. Geez, you shouldn't have.

In the week before they dragged me from my room, the nights had been maybe an hour long. But there were sunsets. I decided to crutch to Koyukuk. Nuna said it was a short flight, whatever that meant. She'd said I could make the hike, even on my crutches. I was weak from months of sitting and lying around. I'd be lucky to manage five or ten miles a day. But that's like not moving at all in Alaska. I did the grim math. My supplies might last a month. Thirty days at ten miles a day, then I'd be out of food completely. Maybe I could do five or so more days after that. So that's four hundred miles, tops. That might be enough to get me to Koyukuk and Nuna. And that was the only thread still holding me to my life.

But where the hell was Koyukuk? I looked around, but didn't see any sort of road. In the waning daylight, I could see the gold foil wrappers of a few PowerBars twinkling in the grass. But they seemed to be sprinkled equally in all directions.

So I had four choices: north, south, east, and west. I couldn't imagine there was much to the north except Santa Claus, and he probably shoots trespassers on sight nowadays. To the south was simply too much stuff. Eastward was Canada, somewhere. So I picked west.

I closed my brain like you would close your mouth and waited for the sun to ease down into the earth. In the long, cool dusk, I got a handle on my situation. I would go west, toward the ocean, and hopefully find Koyukuk and Nuna.

I aligned the compass, found west, then put my foot into my backpack and started crutching into the short night.

51.

The first days, I could only go a few hundred yards before I'd have to stop and sit down. My armpits chafed and my whole body burned and ached. But by the end of the week, I could go for what seemed like more than a mile before I had to sit down and rest. By the second week, my long shadow leapt across the distances like a lean, three-legged giant. I hoped I was ten miles a day, but I had no way to tell.

The grassy plains gave way to a forest and the forest crowded around a big river. Judging from the sunset and the compass on my ivory foot, the river ran southwest. I still hadn't seen a road, a bridge, or any evidence of people aside from the occasional gold foil PowerBar wrapper in the pine needles. If anything out there led to a town, it would be the river, I figured. So I followed it hoping for a town, a shack, or anything that might help me figure out the rest of the way to Koyukuk.

I crutched through the woods for days along the bank of the river, checking my course each day at dusk. The river and I kept going southwest. I nibbled at the PowerBars in the day. And most nights I'd cook up some rice in river water. But mostly, I wasn't too hungry.

It was late summer and there were a lot of animals in the woods—birds, critters, and caribou. I liked the caribou. They'd watch me until they we locked eyes. And after a few seconds, sometimes even a long minute, on some unseen cue, they'd sprint away. Some days, a wolf would follow me from about twenty feet back. It wasn't such a menace. I made a fire each night and it kept its distance. I figured the wolves would be the ones to finish me off when I couldn't crutch anymore. And I hoped they'd be quick about it.

After three weeks, I still hadn't seen a town or a road or anything. The glimmer of PowerBar wrappers in the pine needles became less frequent. But at least I wasn't the first one to head this way.

By then I'd stopped thinking of where I was coming from or where I was going. I stopped imagining what would happen when I ran out of food or when the weather changed. I stopped thinking of what I would do if I found a town. And I stopped thinking of what I would do if I never did. I just kept crutching along the soft, uneven ground by the river.

If a failed gospel writer falls alone in the forest and no one is there to hear it, does he make a sound? And if the whole World falls alone in a forest? It doesn't seem to have made a sound here.

It was weeks of crutching before I even had a dream, back at the same beach house. I was holding a huge dinner party, the house seemed to expand to accommodate it. And the party filled the house's countless cozy and tasteful rooms. The guests included everyone I'd ever known, or even seen. The conversation and the wine flowed freely.

Then the doorbell rang. I answered the door, and there was Nuna. The thousand conversations paused for a second, then resumed. I said hello and kissed her cheek. I took her coat to the coatroom. It was a chilly night, with a strong breeze coming off the ocean, at the very end of summer. I mingled awhile with the guests, and then went into the kitchen to check on some appetizers I had in the oven. Nuna came into the kitchen and tapped me on the shoulder. Her big brown eyes were bigger and darker than before. She seemed to stare at me more directly than she had before, if that's possible.

"Hi," she said.

"Hi."

"I'm sorry I couldn't help you," she said, skipping the small talk.

"Why did you leave me?"

"I had to. It was my mother. But I meant what I said. I will always help you."

"But how will you help me now? Can't you see I'm going to die?"

"I'm gone. But I will always help you. I have to go now."

I will always help you. She said it as if I hadn't understood her the first time. It was like she was aiming the words for the one speck of my brain capable of taking it in.

"Nuna, don't go, please."

"I have to. It's not up to me. None of this is up to any of us. We tried to make it up to us. We did that for a little while. It was

188

good. Don't be sad that it didn't last. We were just too late."

She kissed me on the cheek and left the kitchen.

I was stunned, but not too stunned to take my mini-egg rolls out of the oven and back to the party.

My guests asked me why I was crying. I said I wasn't crying. They said that the tears looked very nice on my cheeks, anyway. I said thank you. We all talked and drank for a long time. But I couldn't find Nuna among the guests. Then, everyone agreed, it was late. They would have to leave, which had never happened at the beach house. No one ever left before.

But now they filed out to their cars. Everyone had a nice car. I shook the men's hands and kissed the women's cheeks, gave them each a light embrace and said good-bye. I told them to drive carefully. I watched their red taillights drift down the driveway and vanish into the darkness.

Dizzy was the last to leave. I said good-bye and we shook hands. On the way to his car, a big Mercedes SUV, he turned and told me something, like an afterthought he had been saving all night for me.

"Hey, just a heads-up—all those people you used to know—they're never coming back."

I knew he was right. And I knew he was doing me a favor by telling me.

I woke with tears on my cheeks. I rose and crutched the whole long day along the river without stopping to rest or to eat. Thirty years of self-portraits fell away with each lurch forward. A million memos to self fluttered off my dirty clothes.

Late in the day, as the sun was easing into dusk, I felt I was being watched. So I stopped and looked up from the river bank. A caribou, a bull, perched on the slope. I'd seen a lot of caribou, but so far only females. The bull was huge, more than seven feet high with his head perked up. His horns reached another four feet into the air. He stared right at me with his big, black eyes. I stared back. He made no move to run away, but just stared, defiant and calm. We stood like that for a few minutes. There was nothing in his eyes, just darkness.

I looked down and kept crutching.

I was starting to wither away. When you're a kid and you make a funny face, adults will say, "stop it or your face will stay that way." They say it to be funny and to make you stop it. But no one warns you about the things you think. And, unlike your face, your mind actually will stick in those contortions. Crutching along, with the near-constant sun riding at the height of my shoulder, my grimace faded. And it seemed like it would be easy to die.

52.

A few days after I saw the caribou bull, I saw the Siberians. At least I think they were Siberians. That's who Mo called them. They looked Polish one moment and Chinese the next and then somewhere in between. Except for their modern shabbiness, they reminded me of some war party of Huns or Khans from a movie.

They were crossing the river in colorful outfits, like pictures of Cossacks or Tibetan llamas. Despite the military demeanor of the caravan, the rifles, artillery, and swords, the pots-and-pans armor on the horses and on the elephants, you could tell those guys were having the times of their lives. This was no military campaign forced on them by necessity, no expedition for survival's sake. They were going to sack the fabled golden cities of the south. They didn't hide their joy.

Some were on horses, some in wagons, some on elephants, but most walked. Some had rifles, some had grenade launchers, and some had bows and arrows. Some carried broken rifles with flat stones or machete blades strapped to their barrels. Some wore hockey pads and carried clubs with nails driven through them. Some had sharpened sticks or colorful flags in the bent barrels of rifles. They were improvising their way back to the Stone Age as they went.

They used big rubber rafts and inflated animal skins to cross the river. There were so many of them that it took a whole long day of sunlight for the column to cross. They were disorganized but enthusiastic. One of them would get swept down the river to his death, and his friends would salute their drowned comrade with hoots and yells, then carry on as boisterous as before. They would break out into a rhythmic, martial-sounding song. There must have been ten thousand of them, splashing and singing and laughing as they went to the next slaughter.

I was upriver, in a clump of undergrowth, and I felt safely hidden enough to watch the whole thing. Their leader rode a white horse, wearing a catcher's apron and a motorcycle helmet with gold jewelry nailed to it, like a sloppy crown. He went up and down the column as it crossed. H was the only one who didn't smile or laugh and the men grew silent when he rode up to their part of the column. They broke into their incomprehensible war song when he gestured in their direction.

At one point, he stopped and looked right at me. I was maybe three hundred feet away from where they were crossing the river. Looking in my direction, he signaled to the men to stop singing. They did so immediately—all of them. The entire war train became impossibly silent. The leader pulled a huge silver revolver from his belt and fired one shot in my direction so quickly that the report from the gun was echoing before I realized he'd fired.

The Siberians were silent for another moment. I turned around to see what he was shooting at, if it wasn't me. There was the huge bull caribou with whom I'd shared a long look a few days before, about thirty or so feet directly behind me, on the top of the hill. He fell forward, into a sphinx-like pose on the pine needles and mud. I could see where bullet had exited through the white fur of his neck, where his spine was blown out. He nuzzled the mud so that only his huge horns stuck up.

The men nearest the leader let out a roar. Then the news spread down the line. You could hear it move along the procession—a murmur followed by a roar, followed by a murmur, followed by another roar. It was twenty minutes before it ended. The leader signaled severely and the men kept going, singing, onward across the river. He continued up and down the line, until all the Siberians had crossed from the north side of the river to the south. He crossed last. I think he saw me as he and his horse crossed. But he didn't seem to care.

53.

Using the rope and a half-deflated raft the Siberians left behind, I crossed the river the next day and followed the path they had left, moving in the opposite direction. It seemed like the best way to find a town. Invaders need pillage as they go.

On their trail I got a pretty good idea of how the Siberians lived. They drank a lot of hard liquor. They hunted, but didn't eat much of what they killed, judging from the swath of dead but untouched or incompletely butchered animals along the way. They also died pretty frequently along the way, violently, or from a sickness that covered their faces with red sores. And they killed a lot of people along the way. I found a number of corpses not wearing the Siberian-type outfits. And it didn't look like they died well. I found what I think was the corpse of the woman who changed my diapers all those months. It was hard to tell because her face was pretty well wrecked by a hammer or a club. She was still wearing her red robe over her clothes. I told her corpse that I was sorry about crapping on her hands, and moved on.

The next day, I saw Mo, naked atop a pile of liquor bottles and fish bones. He had been stabbed through the stomach. After that, I didn't pay the bodies too much mind, except to look for Nuna.

After a week or so, I was far enough away from the Siberians to camp up on a hill and light a fire. I was hoping to see some kind of road or bridge or town from up there. It was a clear day and I was nearly out of food. The sun was still a finger's width off the horizon, which gave me at least an hour before dusk.

The forest below stretched on for miles and I could see where the river I'd been following met another, much larger river. Where they met, I could make out a little town, with houses on stilts and a few roads. A little farther out from the river, there was a larger building, a gas station, and a landing strip.

It was more than I'd seen so far. The nights were getting longer. Winter was coming. And I figured I'd have better luck with the mercy of a town than the mercy of the elements. I decided to eat, get some rest, and crutch down to the town in the morning. I took a deep breath, glad that my life would have one more chapter.

The dusk brightened unexpectedly. I was starting a fire when it happened. A bright star rose quickly over the horizon, silent and nearly as bright as a full moon. It grew bigger and brighter as it crossed the sky. I looked away and went back to setting up camp. Looking back up, it had grown a tail. It was a comet, or a meteor. It was bigger than the moon when it crossed the other horizon.

Thinking the meteor was the real end, the end of the end, I decided not to cook. I took out my second-to-last PowerBar. It was hazelnut-flavored. And since there was nothing to enjoy about the taste of the thing, I just tried to enjoy chewing.

Halfway through the PowerBar, the earth shook in a nauseous, jelly-like shudder that threw me halfway down the hill. I'd been in earthquakes before, and this wasn't that. Trees swayed and cracked. The two rivers below sloshed and jumped their banks. I was on my back, on the side of the hill. I reached back and dug my fingers into the dirt, while the planet buckled and shuddered again.

I saw the sun plummet below the horizon and then spring back up in a different spot. But I had never, in Alaska or anywhere else, seen the sun do that.

A low rumbling sound persisted in the distance, like an avalanche that lasted an hour. Muddy water surged up the big river, opposite its flow. Reaching its junction with the smaller river, it changed the direction of both. The brown surge flooded them to twice their original widths. Some of the buildings in the town below were washed away. A few hours later, the flood receded. The sun was still up, dragging low above on the rim of distant mountains. I could hear big fish flopping to death on the mud below. Then the rivers changed directions, back to their normal courses, then went completely dry. More big fish flopped to their deaths on the sandy river floor.

But in the town below, I heard no voices, saw no flashlights, saw no movement, no light.

It was the first I'd seen of the apocalypse. And it had missed me again. I knew better than to call it luck. I finished my PowerBar and laid out my bedroll. By then, the rivers seemed to have returned to normal. I didn't know what had happened. But I knew that even after all I'd seen and heard about, it was probably the biggest thing of all. I bedded down and waited for the brief evening.

But dusk never came. The sun stayed up, circling just above the nearby mountains. It was a constant bright twilight that lasted for what seemed like an entire day. I didn't have a watch. So I kept track of the sun. It worked its way around the horizon in a slow circle, neither rising nor falling from its place just above the land.

I watched for sunset. And I watched for some sign of life in the town. I was suddenly afraid of what I'd find down there.

Heaven is a place where nothing ever happens
Heaven is a place where nothing ever happens
—Talking Heads, *Heaven*

54.

Koyukuk, AK—The sun didn't set and the town didn't stir. I watched the sun circle close to the horizon. The thing I'd been staying alive for was within reach, but it looked dead. I was eager to go into town, but afraid.

The next day, I ate all my food at once. It was good to feel the bloat of overeating one more time. I went to sleep in the dim sunlight, and when I woke, I was hungry. So I got up my nerve to go down the hill.

In town, the sign on the little public school let me know that I had reached Koyukuk after all. I crutched around, yelling HELLO and NUNA at the top of my lungs. But it was empty. There'd been a slaughter, and a damned thorough one. I found a few Siberians among a pile of dead locals. There were at least a hundred bodies in the pile and more scattered about. It looked like they'd been dead more than a week. The place stank. Big, black flies buzzed everywhere.

Nuna and her mother had made it home in time for the slaughter. I found their bodies, both undressed to some degree, bruised and cut. There was blood and skin under her nails, bruises on her forearms, cuts on her palms, and her clothes were ripped all over. She had been beaten about the head and strangled.

The days were unclear, but it must have taken me a week of hard work and ingenuity—ropes, carts, etcetera to get all the bodies together. I made a huge pile by the river. I burned them all in one big gasoline fire before I could think any better of it. Nuna and her mom, too. I cried, but only a little.

I thought of jumping in to the flames. That would be a clean end. Kill the last witness to the tree that fell in the forest. The idea had its appeal. The end of my life began when I killed Jack in New Mexico. And the funeral fire by the river was the end of the end. It was the final period and carriage return at the end of the paragraph expressing all I thought I cared for and belonged to.

The Dizzy in my dream was right: All those people I used to know, they're never coming back. I cried, and then a strange peace came over me. In the fire by the river, when I thought I could be relieved no further, I was relieved further still.

I got on with the rest of my life. And I had a whole town at my disposal, or most of one. Between the Siberians' fires and the flood, about a third of the town's buildings remained in livable condition.

And for all their thoroughness in slaughtering, the Siberians did a poor job of looting. All they took was canned fish, liquor, guns, and ammo. They left a lot of gasoline and food along with fishing poles and animal traps. That left me with a few months' worth of canned vegetables, as well as bags and boxes of rice, spaghetti, and cereal. And that gave me enough time to get the hang of making a fire, trapping, and fishing. I liked fishing better than trapping. It was less effort, and easier on the nerves.

I moved into Nuna's old house. It was nice there, though lonely. With no one left in the entire World, I was somehow less lonely than I'd been in Long Island or New Mexico or New York City or Redlands or Oxnard. I grew to like the quiet and enjoy the company of the pines and the river, the birds, wolves, and caribou. I never did see another bull caribou again, though.

Whatever remained of my old personality melted away into the moss and the dirt in the long, nightless day and long, seasonless year. The Arctic winter never came. It stayed between forty and sixty degrees all the time, depending mostly on the clouds. And the sun just circled around and around Koyukuk, like an animal who wants to be your friend, but who is afraid.

I hear the mountains are doin' fine
—Neil Young, *Motion Pictures*

Epilogue
55.

I'm older now. And things have changed in Koyukuk. After a long time alone—a few years is my best guess—other people made their way here.

The first was Ted. He's my best friend here. He was working as a forest ranger on the Denali National Park when the World ended. He's handy and has helped fix up most of the wrecked houses here. We're about the same age. We both know more about the World that vanished than anyone else here.

Some of the people who came here were refugees from the nightmare in the south, or from the other nearby cities and towns, which were ruined in their own various disasters. Some were Siberian stragglers who lost interest or showed up too late for the legendary invasion. They came in dribs and drabs and stayed. I was glad to see them all the same.

There was food from the rivers and the woods, and the town started to fill up again.

The days and years elude me. But enough time has passed for that I've had half a dozen sons and four daughters by three wives. One wife and half of the children are still alive. My current wife is a Siberian woman with kind eyes and big hips. After two children and four pregnancies, there's still a language barrier between us, and we both still find it sort of charming. I call her Kate and she likes it. She reminds me of Nuna a little. We live with our daughter and son, but not in Nuna's house.

Some of my older kids have kids of their own now. There are around a hundred fifty of us here. The town is actually getting crowded, which is sort of reassuring.

Because I was the first one to come here after the town was slaughtered, I'm an unofficial town elder, and sit on the town council. It's not as political as it sounds. We meet occasionally to decide on important matters, but there aren't many.

Otherwise, I sleep a lot. I'm known for it, actually. I play with the kids, or talk with Ted, or go fishing the rest the time. My sons do most of the trapping nowadays.

Like me, the other older people in Koyukuk are subdued, reluctant in most matters. We're sociable up to a point, but we don't make any trouble. We've had enough trouble. We're still a bit shell-shocked and always will be.

The kids, though, want excitement. And there's really no dissuading them. One of my sons from my first two marriages stayed in town. But the others have traveled hundreds of miles to meet the few people in the other towns. Most of the old towns are either empty or full of corpses, my son Jason, told me. He and his brothers traveled as far as Nome. He said something really terrible must have happened there. There were corpses that looked as if they'd been paved into the roads, bodies embedded in the sides of buildings or impaled on telephone poles.

Jason was the only one of my sons to come back from that trip. Ronald died from an infection on the way back. And Bobby married a girl in Council, which I understand is doing well, despite being so close to Nome. I haven't seen him since he left Koyukuk.

My friend Ted is an east-coast boy like me, originally from Rockville, Maryland. Living way up at Denali, he knew something had happened mostly from shortwave transmissions. Not long after he came to town, I gave him the details I had. He went off into the woods for a few days to let it sink in. But he came back fine. A few months later, we were fishing, and he asked me how I survived the end, and how I knew so much about it.

I almost never talk about my old life, but I told Ted the story of how I missed my just desserts, the whole story, with the aliens and the ghosts, Dizzy and Mary Beth, Guy and Cinderella, Mo and the gospel. And I told Ted about the library.

198

"So really, the library can't be too far from here. We could probably find it. We could go over there with some of the young guys, get the books and bring them back to town. We could build a big library here, like a centerpiece for the town. It would be great for the kids. You could recognize the remnants of the building, couldn't you?"

"If I ever went back to find the library, it would only be so I could dig it up and burn it."

"You really mean that?"

"Yeah."

"But why?" he asked.

"It doesn't matter. And it shouldn't matter."

"Of course it does. How can you say that?"

"Ted, take a second. I want you to imagine all the dead-ends of history. Imagine the theological debates among the Algonquin Indians, the political intrigues within the Gallic tribes, the zoning committee meetings over a shrine to Apollo in Alexandria. They mattered once. But now they don't. And it's all right that they don't matter anymore. They're not coming back and they shouldn't come back. And that's us: We're over. I don't see the use in imposing all that stuff on the kids. Why make them live under such a big shadow? Why leave them a past to worship or to fear? I say we just stay on our side of the angel with the fiery sword."

"But what about leaving something to our kids—a history, a culture?"

"The kids have plenty up here. They have plenty of food. They have the woods and the mountains and the rivers and each other. We need to forget about what happened before. We need to let it go and just try to live good lives. That's all the knowledge I want to leave my kids. That's all they need. The rest will do more harm than good at this point. What good is Plato in the woods?"

"It might do them a lot of good."

"If they want to know more, let them discover it all from scratch, instead of reading it. It's an opportunity we didn't have. And you never know, maybe they'll do it right this time."

"I just don't think it's fair to leave those kids without all that stuff, especially if we could give it to them."

"Hey Ted, if you loved it all so much, how come you didn't stay back on the east coast? DC, New York, Boston, you could have had your pick of colleges, museums, libraries. Why didn't you stay, if you liked it so much? You don't even have to tell me because I know: Because you hated it. You hated the cities and the suburbs and all the people in them and how they made you feel. You probably didn't even love nature all that much more than me. It was just a place away from all that."

"I dunno. I guess so. But we could just bring so much back, so many of the good things, the medicine, the art. We could leave all the bad parts back in the hole. We could do it right."

"I'm sorry, Ted. But I don't trust myself to do it right. I'm just not into it."

He was disappointed, but not overly so. He understood. And like all the older people here, there's not much that was worth making a ruckus about. Not even for the legacy of the Western World.

The past still looms. And I still fight it on the town council. Whenever one of the youngsters wants to make an expedition to Fairbanks for books and tools, or thinks he can get some distant power plant restarted or something, my answer's always the same. I table the idea. I say we need to look into the pros and cons. We need to talk about it more. They mostly lose interest after a few long meetings.

I've made a few enemies by doing that. I figure if I give it a little longer, most of the books will disintegrate. Then we'll be free of it for good.

As a town elder, my big responsibility is to create a calendar. At least that's what I tell people I'm doing. Since the sun never rises or sets, telling one day from the next isn't as easy as it used to be. People sleep odd hours, but it hardly matters. It actually helps, since the houses can sleep two times as many people.

But without seasons or days to count, it's hard to count the years. That's why I don't know how long I've been here in Koyukuk, or know my own age, or that of my children.

My rough estimate is that it's been around twenty-five years since I got here and twenty years or so years since the others started showing up. There's no real science behind that, though. I figure the twenty years because my kids are having kids.

Actually my kids were probably younger than twenty when they started having kids of their own. But I'll give them the benefit of the doubt.

Tracking time is a pretty simple but boring business. You just pick a spot on the horizon. Each time the sun passes that point, a day has passed. And after 365 of them, you have a year. I'll deal with leap years once I get the regular ones down. The calendar is a novelty, really. We don't need one, since the weather never changes and we don't farm. But at least we could start to celebrate birthdays.

Once I get myself organized, I figure I'll start the calendar at year 30 PA, for Present Age. That will give the young parents here the appearance of some propriety and set a reasonable standard for everyone after to transgress. I decided on Present Age because it won't make our lives here seem like a sequel.

I don't want people thinking about the past too much if they can help it. That's the last real opinion I have left.

Still, it's a lot of work to keep track of the sun every day, and then to mark down each day, and then tally them into years. It's tedious. Not really my bag. The women, with their menstrual cycles, probably have a better feel for time than me. Maybe I should fob the calendar off on one of them. They seem more serious about things than me, or any of the men here, really.

But if a life of profligate laziness has taught me anything, it's this: Look busy. Whenever anyone asks me how the calendar is coming, I say it's going well. I say I still have more calculations to work out. And I always like to work out my calculations while I'm fishing, or in my bedroom with the curtains pulled.

There's no rush on this thing. No one really seems to mind not knowing what day it is, or how old they are, or how long it's been since the thing that nobody really wants to talk about.

So maybe I'll just let it slide a little longer.

THE END

Other Books by Colin Dodds

Poetry

Last Man on the Moon

The Blue Blueprint

Heaven Unbuilt

Novels

Fun's Monsters

What Smiled at Him

Another Broken Wizard

WINDFALL

Screenplays

Refreshment — a tragedy

But Let's Not Talk about Work

About the Author
Colin Dodds grew up in Massachusetts and completed his education at The New School in New York City. Dodds' novels *What Smiled at Him* and *Another Broken Wizard* have been widely acclaimed by critics and readers alike. His screenplay, *Refreshment – A Tragedy*, was named a semi-finalist in 2010 American Zoetrope Contest. Two books of Dodds' poetry—*The Last Man on the Moon* and *The Blue Blueprint*—are available from Medium Rare Publishing and his writing has appeared in a number of periodicals, including *The Wall Street Journal Online*, *Folio*, *Explosion-Proof*, *Block Magazine*, *The Architect's Newspaper*, *The Main Street Rag*, *The Reno News & Review* and *Lungfull! Magazine*. He lives in Brooklyn, New York, with his wife Samantha.

46690662R00124

Made in the USA
Middletown, DE
06 August 2017